"A no-frills tale that
detective work and
likely to see this se

"Clean, springy action and a colorful cast of
supporting characters."
— *Publishers Weekly*

"Delilah is a no-nonsense woman..."
— *Brazosport Facts*

"Maxine O'Callaghan doesn't make one false
move..."
— *Fort Lauderdale Sun-Sentinel*

"This mystery comes together perfectly at the
end."
— *The Sunday Oregonian*

"The pace of the book...never slows up."
— *Mystery News*

DOWN FOR THE COUNT

Maxine O'Callaghan

WORLDWIDE®

TORONTO • NEW YORK • LONDON
AMSTERDAM • PARIS • SYDNEY • HAMBURG
STOCKHOLM • ATHENS • TOKYO • MILAN
MADRID • WARSAW • BUDAPEST • AUCKLAND

DOWN FOR THE COUNT

A Worldwide Mystery/December 1998

First published by St. Martin's Press, Incorporated.

ISBN 0-373-26294-9

To Jill Morgan, Patricia Wallace and Marcia Muller, who can always be counted on to provide lots of encouragement and boosts for my ego.

And to Gary Bale for sharing his expertise in the field of law enforcement, for demanding my books—loudly—in every bookstore in Orange County, and for being one of the growing numbers of men who let me know that a Delilah West novel is not "for women only."

ONE

CATASTROPHE is a part of life. We all know that. But on some of the major stuff, at least we get a little warning. Tornadoes are predicted by storm clouds and lightning. Hurricanes spin their way up to howling fury so they can be tracked and we can batten down the hatches. Even earthquakes give off some kind of subsonic vibration that we might feel if we were as sensitive as dogs and horses.

But when your life goes suddenly and completely to hell, what do you get?

Nada.

Unless you are lucky, you will be caught out in the open with no refuge in sight. And guess what?

My luck was about to run out.

THE WHOLE THING BEGAN on the day after Christmas with a shopping trip—something I normally avoid. Yet there I was, circling the parking lot outside Main Street Mall, all because nine-year-old Isabel Sanchez knows I'm a sucker for her big, pleading eyes.

I'd had Christmas dinner with the Sanchezes and several dozens of their relatives. Since both Jorge and Consuelo were scheduled to work on the 26th, somehow I found myself promising to take Isabel out to spend the thirty-two dollars she had accumulated from her aunts and uncles.

Well, private eye work was slow to nonexistent, and with Erik off in Vermont, Lord knows I had nothing else to do.

"There!"

Isabel pointed to a pickup backing out of the space right up at the head of the aisle.

A Honda stopped, letting the pickup exit the aisle. Good manners? Oh, sure. I knew what the driver had in mind: He'd enter the wrong way and whip into the space before I could get there. Well, it's what *I'd* do. And he had a good chance of beating us out because we were still about ten car lengths away.

A quick scan for strollers and bargain-laden shoppers, then I goosed the Astro van, accelerating like a crazy woman, and wheeled into the space as the Honda stood on his brakes and honked indignantly.

"Yes!" Isabel said and beamed her approval.

I gave her a modest, shucks-it's-nothing smile and ignored a last blast of horn from the Honda as the driver took off in a huff.

As we got out of the van, I thought briefly about the .38 locked in the glove box. Auto break-ins are as common as fake holly this time of year, and a handgun is one of the thieves' favorite prizes, being always in demand on the street and sure to bring enough money for a quick fix.

But the temperature outside was a balmy seventy-eight degrees, and we were dressed accordingly. Isabel wore what looked like plaid flannel boxer shorts and a red T-shirt with a silly-looking cat wishing everybody a MEOWY CHRISTMAS. My short-sleeved denim shirt was tucked into jeans. I could stick the weapon in my waistband in back, but then I'd have to wear a jacket to hide the lump. Too warm for a jacket, I decided, so I left my vehicle and its contents to the vagaries of fate and hurried after Isabel into the mall.

Inside Robinson's-May the tinsel garlands and plastic wreaths were looking a little seedy. The noise level guaranteed a headache, and "Jingle Bells" over the music system made me wish I'd brought along the .38 to blast the damn speakers. However, the crowds were merry enough, like smiling sharks during a feeding frenzy.

Isabel had her orders. One eye on me at all times, or we aborted the mission, pronto. Although she was good about following my mandate, I wasn't taking any chances and tracked her like radar. She's tall for her age, but still short enough to lose in a sea of people. I kept my eyes glued to the bobbing ponytail and the bright red shirt while I fulfilled my most important functions: carrying Isabel's finds and providing safe transport for her funds.

Of course, having served a stint as a store detective, I noticed things going on around me as we moved through the various departments, things most people would miss. So I saw a well-dressed middle-aged woman slipping a wallet down into the paper stuffed inside a purse before she bought it, and two teens working the jewelry counter, a unisex pair in short hair, jeans, nose rings, and black motorcycle jackets replete with lots of zippered pockets. One distracted the already harried clerk while the other took two Guess watches and some gold earrings in the shape of a cross.

Another guy caught my attention: short and thickset with expressionless eyes, carrying a gym bag. I figured he was out for major loot, but either he didn't take anything or he was awfully good at his work.

Or maybe I just have a suspicious mind.

Which I do.

No denying that.

"Look, Delilah." Triumphantly Isabel bore her latest find: a pair of purple shorts that couldn't have measured more than eight inches from waistband to cuff. *"Four dollars."*

"Hey, great." At fifty cents an inch I guess it was a buy.

"Now how much do I have left?" she asked.

"Let's see—thirteen dollars and forty-nine cents." I dodged a woman flying blind behind a bag containing a king-sized down comforter. "How about it? Can we get out of here?"

"Yeah, let's hit the mall shops."

I was thinking more in terms of sitting down with a cup of coffee, but my little bargain hound had her nose to the ground and was tracking. Among her next buys were some poisonous green bath crystals and a candle shaped like Elvis, complete with guitar and blue suede shoes. Well, I was along to serve as packhorse and chauffeur, not as a member of the taste police.

The mall's center promenade wasn't as claustrophobic as the department store, but the crowd noise was louder, echoing off the roof. A refurbishing a few years back had opened up the ceilings so now you had a view of pipes and ductwork, all painted and clean, some of it functional, I suppose, although it looked like a carefully planned stage set to me.

While I trudged behind Isabel, I noted there didn't seem to be any more security guards than normal, but that the fuzz-faced youngsters you commonly see had been replaced with older guys, tougher, armed, maybe ex-cops. Although the mall liked to bill itself as the Rodeo Drive of Santa Ana, it sat slap-dab in the middle of a high-crime area. And, come to think of it, I remembered hearing about a gang incident here recently. So I kept a wary eye out.

The streams of people contained a mixture of every age and race, but nobody in gang colors or dress, as far as I could tell. I did see the guy with the gym bag again, standing outside a jewelry store window, staring in, and won-

dered if he was debating the logistics of a heist. I decided
the crowd would be both cover and obstacle, and that per-
sonally I'd wait for another day.

What can I say?

This is just the way my mind works.

A half dozen stores later I finally demanded a time-out.
Isabel and I were a long way from the food court, so I
agreed to stop at a counter that offered hot dogs and lemonade made from real lemons squeezed by a young woman
with frizzy red hair who jumped on a contraption that
looked like a pogo stick inside a barrel. The bright yellow
decor and the overpowering tangy smell mixed with the
order of cooking hot dogs quickly put me into sensory
overload.

While we waited in line, Isabel said, "Delilah, are you
and Mr. Lundstrom having a fight?"

It was a bit of a jolt having her mention Erik's name
when I'd been expending a lot of energy putting him out
of my mind.

"No," I said. "We're not having a fight. Why do you
think that?"

"I heard Mama and Papa talking. Mama said you must
be having one, otherwise he wouldn't have left you all
alone at Christmas."

"Oh—well, he went back east to spend the holidays
with his daughter. He asked me to go along."

*"You'll love it, Delilah. I always take Nicki skiing and
we stay at this wonderful old inn. They have a fireplace in
every room."*

*"Erik, one thing you need to know about me. I avoid
snow at all costs."*

*"Seems to me snow's not the main thing you're avoid-
ing...."*

"So why didn't you go?" Isabel was asking.

"What? And miss shopping with you?"

I paid for our drinks and looked around for a place to sit. There were a few small tables, all of them occupied. At one, a young boy, maybe ten years old, sat alone, reading a *Judge Dredd* comic book.

"Let's ask if we can share," I said.

Isabel looked horrified. "No way. He might think I wanted to sit there. With *him.*"

"Oh," I said. "Right."

Lord, it does start early, this male-female thing.

We parked ourselves about five feet away from the boy on the edge of a planter. Close enough so when a security guard stopped at the table, I could hear what was being said.

"You been here sittin' around here a long time, kid," the guard said. He was about fifty with a compact body, blunt features, and a flat-top. Former marine? Lots of them around these days, retired early with the closure of the El Toro base looming.

"Like I told you before," the boy said, "I'm waiting for my mom."

"Yeah, well, five minutes, she's not here, you be on your way."

"Okay, okay," the boy muttered, slouching down in his chair.

He saw me watching and quickly brought up the comic book like a shield. He had shaggy brown hair and wore an oversized T-shirt and baggy pants. The outfit has turned into standard dress for kids and didn't necessarily mean he was hiding a switchblade or a spray can.

Isabel leaned close to me. "Mall baby."

That was my guess, too. It's cheaper to give a kid a few bucks to hang out in a shopping center than it is to pay for child care, and the place seems safe, although I know for a fact that's not always the case.

"Delilah, are you hungry?" Isabel looked at me hopefully, too well trained to ask me outright to buy her something.

"I was thinking those hot dogs smelled awfully good," I said.

We got up to rejoin the line, now long enough so it snaked back between the tables near where the boy was sitting, playing out his full five minutes and watching the guard, who was moving away.

A man shouted something, too far down the mall to distinguish the words but no mistaking the rage. Then I heard two loud booms, and a big glass cooler of lemonade exploded on the counter ahead of us, showering us with glass shards and syrupy liquid.

There was a second of frozen terror before pandemonium broke loose, a moment while people processed what was happening. I know gunfire when I hear it and reacted instantly.

I grabbed Isabel and shoved her under the table where the boy was sitting, seized him, and thrust him under it, too. Then I dived in, putting an arm around each of them and covering them with my body the best I could.

Around us people screamed and began running. Two more gunshots and somewhere a window shattered. Somebody shrieked in pain. The table was jounced by the stampeding mob, but stayed upright. We were behind the planter, but near the corner of it, and there was no way I could pull us back farther behind it, not without risk of being trampled.

A different man yelled, maybe the security guard, the shout abruptly cut off by another burst of gunfire.

The two children burrowed close to me. Little bits of

glass shone in Isabel's dark hair, and she smelled of lemon. I felt something trickling down my temple and hoped to God it was juice and not blood.

Then movement stopped as the promenade emptied. Everybody had scurried into shops, maybe finding back doors to the outside. We were the only ones left huddled behind the planter, trapped.

Brilliant move, Delilah.

What was going on? A robbery? A gang shooting? The mall must have some kind of security plan. Surely, the police had been called. The incident seemed to be lasting a long time—Jesus, an eternity—but I knew it had really been only a matter of minutes.

Another *whump-whump* broke the ominous silence, like cherry bombs going off, followed by the splintering of glass. Closer now. Definitely closer. Sure, the police would be coming soon, but how soon?

Carefully, I began to inch backward toward the planter, taking the two kids with me, until I felt they were safely out of the line of fire, at least for the moment.

"Stay down," I whispered fiercely. "I have to take a look."

Another explosion, near enough to jar the bones in my ears.

"Delilah, no—" Isabel said, clutching me like a limpet.

"Isabel, honey, I'll be right back. I promise you."

Reluctantly, she let go.

"Don't either of you move," I cautioned as I crawled back to a point where I could peer over the top of the planter and get a view of the promenade through the foliage.

No sign of the shooter at first; then, suddenly, there he was, coming out of a dress shop across the mall about six stores down. I recognized him immediately: the man with the gym bag. He had the bag slung over his left shoulder, blue nylon and roomy enough to hold the gun he was now carrying. As I watched he ejected a magazine from the big semiautomatic, reached into the bag for a new one, and slid it into place.

I counted four bodies that I could see, including the security guard who had just been talking to the boy; there were probably more in the dress shop. Where the hell were the other guards?

In addition to the .38 out in the parking lot locked in the glove box of my van, I own a Beretta mini-automatic, but it was at home. Well, I was going *shopping,* for Chrissake. Of *course,* I wasn't armed.

The gunman started walking, warily, up near the wall. The guy might be crazy, but he was not devoid of caution. He was coming straight at us but keeping, so far, to the opposite side of the mall. He skipped a tobacconist, paused in front of a Hallmark's. Turned abruptly and went inside. Only three shops away. Was there some method to what he was doing? I didn't think so. I'd been a cop once and this was a cop's worse nightmare, a madman loose in a public place crowded with people, shooting at random.

I went back and yanked the kids up. Glass crunched beneath our feet as I hustled them over to the lemonade counter, urging them to stay low and hurry as we headed to a door behind the counter. Through a small window in the door, I could see a light was on. I opened the door and saw at once there was no back exit, that the room was simply a small area for storage. As I shoved Isabel and the boy inside ahead of me, somebody bleated in surprise and terror, the red-haired young woman who had been crushing the lemons, one of two employees hiding back there behind some boxes. I pushed the children down beside them and dropped on my heels.

Isabel was crying now as we heard screams and the *whump-whump* of shots, only slightly muffled.

"Where's the phone?" I asked the two young women.

One just stared at me, dark eyes wide and glazed, skin pale as milk inside the frame of her black bobbed hair. The redhead said, "Outside."

"Did you call nine-one-one?"

"Yeah, right." She was shivering. "Are you *crazy?*"

"Stay there," I said to the children and went back to the window in the storage room door, pausing to flip off the light before I peered out.

The view was restricted, but since the action was on the opposite side of the promenade, I could see what was going on. And what I saw was movement off to my left, a security guard approaching, gun drawn, staying close to the wall. Just then, to my right, the shooter backed out of the Hallmark's. Garbled shouts, a shot. The man with the gym bag clutched his left arm, hit, staggering, but not going down.

The guard rushed him, yelling hoarsely, firing again, missing. That distinctive *whump-whump* from the shooter's semiautomatic and the guard threw up his arms and pitched face-forward. The gun flew out of his hand and came skating across the shiny hard tiles of the floor at an angle, spinning around and around.

It stopped just in front of the lemonade counter, right in the middle of the promenade, tantalizingly close.

Dammit, dammit, why was I even here? Why wasn't I at work, or freezing my ass off in fucking Vermont? If I hadn't come with her, Isabel would be safe at home. Of course, the boy would have been here, and the two young women huddling behind me, and God knows how many more hiding in the shops along the gunman's route.

He was leaning against the wall out in front of the card

shop. His left arm hung limply. The gym bag had slid off his shoulder and lay on the floor. Maybe he'd give up, see it was hopeless. Put the gun to his own head. No, he squatted to retrieve the gym bag, stood up, and slung it over his good shoulder, then moved off slowly but doggedly. He raised the gun and took a shot down the mall. Maybe at another guard. I couldn't see. Nobody fired back. Five more steps and he was in front of a luggage shop.

The police would arrive any minute now with a SWAT team and sharpshooters, might already be in the parking lot establishing perimeters and a command post and doing all the other things necessary to lock down the situation. Maybe they'd come in time, at least for us, because the shooter was still working his way down the opposite side of the mall. If he continued that course, he'd go right on by.

But even as I thought this the gunman stood, swaying for a second in front of the luggage shop, then turned and headed across toward our side of the mall, his movements deliberate and robotlike.

The guard's gun lay out there, a revolver, light glinting off a steel barrel. I thought the guard had only fired once, maybe twice, but was I willing to bet my life—our lives—on it?

I hurried back to the children.

"Is he coming?" Even in the dim gloom of the storeroom I could see Isabel's eyes, big as saucers.

"Isabel, I want you to listen to me. I'm going to have to leave you here."

"No—*no,* Delilah. I want you to stay, please."

"I wish I could, sweetheart. Can you lock this door?" I asked the red-haired girl.

She shook her head.

"Okay, then. Isabel—both of you"—I included the

boy—"get as far back in the corner as you can. Lie down flat. Don't get up until you hear me or the police tell you it's safe. Understand?"

The boy nodded. Isabel gave me a quick hug, and the two did what I said. The redhead muttered something, her tone telling me she knew I really had flipped out, but she crawled back, too. The other young woman stayed where she was, all curled up in a tight little ball.

I hastily pulled boxes of paper cups and napkins in front of them before I went back to the door. I couldn't see the shooter from the window—which didn't mean he wouldn't see me as soon as I stuck my head out. I took a deep breath, cracked the door, and slipped outside. Staying down behind the counter, I duckwalked to the end so I could peer around it. The gunman was just going into a shoe store two doors down.

Huge windows fronted display cases, taking up maybe two thirds of the entrance, big sale racks down the middle of the store. The shoe store was so open he was sure to look out and see me.

Whump-whump. Mirrored walls shattering.

One more store between us. A Gap. Even more wide open.

Now or never.

I jumped up and bolted—and found I had no edge at all.

He was already coming out of the shoe store, pulling the trigger the instant he saw me.

I felt the air above me split with concussion. My head rang with the explosion, but I was already down, diving, willing my body to slide, slide across a good thirty feet of slick tile mined with fragments of glass and sticky with lemonade to the security guard's gun.

TWO

"AIM TO STOP," that's what the firing instructor at the police academy had told us, although even the thickest among us knew we were dealing in euphemisms. Hitting the middle of that series of rings in the silhouette on the paper targets at the range was teaching us not only to stop somebody, but to drop them stone cold dead. So when I put two bullets as close as possible to the middle of the gunman's blocky torso, I knew what I was aiming to do.

I was close enough to see the man's body jerk with the impact and to see the surprise on his face. Then he seemed to hang suspended for a long, stretched moment before he fell, pitching forward as he went down.

Well, I'd stopped him, all right, and I was fairly sure I'd killed him, but I wasn't ready to deal with *that* nasty little reality just then. Too many other things flashed rapidly through my mind. Like the prospect of all the statements and questions and hassling by the police, and the media—Jesus, they'd be swarming like flies.

Today I'd be a hero, tomorrow courted by Oprah and Geraldo, and the day after that most likely be sued by the gunman's family for ending the poor, misunderstood sucker's life.

And, although I don't much like to admit it, my relationship with Erik Lundstrom weighed in, too. Somehow I didn't think sensationalism was going to help, and there was no way to escape that kind of attention now that some society columnist had dubbed Erik Orange County's Most Eligible Bachelor.

No time for second thoughts. Ignoring my appalled conscience's objection to compromising a crime scene, I sprang up, quickly wiped the gun on my shirttail, dropped the weapon, and kicked it back toward the dead guard.

If there were any eyewitnesses to what had just happened or a security camera taping the scene, I was going to be in trouble, but I was pretty sure everybody had been busy keeping their heads down and I couldn't spot a camera. There would be questions about the trajectory of the bullets and the lack of prints, but if I got lucky, in the end the guard would get the credit for taking out the gunman. I sincerely hoped so as I raced back to the storeroom behind the lemonade counter.

My arms were oozing blood and stinging like crazy, the undersides full of cuts from the broken glass on the mall floor, and the cuts full of lemonade. However, at that moment, the wounds were the least of my worries.

I opened the door, flipped on the light switch, and called, "Isabel, come on."

She peeped out cautiously from the boxes, as though she couldn't trust her hearing to know it was really me. Her face lit with relief as she scrambled to her feet. The boy popped his head up, and I added, "You, too. Hurry."

"What happened?" Isabel said. "Is he gone?" Then: "Delilah, you're bleeding!"

The young woman with the frizzy red hair stared at me. I said quickly, "It's just catsup." Plausible enough, I hoped, since there were packets of the stuff around for the hot dogs. "I think the guard shot the guy," I said to the redhead, "but wait a few minutes before you leave."

Then I hurried the two kids out, blocking as much of the gory view in the promenade as possible, and hustled them to the nearest exit.

There was chaos out in the parking lot. Fleeing shoppers

were pouring out; patrol cars, fire trucks, and paramedics were pouring in along with a SWAT van. Two helicopters thrummed overhead, one police, one with a Channel 4 logo. CNN and the rest of the media pack couldn't be far behind.

I made an end run with both children in tow down to the van where I quickly slipped into a jacket to cover up my arms. There was blood on my shirt and my jeans, but I hoped Isabel had bought my catsup story.

I did a visual check of the two kids. They seemed fine except for messy hair and clothes. Isabel looked a little pale, but her eyes were bright with excitement. While I tried to maneuver us out of the parking lot without getting the van smashed up, she said, "You did something, didn't you, Delilah?"

"Me? No," I lied.

"What could *she* do?" the boy asked with young male scorn in his voice.

"You'd be surprised," Isabel proudly declared. "Delilah's a private eye."

Like I needed a press agent just then.

"Yeah, sure," the boy muttered.

"She *is*." I'd brought along some business letters to mail; they lay on the floor between the seats. Isabel picked one up and shoved it at him, pointing to the return address, which reads WEST INVESTIGATIONS. "See?" Then, unwilling to let the subject go, she turned back to me. "Did you shoot him?"

"Sorry," I said. "My gun was here in the van."

Isabel looked a little crestfallen, but said loyally, "Well, I bet you *would* have shot him if you had your gun."

Oh, Lord.

Even children know me well.

Changing the subject, I found out the boy's name was

Brian Hall and that he lived in Orange. Since we were closer to the Sanchezes and I was afraid Consuelo might have heard about the shooting, I drove there first. On the way, I had Isabel try to call home on the cellular phone, but even the cell lines were jammed.

When we arrived, Consuelo came running from the house to meet us, speaking in rapid-fire Spanish. I caught "Main Street" and "televisión." I had to make a lame attempt to explain with my limited vocabulary—*muy bueno, es okay, no problemo*—because as soon as her mother's arms closed around her, Isabel regressed to clingy, wordless babyhood and began to cry.

"Telefono Jorge a Mom's," I said, hoping Consuelo understood I planned to call Jorge at the restaurant where he worked to explain. I kissed the top of Isabel's sticky head, got back in the van, and drove away.

Brian moved up to sit in the seat beside me, but didn't say much except to give me some general directions. He just kept giving me quick probing glances like he was trying to catch me off guard and read my thoughts.

"You can try the phone again," I offered. "Call your folks."

"That's okay. My mom's at work."

He didn't say where his father was, and I didn't ask. I concentrated on driving, set my teeth against the burning pain in my arms, and tried to ignore the fact that my knees hurt, too, where the fabric stretched tight. The jeans weren't torn, but I'd bet I was going to find some skin peeled off because fresh blood was seeping through and staining the fabric.

Off the 55 Freeway, Brian directed me to Cedar Creek Apartments. One-story units, built around an artificial babbling brook, tried for rustic and charming, but instead the place only looked cheap, run-down, and tacky.

It occurred to me just about then that I was tracking on instinct, and that my thought processes were lagging way behind my physical movements. As I pulled into the parking lot, I realized the boy might also be suffering from delayed shock, and it might not be such a good idea to leave him alone.

But a man was getting out of a pickup truck a few slots away from the one Brian pointed out for me to use. He spotted Brian in my vehicle, obviously recognized him, and began walking over. My age—edging forty—lanky and tanned, he had thinning mousy-brown hair going gray, long enough to pull back in a ponytail, and a pale, coarse mustache.

"My mom's boyfriend," Brian explained briefly, his tone carefully detached in a way that told me more than if he'd stated his dislike for the guy.

Instead of reaching for the door handle, Brian hesitated, then asked, "Are you really a private detective?"

"Yes, I really am." I didn't add that sometimes it's the last thing I want to be.

The boyfriend arrived at the passenger side of the van. He opened the door and said, "Yo, Bry. Thought I was picking you up at the mall. What're you doing? Hitching rides?"

"Some guy was shooting up the place," Brian said with the aplomb of a true child of TV land. "This lady brought me home."

"Get outta here." This was said with slack-jawed astonishment. "Is that really true?" He was bending to stare in at me as Brian climbed down from the van.

"I'm afraid so." I draped my left arm across my knees to hide the bloodstained jeans. "I think Brian's okay, but you might want to keep an eye on him."

"I will. Say, listen, thanks a lot, Miss—?"

"West," I said. "Delilah."

"Delilah. I'm Larry. Larry Vogel."

He stuck his hand in through the door and across the passenger seat. Nothing I could do but take it. Stretching my arm out hurt like hell. Through the pain, I got an impression of slightly callused skin and masculine strength transmitted by a hard squeeze.

"Really appreciate your taking care of the boy," Larry said. "I know his mom does, too. Not many people would go out of their way like that."

"Glad to do it. Brian, you'll be okay?"

"Yeah."

"Take a shower," I said. "Wash your hair good. I bet you got glass in it. I know I did."

"Okay."

Suddenly, he looked reluctant to leave me. Another second and I think he might have climbed back in, but Larry said, "You take care," closed the door, raised one hand in good-bye, and dropped the other on Brian's shoulder.

Brian stood there, a trapped look on his face, watching me drive away.

Ordinarily I would have been speculating on the boy's home situation. A pessimistic assessment, no doubt. Life has skewed my thinking that way. Today—well, to tell the truth I didn't give it a whole lot of thought.

My brain had come up with a inventory of things I had to do and I was ticking them off, one at a time, keeping a tight focus. Right then getting home was the next item on my list. I drove there with patience, courtesy, and skill. I did *not* turn on the radio. At my complex I parked. Remembered to lock up. Walked to my apartment and opened the door. I swear my hands weren't even shaking.

However, closing the door behind me was like throwing a switch. Talk about your delayed reaction. My knees folded up. I didn't even make it to the couch, just slid down the door and sat there, trying to catch my breath and thinking if I was in the ER somebody would be yelling for a crash cart.

I know about flashbacks. I've had a few. This one was a doozy. Suddenly I was back there in the mall with the screams and the gunfire, the acrid stench of nitrates and the sweet-sour odor of lemonade. I slid across the floor with bits of shattered glass digging into my arms, grabbed the gun, squeezed off two rounds, looked in the gunman's face as he jerked and fell.

All during this replay, a little voice of reason kept reminding me that I'd done what had to be done, that I had taken out a psycho who might very well have killed me, two children, and the two young women in the storeroom as well as God knows how many others, and that I was absolutely not under any circumstances going to become hysterical.

Slowly, I stopped hyperventilating. When I could finally stand up again, I fumbled my way to the kitchen, drank three swallows of brandy straight from the bottle, then stumbled into the bathroom.

I managed to get my jeans off with a minimum of pain to reveal the skinned knees I expected. But the blood on my arms had dried just enough so the jacket fabric was sticking. Rather than rip it loose, I got into the shower with the thing on, let it get good and wet before I pulled my arms out. That meant my shirt and bra were drippy, too.

Hell.

It hurt some more when I soaped my arms, but at least none of the cuts looked deep. If they left scars, it was going to look like I did a really botched-up job of attempted suicide with a butter knife.

Clean, with some antibiotic-cortisone cream soothing the

cuts, I eased into sweats and went to call Jorge, who had already talked to his wife. I accepted his profuse thanks for bringing Isabel home safely, said that yes, I was just fine, and no, I didn't want company. No need for him to pick me up and take me to the Sanchez house to spend the night.

Just as I hung up, the phone rang. It was my assistant, Danny Thu, a connection full of static from a pay phone in Ensenada. He had taken the week off to go on a bicycle marathon down in the Baja. When he checked in with his mom, she told him the news passed on by Jorge earlier.

I repeated my assertions that I was okay and didn't need Mr. and Mrs. Thu to come and take me home with *them*.

Of course, I'd lied to both Jorge and Danny.

I was a long way from being fine, and the last thing I wanted was to be by myself, but I didn't want to be with the Sanchezes or Rita and Farley or anybody else except the one person who wasn't in town. Who was as a matter of fact three thousand miles away in a place that also contained his eighteen-year-old daughter.

And snow.

Nevertheless, I stuffed some clothes into a carry-on bag, grabbed my purse, and headed for John Wayne Airport. Was I giving any philosophical thought to the way love breeds dependency, or taking a hard look at how I keep running off to Erik in times of stress?

Not then I wasn't.

Anyway, what's the good of loving somebody if you can't hide under the covers with him when the world becomes a scary place?

Airline agents clearly thought I was nuts to start my traveling so late in the day, but ticketed me through to Burlington, Vermont, at a fare that could probably get me to China from LAX. The trip involved three flight segments and a long layover in Dallas, a deserted, cavernous place in the middle of the night that reminded me of an Edward Hopper painting. There I had some truly terrible coffee and even worse food and watched a cold rain lash the big windows while news reports about the shooting at the mall back in Santa Ana played endlessly on television monitors throughout the terminal.

These preliminary reports were all confusion with "informed sources" guessing there had been a shoot-out between the security guard and the gunman. I wished the news item made me feel better but it didn't, even after I heard the body count was up to fifteen and that it surely would have been higher if the gunman hadn't been killed.

Jet planes got me just so close to the ski resort where Erik was staying. A train and a four-wheel-drive courtesy vehicle were required to take me the rest of the way. I arrived shortly after 1 p.m. much the worse for wear. I'd had very little sleep, lousy meals, and lots of time to reflect on the folly and expense of my cross-country dash.

Somehow, though, I hadn't considered the fact that Erik might not be in his room at the lodge when I arrived. While I stood at a house phone and listened to the unanswered ringing, I watched all the beautiful people laughing and talking, going for a late lunch or back to the slopes, wearing wealth like a perfume; meanwhile, I was getting the eagle eye from the bell captain, the desk clerk, and the concierge.

I knew what they saw: a thirtysomething—well, okay, a nearly forty woman in a beat-up old quilted parka and dirty sweats. Bloodshot brown eyes and cinnamon brown hair, shaggy on the shoulders because she'd missed her last two hair appointments, with some gray strands she'd rather forget.

That was the point when I began thinking that I'd sit

down on the floor again and this time really have hysterics, and I might have done just that, except for the fact that across the lobby I saw the elevator doors open and Erik walk out.

It gave me a momentary wrench as it always does to see just how perfectly Erik Lundstrom fitted into this kind of setting and know that I didn't and never would. Then, also as usual, I put the thought aside and tried to get to him as fast as possible.

Jet lag and fatigue slowed me down so Erik reached me first, long strides bringing him swiftly, with just enough time for me to note that he looked lean and elegant even in the casual ski clothes and how the blue of his jacket accentuated the blue of his eyes.

Then I was in his arms and whatever time and discomfort it had taken to get there seemed worth the cost—at least for a few seconds.

Standing the way we were I could see past him in the direction of the elevator. Although I'd never met his daughter, I had seen pictures, and, anyway, would have recognized Nicole Lundstrom because she looked so much like Erik. The same blue, blue eyes, a feminine version of Erik's face, and blond hair that would undoubtedly turn the same shade of premature silver as her dad's.

Besides having no desire to slide down mountains on two skinny pieces of fiberglass, I'd had good reason to decline Erik's invitation to join their annual Christmas stay.

For one thing I was sure Nicki wouldn't appreciate having me butt into this ritual. For another, I know Erik's been involved with other women. Nicki must have seen them come and go over the years. I had no desire to be viewed as just another of the passing parade.

Bottom line, though, I guess I was stalling off a meeting because I was afraid we might not get along.

Now, reading Nicki's face, I knew I'd been right to worry.

Erik's daughter hated me on sight.

THREE

HOO BOY, I thought, gauging the naked malice in Nicki Lundstrom's beautiful blue eyes. Forget friendship. I'd be lucky to even get to the politely tolerant stage with this one.

She had that special shine, that careless air of expectation that comes from always having money available to oil life's squeaky joints and pave the rough spots. Her ski outfit, white with turquoise trim, showed off a slender, athletic body that looked taut now with anger.

"This is a wonderful surprise, darling," Erik said, hugging me and laying his cheek against my hair. "But you should've called. I'd've sent the plane back for you—" He broke off as he released me enough to get a look at my face. "What is it? What's wrong?"

"Just tired," I said since I wasn't about to go into hostile daughters, not to mention mall massacres. "Long trip when you fly the old-fashioned way on commercial jets."

He didn't believe a word of it, but Nicole had reached us and was standing there, shuttering the hatred in her eyes, so he didn't press.

Instead he said, "Sweetheart, Delilah's come to join us after all."

"How nice," she said. A good two inches taller than I was, she could look down her perfect nose at the same time she gave me a cool, polite little smile.

I wanted to back off from her father, but he had one arm firmly locked around me, and, anyway, I might have fallen on my face if I'd pulled away. So I tried for sincerity and said, "Nicki, I'm happy to meet you at last. Your Dad's told me so much about you."

"I've heard a lot about you, too, Delilah," she said sweetly.

Not all of it from Erik, and not all of it good, I'd bet. Maybe she'd had somebody run a check on me. Maybe Charlie Colfax. Charlie's an old acquaintance—notice I didn't say friend—heads up his own PI firm, and is on retainer with Erik. Oh, Charlie could give her an earful all right.

Then again, after what had happened the day before, maybe I was just a little bit paranoid. Still, at that moment, any residual guilt vanished, and I was sincerely thankful that I'd had presence of mind enough to cover my actions.

"Dad and I were heading out to the slopes," Nicki said. "I'm sure you'll want to go get cleaned up and maybe take a rest."

Somebody opened a big door, letting in a blast of frigid air. I hadn't been warm since I left California and now I began shivering.

"That's just what I want to do," I said. I quickly ran through some nonsense in my head about getting myself a room, but that was ridiculous, so I added, "Erik, if you'll just give me a key—"

"Don't be silly," Erik said. "I'll come up with you."

"No, you don't have to. Nicki shouldn't go skiing alone."

"Nicki knows lots of people here. She won't mind if I skip a few runs—will you, Nick?"

"Oh, no," Nicki said with a flash of perfect white teeth. "I'll catch up with you later."

Totally pissed was my opinion as she moved off swiftly, calling out to some young people just exiting the lodge, melding into the small group without a backward glance.

The bellman, who had been looking down his nose at me and my scruffy luggage, now came running as Erik reached for my carry-on bag, but Erik waved him away, picked up the bag himself, and bundled it and me into the elevator.

"Well, that was a bust," I said bleakly as the doors closed, leaving us alone for the trip up to the third floor of the lodge. "Talk about getting off on the wrong foot. Two wrong feet."

"It was just awkward," Erik said. "Things will get better. You'll see."

I knew he was dead wrong, but there was no point in arguing about it. Anyway, I had other things to worry about because I knew that fairly soon I'd be taking off my clothes—which is a thing I commonly do around Erik— and then I would have to explain my skinned knees and all those cuts on my arms.

Inside the spacious suite, I tried to stall off the moment of reckoning by exclaiming about the beautiful appointments and the gorgeous view. Well, it *was* breathtaking, dark green trees with a lacy touch of snow set against an intensely blue sky.

Erik stopped my babble by sitting on the big, overstuffed sofa and pulling me down beside him. I winced as his fingers closed around my arm and hoped he wouldn't notice, but Erik doesn't miss much.

"You're hurt," he said.

"Not really. Scratches, that's all."

"Let me see," he demanded.

Reluctantly, I took off my jacket, unzipped my sweatshirt. I had a short-sleeved T-shirt under that. Layers, supposed to keep you warm, and what a crock that was.

"*Jesus,*" Erik said when he saw the maze of cuts on the outside of my forearms. "How did you do this?"

"Do you know what happened at Main Street Mall yesterday?"

"Christ, yes, I saw a report on TV this morning. You mean you were there?"

I nodded. "With Isabel Sanchez. The nine-year-old. And it was nothing like TV."

"My God," he said. "Is she—?"

"Fine," I said quickly. "She's fine. Scared, that's all. It was damned scary, Erik. This crazy man shooting up the place—people screaming and running. There was broken glass everywhere. I wasn't sure we'd get out alive, so I—"

I faltered, wanting to come clean and tell him everything. But I felt trapped by my lie, and too damn tired to decide what was the right thing to do.

"I just tried to keep us down, out of sight," I finished, salting my explanation with half-truths. "There was glass on the floor." I slid up against him and laid my head on his chest.

He sighed and I knew that if he had any doubts, he was letting them go for now.

"God, I'm cold, Erik," I whispered. "I don't think I'll ever be warm again."

It took awhile, under a down comforter, before I knew I was wrong about that.

TWO DAYS LATER we were in Erik's Gulfstream IV-SP, heading back to California, a cozy threesome in the luxurious cabin with its sofas and big soft recliners, deep pile champagne carpeting, and gold fixtures in the bathroom.

Forty-eight hours of hiding out with Erik had been more than enough to start healing my skinned knees and the chicken-track cuts on my arms and to soothe my jangled nerves. The fact was, I was going stir-crazy.

At my insistence, Erik split his time between me and his

daughter. This left me with long hours cooped up in the lodge because when I ventured out, the wet snow immediately soaked into my thin leather running shoes, and the cold air sank icy claws into my lungs.

No, thanks.

Mostly, I holed up in the room and watched CNN. The mass killings at the mall quickly became old news, but now and then I'd catch a snippet. The police back in Orange County might still be noncommittal about who had killed the shooter—now identified as George Howard Mendel, an unemployed aerospace worker. But the media had declared the security guard, Edward Earl Daley, a hero who had died taking down a madman.

Countering this were brief clips of George Mendel's grieving, bewildered mother and his brother Albert, who looked enough like George to be a twin. Albert's grief was redirected to anger over the fact that his brother had been shot down like a dog.

Never mind. The media gave these two short shrift in their coverage because if there was ever a man cut out to be a hero, it was Ed Daley. During twenty years with the Orange County Sheriff's Department, he'd never used his gun in the line of duty. He'd been married to the same woman for twenty-three years, had two sons, one still in college. He was a Little League coach and volunteered at a local animal shelter, cleaning cages and walking lonely, abandoned dogs.

Well, as far as I was concerned, Ed deserved his hero status. He'd done his best to kill Mendel; I'd just finished the job. When I saw his family's grief tempered by pride and heard about the money pouring into an Ed Daley Memorial Fund, I told myself that I really had done the right thing back there in the mall, after all.

I just hoped the cops wouldn't be waiting to ask some pointed questions when I got home.

Now, looking down from 47,000 feet, way above the commercial jets, I had no idea where we were, just someplace over that great, sprawling heartland of the country. I sat in a big recliner, my face toward the window, pretending to nap and listening to Erik and Nicki talk. Their conversation was peppered with references to people I didn't know and places I'd never been, as alien as the vast frozen landscape below.

"I think the New Year's Eve party is going to be great this year," Nicki was saying, so wistfully I suspected she knew my sleeping act was a sham.

"I'm sorry you'll miss it," Erik said. "I told you, you didn't have to come home with us."

"Oh, that's okay. It wouldn't be the same without you, Dad. I just wished we could've talked Delilah into staying. She was welcome to wear some of my stuff if that was the problem—I mean, if she could fit into any of it. Or she could have just gone casual. That seems more her style."

Oh yeah, she knew I was awake, all right.

I wished now that I'd sneaked out while they were on the ski slopes, going back the way I'd come. But luxury is a seductive thing, and a trip in a private jet beats three plane changes and a layover in Dallas, hands down.

Of course, as soon as I said I was going home, Erik, still worried about me, insisted on coming along. And Nicki wasn't going to be left behind. So here we were—and I for one was definitely not having fun yet.

During the year that Erik and I had been together, I had ducked all events involving his close friends and family. Once, last summer when Nicole was in town, I'd volunteered to go to Bakersfield on a job for a PI friend of mine. If you'd ever been in Bakersfield in August, you'd appreciate the lengths I'd go to to avoid his daughter and further entanglements.

"You want him in your bed but not in your life," my friend Rita Braddock said once. "Is that really fair?"

I guess it wasn't, but I'd never been sure I could handle much more than the bed part, and now I thought I was right.

Determined not to let Nicki get to me, I made an effort to block out their conversation. Pretty soon I really was drifting off, their voices a distant drone. It was a harsh shift in Nicki's tone that snapped me suddenly awake.

"But I don't *want* to get to know her better, Dad," she was saying, and there wasn't a doubt in my mind who she was talking about. "Why should I? I mean, you're not going to *marry* her or anything—God, Dad, you're not, are you?"

I froze, waiting for the answer to that one myself, but just then the plane lurched and the pilot came on to announce we'd hit some turbulence and had to fasten our seat belts. No way to play possum with Erik nudging me to make sure I was properly belted in.

Oh, yeah, I thought as I looked past Erik and saw Nicki's angry indignation. We'd run into turbulence all right, and it would still be going on long after we landed.

SINCE I HAD LEFT my van at the airport, I could skip the ride in Erik's limo. I collected a good-bye kiss, made vague promises to call, and beat a hasty retreat. On the way home I really tried not to think about it, but Nicki's words keep ringing in my ears.

"You're not going to marry her or anything?"

Uh uh, no way, I told myself.

I was not ready to think about marriage again and certainly not to Erik. He probably wasn't considering matrimony either. It was just Nicki, jumping to conclusions.

There were none of Orange County's finest waiting at my apartment and nothing on my answering machine except concerned messages from friends—the grapevine working overtime.

Headlines shrieked from the newspapers accumulated outside my door. The rest of the nation and the world had been quiet, so in Orange County the mall massacre was front-page news all week. I scanned the stories quickly. Lots of unanswered questions, but none of the speculation included a mention of me.

I stacked the newspapers in the recycling bin, dumped my dirty clothes, took a quick shower, and changed into jeans and a light cotton long-sleeved sweater. At three-thirty in the afternoon, the temperature was starting to slide down to about sixty degrees, cool for here, downright balmy compared to where I'd been.

I'd taken off without much thought for my business. I had a few cases pending but nothing urgent. With Danny in the Baja, the office had been closed. I knew I ought to go over and put in a few hours. If nothing else, it would take my mind off Erik and his daughter's unanswered question.

When I arrived, Harry Polk was out in back of the office building, cleaning graffiti off a block wall. "Damn kids," he muttered as he limped over to say hello.

He said nothing about the episode at the mall, which meant he must not have heard that I was there with Isabel. Thank God for that much.

Harry's the building janitor, a scrawny little man with thin gray hair, rounded shoulders, and a slight potbelly, who takes far too much interest in my business. He's developed a touch of arthritis in his hands and his hip that bothers him when the weather cools off. If he lived in Vermont, he'd probably be using a walker.

"I know who done this, too." Harry scowled, gesturing to the wall. "Seen 'em hangin' around. Know it's them, but cops say I got to catch 'em in the act. Almost did catch one of 'em. He was in the building. Right outside your office, Miz West. Little kid. Nine or ten years old. Tried to grab him, but he got away."

"Well, if it happens again, just call the cops," I said. "Or me if I'm here. He might be carrying more than a spray can."

Harry could be a pain in the neck, but I didn't want him hurt.

Upstairs, I sorted the mail, tossing the junk and stacking the rest—all bills, I suspected—while I listened to phone messages and turned on the computer to answer my e-mail. I like e-mail. It's a California kind of thing—short, quick, and casual.

At least there were no emergencies while I was away. I would be finished quickly and out of here. I could call Erik and—no, I would not call Erik. I'd call Rita instead. She'd left several anxious messages, both here and at home.

I was reaching for the phone when I heard loud voices in the hall, two people, one of them Harry, the other very young, male, and indignant.

I hurried through the outer office and went out the door, visions of switchblades dancing in my head. But I knew I could relax because I recognized the boy who squirmed in Harry's firm grip.

I said, "It's okay, Harry. Let him go. I don't think he's one of your vandals."

"You know this kid?" Harry asked.

"Of course she does," Brian Hall said. He yanked his arm free as soon as Harry loosened his hold.

"Well, if he gives you any trouble, just holler." Harry scowled at the boy. "I'm gonna be in yellin' distance."

"Thanks, Harry."

I held open the door for Brian, then led the way into my office.

Brian flopped down in one of the chairs I have for clients. He'd gotten a haircut, one of those jobs that looked like somebody put a bowl over his head, cut his brown hair at ear level, then shaved his head below that line.

He said, "Man, what's that old dude's problem? I came here the other day and he chased me out."

"Harry takes good care of things around here," I said. "He doesn't like graffiti. He thought you were with some kids who messed up the wall outside."

"Well, I wasn't. I just came to see you."

I kind of half sat, half leaned on the edge of my desk and looked down at him.

"Does your mom know you're here?"

He shrugged. "They closed the mall for a few days, but it's open again. I don't much like going there. It's kinda creepy. So Larry took me to the movies. I was supposed to see a coupla shows, but I got bored. I took the bus down here."

In other words, his mother had no idea where he was.

"Are you okay?" I asked.

"Yeah, I'm cool. Had some bad dreams, that's all."

"Me, too," I said. "Do you want to talk about it?"

He shook his head. Hesitated. Taking his time about telling me why he was here.

Finally, he said, "Private detectives look for people and stuff, don't they?"

"That's one of the things we do." I eased up and went around to sit behind my desk.

"Larry says you're all rip-off artists."

"He does, huh?"

"Yeah. I guess you charge a lot—to look for people, I mean."

"Sometimes. It depends. Who is it you want me to look for, Brian?"

"My dad," he said, suddenly looking small, sad, and very young. "He lives in Texas now, and he drives a truck, so I only see him once in a while. But he didn't send Mom a check for two months now, and he missed Christmas. Mom says he's just got a new girlfriend and forgot about us. But he always comes for Christmas, always."

Brian ducked his head, fighting for control, and when he looked up his eyes had a wet shine. He said, "I've got twenty-five dollars saved up for RollerBlades. And maybe I can do some stuff for the neighbors to make money."

Well, so I'm a sucker for a kid's pleading eyes; we already know that. Anyway, what could it hurt to make a few phone calls?

"Tell you what," I said. "Give me ten dollars for a retainer. We'll settle up the rest later."

"You mean you'll do it?" he asked.

"Yes, but I want you to tell your mom," I said.

"Do I have to?"

"Afraid so. I'm going to need your dad's Social Security number, his driver's license number, any credit cards she knows about—things like that."

He agreed reluctantly, then took money from his pocket and counted out ten grubby one-dollar bills. I wrote him a receipt.

"Can I call you tomorrow?" he asked.

New Year's Eve, but I really wasn't planning anything If Erik was, Nicki was sure to be involved. Did I want to be with him that badly?

Don't answer that, I told myself.

To Brian I said, "Why don't you give me some time? I won't be able to do much about finding your dad until after New Year's. And don't expect instant results, Brian. This could take awhile."

He said he'd talk to his mother and call me, then he went off to catch the bus back to the movie theater.

After he'd gone, I sat, fingering the ten one-dollar bills, getting a sudden chill because I was reminded of holding Isabel Sanchez's money and all that had followed. I shook off the feeling, because what was the chance of something really bad like the thing at the mall happening again?

At that point, of course, I had no idea that all I'd had was the curtain raiser, and the main event was yet to come.

FOUR

I TRACKED RITA DOWN at Ultimate Fitness in Aliso Viejo, a second health spa she and Farley Truitt had opened recently in south county.

"Where were you?" she demanded. "We were all worried sick."

I've come to the conclusion that my friends operate a telephone tree. Details about my life get passed around at speeds that rival those on the Internet. Naturally, Rita would know about the incident at the mall. Well, she wouldn't know *everything,* just what Jorge and Danny knew.

I said, "I decided to get away for a few days."

"You went to Vermont."

"Geez," I muttered.

"What?"

"I said *yes,* I went to Vermont."

"I'm glad you did," she said. "Lot nicer than sitting around brooding by yourself."

"Oh yeah, it was nice, all right."

"I see. That good, huh?"

"I'd really rather not discuss it."

"Well, how about we not discuss it over dinner? If you can stand the commute traffic, that is. I'm stuck down here."

When Jack and I first opened West and West Investigations, we used Rita Braddock's answering service. That business association turned to friendship after Jack's death. Since then, Rita's seen me through the grief of widowhood, the near collapse of the agency, the ups and downs of my relationship with Erik.

We have lots of history, so I know she's incapable of minding her own business. Still, I suppose I was desperate to see a friendly face.

"Okay," I said. "Where should I meet you?"

WONDERING IF RITA was already disseminating the news about my trip back east, I joined the thousands of cars hurtling south on I-5 in the early winter darkness.

Most of the construction is complete on the Santa Ana Freeway from the junction with the 57—known locally as the Orange Crush—down through Irvine. The speed limit is up to sixty-five, which means traffic flies along at seventy-five plus when possible—only to come to a screeching halt in Irvine when the Santa Ana merges with the San Diego Freeway at the infamous El Toro Y.

Here ten lanes of cars funnel down to four, the bottleneck further complicated by a massive restructuring of the interchange. About the time the construction is complete, rumor has it that the whole road will have to be torn down and moved over so the runways at El Toro can be lengthened to accommodate commercial jets.

A new toll road skirts the junction to the west. Promising relief, it has only piled up cars in Laguna Canyon and cut a deep wound in the heart of the coastal mountain greenbelt.

By the time I got to Antonucci's in Mission Viejo, Rita was already working on a bottle of Chianti. She poured a glass for me as soon as she saw me coming in the front door, handed it to me silently as I sank into a chair across the table from her, and waited while I drank a few sips to settle my frazzled nerves.

This was my first visit to the restaurant, which was

tucked into a strip mall a couple of traffic lights off the freeway. The place was small and homey and, Rita had assured me, offered great food and the best of friendly service. If the wonderful smells of tomatoes, garlic, and Italian spices were any indication, dinner should live up to her promises.

It did.

Her assurances about noninterference were, of course, not nearly so reliable.

She gave me until the homemade pasta arrived—penne alla bettola for her, mostacciolli calalora for me—before she asked, "So why aren't you with Erik? Why did you bail out and head for home?"

Well, at least she'd homed in on Erik and not the shooting at the mall.

"I didn't bail out," I said. "We flew back together."

"So what happened?"

"Nothing much. Mostly it snowed. That's what it does in Vermont."

"Come on, kiddo. I know something went wrong."

What's the line? Nibbled to death by ducks?

"I met Nicki Lundstrom who despises me and she came back with us and I'm afraid Erik's going to propose and if he does and if I was insane enough to say yes—which I'm not—but if I did, it means that I'd be that bitchy little snob's stepmother."

Her eyes lit up. "You're getting married?"

"Jesus," I said and urgently signaled the waitress for another bottle of wine.

PLEADING NONEXISTENT WORK to catch up on, I bolted my pasta and left Rita to go find a Starbucks and try to sober up from the Chianti. Then, not trusting my reflexes, I drove home using surface streets rather than attempt to keep up with the breakneck speeds of the freeway.

I have a timer that turns a lamp on at dusk, so the strip of light under my apartment door didn't set off any alarms in my head. I was inside, closing the door, before I realized there were *two* lamps on.

Freezing in the act of turning the deadbolt, I cursed myself for the fact that both my guns were in a drawer in the bedroom where another light blazed, the weapons left there when I took off on my impulsive cross-country trek and not returned to car or purse.

I was unlocking the bolt, ready to beat a hasty retreat, when I realized that lights were also on in the kitchen, and at that moment a smell of brewing coffee wafted out.

"Delilah?" Erik came through the arched doorway separating the two rooms. "Great timing. I just started the decaf, and I brought raspberry tarts."

Jet lag and fatigue usually raise havoc with a person's looks. On Erik these things just add a note of vulnerable appeal: crinkly little lines around the blue eyes, a weary sag of the shoulders that make you want to hover.

Just then, however, I was thinking about what might've happened if one of my guns had been handy, that horrifying thought quickly followed by one almost as unnerving.

"Erik, what are you doing here? Is Nicki with you?"

I darted a glance at the bedroom, where I'd left a mound of dirty clothes when I dumped my suitcase on the floor, then to the bathroom that was equally messy.

"She went to a party up in L.A. with some friends." He came into the living room and stood in front of me, looking a little hurt. "You don't seem very happy to see me."

"Sorry, I just wished you'd called."

"I did."

He tilted his head toward the answering machine, where a green light blinked. Sitting next to it was my cellular phone, forgotten along with the guns.

"You gave me a key," he said. "I thought that meant I could use it."

"It does. It's just—"

"What?" He reached out to brush the side of my face with the backs of his fingers. "I'd be happy to fight with you, darling, if I knew what we were arguing about."

I wrapped my arms around him and laid my head on his chest. "I don't want to fight."

"Good." He hugged me tightly. "Talking's better."

Mellowed on wine and wired on coffee, I didn't trust myself to hold a conversation, especially if we got into questions and answers.

"I don't want to talk either," I said, lifting my mouth for a kiss.

ERIK HAD ASKED ME only once to move in with him. When I said no, he hadn't pushed. He'd just said the offer was always open.

His huge mission-style house sits in beautiful isolation on a hill overlooking the ocean, about halfway between Laguna Beach and Corona del Mar. It comes with impeccable decor and a staff to attend to your every whim. So what the hell was I doing in my cheesy little one-bedroom apartment in a neighborhood where the sound of gunfire is not uncommon?

Well, to tell the truth, I don't much like staying at Erik's place overnight. All that space and luxury make me uneasy. I count the empty rooms and think of families jammed into tiny stucco homes in the barrio. At night from the wide windows I see the coastal hills becoming ever more encrusted with lights and think about how many acres of wild land are daily lost to the bulldozers operated by developers like Erik Lundstrom.

Which all goes to show how preposterous the idea of marriage is.

I hadn't explained any of these feelings to Erik, of course. Still, smart as he is, he has to know. Men like Erik who operate from power and money just assume that eventually they will get what they want, if for no other reason than their staying power. So he puts up with my excuses and mostly he comes here, and usually he stays over, but not this time.

At midnight Erik was getting dressed to go home, sitting beside me on the bed, putting on his shirt. He hadn't even left yet and already I felt lonely.

"When Nicki's three thousand miles away, I don't worry about her," he had said by way of explanation and apology. "But as soon as she's with me, I can't rest until I know she's home and safe in her bed."

After that I'd turned down offers for breakfast, lunch, and dinner. Now we were down to the New Year's Eve party.

"I'm not giving you an option," he said. "As long as we're in the same state, we're going to be together. I'll pick you up at eight-thirty." He stopped buttoning his shirt to study me with a worried look. "I don't like leaving you here alone. I wish you'd change your mind and come home with me. Even if you won't admit it, I know you're still upset about what happened at the mall."

I had slipped into a flannel nightshirt when he got out of bed, and now I shivered, hugged it around me, and said, "I'm fine, Erik, just too tired to get dressed and go out. Maybe you don't suffer from jet lag, but I do."

He sighed. "You're not fine, Delilah. If you won't talk

to me about what happened, then please, go back and see that therapist you went to last year.''

A year ago I had shot a man up near Lake Arrowhead, defending myself and a young girl I'd been hired to find. At Erik's insistence I'd gone for a few therapy sessions. I suppose they helped. Mainly I found I just didn't like somebody poking around in my head. And when the therapist began prying into the personal stuff, I vamoosed.

''I'll think about it,'' I said.

Erik shook his head and leaned down to kiss me. ''Liar.''

''Always was,'' I said lightly. ''Go on home, Erik. Worry about your daughter. She needs it more than I do.''

''I doubt that,'' he said.

Nevertheless, he left me.

I spent my first night alone since the shooting, curled up in a knot with all the lights on. It was almost dawn before I went to sleep.

FIVE

IT WAS TEN O'CLOCK the next morning by the time I got to the office. There was one message on my machine, not from Brian Hall, but from his mother, Gloria.

After identifying herself she said, "This stuff with Brian and his dad—it's just too bizarre. We need to talk about it. Can we get together on the second? Like ten o'clock?"

She added that I couldn't reach her at work, to leave a message on the answering machine at home. "Oh, and listen, thanks for taking care of Brian that day at the mall."

I called, leaving a message to confirm the date and time, wondering if Brian was at the mall again and what he did, day after day, to pass the time there. I didn't much like the images that came to mind.

The mail hadn't come yet. Nothing on e-mail. I flipped through the unpaid bill file—just to make sure I was good and depressed—and decided to hell with it. Tomorrow was another day—actually, another year.

Then the door in the outer office opened and closed. Danny sang out, "Don't shoot. It's only me."

"Danny? What are you doing here?"

"Just thought I'd check in."

Oh, sure.

He sailed into my office looking even leaner after the bike trip, his sleek black hair newly trimmed and very short. All guileless smiles and crackling energy, he sought reassurances that I'd bounced back from the mall incident and gave me a report on the trek to the Baja and his plans for the holiday evening. Meanwhile he kept sneaking glances at my hands.

I finally held up the left one and wiggled my ring finger. "Look, no diamond. Pass it on."

He grinned. "Sorry. PI in training."

I worry about Danny. He's going for a double major in business and computer science at the University of California in Irvine, but he took fewer classes last semester so he could put in more hours here. And one day he asked casually if I'd ever considered making the agency, once again, into a partnership.

Now I scowled back at him. "You're *not* a private eye. You're a brilliant student who's going to make Bill Gates look like a struggling know-nothing. Now go home. Study."

"Okay, I'm outta here." But at the door he paused. "Just one question from my mom. She's dying to know. What are you wearing to the Yacht Club?"

SOMETIMES I THINK everybody in the world except me has a little black dress in their closet that fits perfectly and makes them look like a million bucks. All of my stuff might as well have a sign reading RED TAG SPECIAL.

Feeling reckless and desperate, not to mention pressured by the expectations of Mrs. Thu and the others, I steeled myself against the bad vibes now and forever associated with shopping malls and blew two hundred dollars at Nordstrom's on something short and clingy with long sleeves to cover up my scabs. And yes, on sale and black with a few silver threads woven in.

Mistake.

Erik's eyes registered approval when he picked me up, but then we all know love is blind. Nicki, who had waited in the limo, didn't see what I was wearing under my old

London Fog until we arrived at the party. As soon as I took off my coat and she sized up my outfit, her disdainful smile told me the dress was meant for somebody twenty pounds skinnier and twenty years younger.

This pretty much set the tone for the evening. Nicki, stunning in a slim, shiny blue tube of a dress with a high halter neck, was skillful at corralling Erik for herself. "Daddy, look who's here," she'd cry, and sweep him away to talk to old friends or parents of friends. These conversations caused them to huddle closely to hear each other over the music of the near-famous rock group who kept upping the volume.

As a result I did a lot of standing around, feeling as though I was invisible. This was fine with me because it helped me escape the reporter and the cameraman who worked the glittering crowd of beautiful people in their tuxedos, designer gowns, and tasteful jewelry that cost more than the average car.

Dinner had been a Lean Cuisine from the freezer, so whenever possible I hung out near the buffet table with its sumptuous spread. In addition to mounds of appetizers, there were great piles of shrimp, lobster, and calamari and an enormous platter of sushi. I prefer my fish cooked, thank you, and liver is still liver even when it's called pâté. So mostly I stuck to the shrimp and the fruits and vegetables I knew names for, and pretty much had the spread to myself.

This bunch didn't eat, they grazed, a nibble here, a nibble there. No, mostly what they did was drink from an endless supply of champagne poured by the waiters and from the three fully stocked bars. And as the night progressed, they got just as drunk and stupid as if they were guzzling Thunderbird while wearing old T-shirts and ratty jeans.

I knew I'd probably omit that last bit from the report that would be expected by my friends. My cheering section has cast me as Cinderella. They don't want to know that the slipper not only doesn't fit, the damn thing's made out of plastic.

Eventually, head pounding from the champagne and the loud music, I escaped out on the deck that was built over the water, wishing I was at the Sanchez house drinking Dos Equis and eating Consuelo's tamales, everybody watching the delayed celebration in New York's Times Square and counting down the seconds in Spanish: *nueve, ocho, siete…*

Somewhere across the bay toward Balboa Island a sky-rocket went up and burst into silver spangles. More rockets flowered in red and gold, bringing a crowd of people spilling out, oooing and ahing.

I had no idea what time it was, but it had to be approaching midnight. Inside a drumroll started, then a count-down began, but not in Spanish, of course. There was now a wall of people between me and the big glass doors, and Erik was nowhere in sight.

I retreated back against the railed porch into a cold, raw wind that skirled along the outer edges. Below, black water growled at the deck supports, and I was freezing in my ridiculous, skimpy dress, alone as midnight arrived with horns and whistles, cries of best wishes, hugs and kisses, a flurry of balloons filling the ballroom and escaping outside to float away in the darkness.

Seconds later Erik plowed through the crowd. I couldn't hear what he was saying because everybody was yelling and the band had started a hard-rock version of Auld Lang Syne. I saw the concern on his face, however. He put an arm around me and quickly pushed a path back inside where Nicki was waiting.

From her malicious little smirk I knew that Erik had been with her on the stroke of midnight, that she had made sure of it. I also knew I was getting damn tired of this stupid game.

"Mr. Lundstrom," somebody cried, and before I could duck away a camera flash strobed, recording our happy little group.

Enough.

Erik didn't argue when I said I was going home—except with Nicki, who was determined to stick by her father's side.

"Let's make it easy," I said. "I'll get a cab."

"No, you won't," Erik said. "You're staying here, Nicki. Enjoy the party. I'll be back after I take Delilah home."

His authoritative, I'm-the-dad tone brooked no argument. I might have felt a tad smug except for the glint in Miss Nicki's eye that promised retribution.

Taken by surprise, Victor, the chauffeur, didn't have time to warm up the limousine. The inside was cold and cavernous.

I confess Erik and I usually break the seat belt law. Limos are made for snuggling, among other things. Tonight I sat next to the window and belted in; Erik sat on his side, and there was a mile of plush leather between us.

I knew I probably owed him an apology. Not his fault if his daughter was a little brat—well, yes, it probably was, come to think of it. And damn it, I'd been the one left standing out in the cold.

"I'm sorry you had a lousy time," he said, "and I'm sorry about Nicki. She's being such a pain in the ass right now, you'd never know how sweet she can be."

"Fooled me all right," I said.

"If you could spend some time with her—I don't know.

Take her shopping, maybe. Go up to Rodeo Drive. She'd like that.''

Oh, yeah, I could see it now. Me and Nicki dropping a few thousand bucks at Gucci's for a handbag or a pair of shoes.

"You've got to be kidding," I said. "Anyway, I don't have time. I have a case to work on."

"Well, if you're too busy," he said, his voice full of quiet disappointment.

Bloody hell.

"I suppose we could have lunch—if she wants to."

That seemed safe enough to offer. I couldn't imagine Nicki voluntarily spending five minutes with me.

"But one thing," I went on. "I don't like competing with her, Erik. She deserves to have time with you. So give it to her and back off on this togetherness bit. And stop hovering. I'm okay. Really."

"Yeah, sure," he said. "You're a tough lady."

"You bet," I said, wishing I felt tough instead of just tired, cold, and guilty as hell for being such a snot when he was being so nice. Wondering what he'd think of me if he knew I'd not only killed somebody a few days ago, but lied through my teeth about it.

I hadn't been paying attention, but now the limo pulled to a stop right outside my apartment house door. So soon, and all that distance still between us. Victor waited for a signal, being discreet. Probably thought we were making out back here.

Little did he know.

"I'll come up," Erik said.

"No, go back to the party." I fumbled with the seat belt. "I'll call you."

He caught my arm just as I reached for the door, unlatching his own seat belt and sliding over. "A little late, but Happy New Year, darling."

His kiss left me dizzy and breathless. What could I do? I dropped all notion of anger and kissed him back. If he'd asked to come up again, I'd've caved in this time, no question.

"My daughter has good instincts," he murmured. "She knows I'm crazy about you."

"Erik—"

"Shh, not now. Later, after Nicki goes back to school, we'll have lots to talk about."

He kissed me again and then Victor was there, opening the door.

Oh, my God, I thought as the limo purred away.

We'll have lots to talk about.

My panic grew as I went upstairs, took a hot shower, put on some flannel pajamas.

I could stall, say I wasn't ready, which was certainly true. But Erik was patient. Relentless. Jack had been that way, too. What the hell was the matter with these men? Didn't they know they were supposed to avoid commitment like normal males?

In bed, I reminded myself I'd had major doubts about marrying Jack, leaving the LAPD, and starting the agency in Orange County.

Jack...

Thinking about our love, our life together, had gotten me through a lot of long nights. But now for the first time I couldn't remember the smell of his skin, the way his hands felt on my body, the sound of his voice. The memories were nearly gone, fading like old pictures kept too long in the light.

SIX

I GOT UP LATE and moped around the apartment, nursing a headache that was caused by the champagne and another bad night. When the phone rang, I let the machine pick it up. It was Rita, checking in for the party report. The others couldn't be far behind.

Sure enough, within five minutes the phone rang again. I swore loudly, snatched it up, and snarled hello.

"Delilah?"

The male voice was unpleasantly familiar.

"Gary," I said.

Gary Hofer was an investigator for the Orange County Sheriff's Special Assignments Unit. Never my favorite person, especially now.

Somebody must have identified me as being at Main Street on the twenty-sixth. Security camera? Media coverage? Whatever. When Gary wasn't playing department politics, he was shrewd enough to put two and two together and come up with my number. Only why was he involved? Wasn't the mall in Santa Ana's jurisdiction?

While my poor hungover brain was wrestling with this, Gary was saying, "Hey, great picture. Sunni and I hated to miss the Yacht Club, but with her being on the Getty board, we had to come up here to Beverly Hills. Gave us an excuse to stay over, which is nice, but still—"

"What picture?"

"The *L.A. Times.* You didn't see it yet?"

I remembered the strobe of camera flash, capturing Erik, Nicki, and me just before I made my escape. My irritation was mixed with relief because of course Gary wasn't calling to haul me in to question me about the shooting. Gary had married into Orange County's elite and had turned to social climbing with relish and determination. When he found out I was connected to Erik, suddenly he'd become one of my dear old pals—and never mind that our dislike had always been mutual.

"No, I did not see the picture," I said.

"Glad I called, then," Gary said. "Hey, don't forget we were going to get together for dinner with you guys one of these days soon."

"Oh, I didn't forget."

"Good. Delilah? You have to settle a bet between Sunni and me. I say you got a diamond for Christmas. Sunni says Erik will wait for Valentine's Day."

"Well, you both lose," I said. "Gotta go. I have another call."

I didn't, but I would soon. I'd bet Rita was already passing the word.

THERE ARE PSYCHOLOGISTS who claim that they can tell a lot from photographs. Well, you didn't have to be a professional to analyze this one.

In the society column photo Erik and Nicki were closer to the camera, gorgeous and relaxed the instant a lens pointed their way with no sign that we were in the middle of an argument. I was between them, ever so slightly out of focus, looking surly and ill at ease.

I wondered why anybody would believe the reporter's hints that Orange County's most eligible bachelor might be headed to the altar with a certain private eye. However, only Rita noticed all had not been well.

On the phone she said, "You picked a fight last night."

"I did not."

"Erik's daughter's very important to him, Delilah. Don't make a mistake and alienate her completely."

"I already made a mistake. I got mixed up with Erik in the first place."

"Uh-huh," she said. "Just one thing. When you get engaged, I'd better be the first one you tell."

I'VE GIVEN UP on New Year's resolutions, but I made one in the van on the way to the Sanchezes for lunch. I vowed I would get my life firmly back in control. That included accepting the decision I'd made at the Main Street Mall— right or wrong—and doing the smart thing by breaking off with Erik now, before it got any harder.

Isabel seemed subdued during the meal. Afterward she and I went to sit in an old glider on the patio while the others watched the Rose Bowl game on TV. Nourished by winter rains, the grass in the backyard was a vivid green, and sweet peas climbed the fence, a tumble of red and pink and purple blooms. New Year's Day is traditionally gorgeous in Southern California. I think the Chamber of Commerce has had it written into law.

"Still having bad dreams?" I asked.

Isabel nodded.

"Me, too," I said.

She pressed against me with a shiver, saying, "Don't tell Mama, she'll just worry," like I could anyway with my limited Spanish, and we sat silently for a moment, both seeing ugly things overlaid on the sunny yard.

"I wonder if he's all right," Isabel said.

I knew who she meant. I said, "Brian seems okay."

"You saw him?"

"He came to my office. He didn't hear from his dad at Christmas and he's worried."

"Are you going to look for him?"

"I think so."

"Good, I'm glad, because everybody needs their dad, Delilah."

"You're right about that," I said, suddenly missing my own father, dead all these years, and for the first time feeling a little sympathy for Nicki, who was so scared of losing even a little part of hers.

Later, back at my apartment, I ignored the blinking light on the answering machine, figuring the call had to be from Erik, and went to bed early. The clock said I'd only been asleep for an hour when I bolted up, awakened by a vivid nightmare. In it I skimmed across that glassy-tiled floor at the mall on my belly with broken glass digging into my arms, a long, endless, desperate slide with the revolver always out of reach.

I'd left the light on in the bathroom again. Easy to see the phone to punch out the number that would ring beside Erik's bed.

"I was hoping it was you," he said. "You must have stayed late at the Sanchezes."

"What? Oh, yeah," I lied, "just getting in."

"I missed you," he said. "How's Isabel?"

"Better, I think."

"That's good. Darling, I hope you don't mind but I told Nicki you'd call her about lunch. Okay?"

"Sure," I said. "Fine."

"Delilah? What is it?"

"Nothing."

"Don't tell me that. Listen, I'm coming over."

"No, you don't have to—"

"I'm leaving. I'm on my way."

"Hurry," I said.

So much for New Year's resolutions.

DANNY WAS ALREADY at the office when I arrived, and he had actually fielded calls from a couple of real live clients. These would involve two background checks, one on a prospective nanny, the other an in-depth look at a man a female client had met over the holidays who seemed too good to be true. In my pre-Erik experience, I would've said her feelings about the guy were probably right on. Now, well, I'd have to concede there may be a few Prince Charmings around.

It's getting damned scary how much information can be obtained via computer these days. Equally stupid not to take advantage of what's out there, especially when you have a computer whiz on hand. While Danny got busy, Brian Hall showed up with his mother—and with the boy-friend, Larry Vogel.

Larry had dressed for the occasion, adding a sports jacket and a tie to casual pants and a button-down shirt, everything in varying muddy shades of brown. His graying mousy hair was neatly combed into a ponytail. A small gold hoop shone in one ear.

He took charge, saying hello and nice to see you, intro-ducing Gloria, and insisting on carrying an extra chair into my office.

When Brian tried to take a place on the other side of his mother, Larry said, "Here, Bry," put a hand on the boy's shoulder, and steered him into the position between the two adults.

Brian endured the touch with his face set in a stoic, mutinous look and fastened his gaze on the middle of my desk.

I went around to take a seat across from them, using the moment to study Gloria Hall.

With leisure and uncomplicated love Gloria might have been a beautiful woman. Instead, she had the tense, hunkered-down look of somebody whose life is constantly imploding around her. Wary light blue eyes watched from a taut face. Shoulder-length platinum blond hair was the wrong shade for the fine, pale skin. So was the dark mauve blouse and midthigh skirt.

While I wondered if she realized how much her son despised Larry and speculated on what Danny would turn up in cyberspace if he checked out Mr. Vogel, Gloria consulted her watch and gave Larry a worried frown.

"Don't worry, Glo," he said. "We'll make sure you get out on time. Gloria's got to go on to work," he explained. "She can't stay long. So, first off, we want to say how much we appreciate the way you took care of Bry the other day, don't we, Glo?"

She nodded. "I just don't know how I can ever thank you—"

"I already did, hon," Larry said, his tone the one you'd use for a slightly retarded child.

"No problem," I said. "I'm just glad I was there."

"Well," Larry said, "you sure made a big impression on the kid."

Larry's eyes had been busy doing their own inventory of me and my crowded surroundings and clearly he did not share Brian's opinion. What was it he'd told Brian? Private detectives were all rip-off artists.

"He even thinks you mighta taken out that guy at the mall. The shooter, I mean." Larry gave me a grin that was equal parts derision and disbelief beneath the pale mustache.

"*She* thought Delilah did it," Brian said with some sullen heat. "That's what the *girl* said, Isabel. If you'd *listen*—"

"Brian, don't be mouthy," Gloria said. "And mind your manners. It's *Miss* West."

"Oh, first names are fine," I said, adding for Larry's benefit, "Kids have a great imagination."

"Just what I was thinking," Larry said. "Now about this deal with Brian's dad. Tell you the truth, it kinda blew our minds when we heard Brian came to you about it. We know old Travis, don't we, Glo? Wasn't exactly a surprise him not showing up for Christmas."

"Excuse me," I said. "Gloria, Brian tells me his father usually gets in touch over the holidays, at least a phone call. Is that true?"

"Well, most of the time, in the past."

"No, Mom, he *always* does," Brian burst out. "You *know* that. And he sends us money. He's not a deadbeat dad."

"Hey, Bry, chill."

Larry dropped a hand on Brian's neck. The long, bony fingers just lay there on the boy's shaved nape, but the way Brian flinched, I'd bet they often dug in for a cruel pinch. When he saw me taking note, Larry removed his hand, turning it into a lift so he could look at his watch.

"Honey, you better scoot," he said to Gloria.

"I don't know," Gloria said as Brian gave her an imploring look. "Maybe I could call—"

"No, babe, they were already pissed when you said you'd be late. Go on. I can handle things here."

"Well, okay." She got up, gave Brian a little good-bye pat on the shoulder, and edged around the chairs. "Sorry, Miss West. Thanks again. Larry, you'll call me?"

"Sure," he said, getting up and going to the door with her for a kiss, some last-minutes words I couldn't hear, and a folded piece of paper she removed from her purse.

Brian just sat, his lips compressed into a tight line, staring fiercely at that midpoint of my desk.

Larry came back and sat down, running those thin fingers along the crease in the folded piece of paper. "About Travis, he's not a bad guy, Delilah, but he's not exactly Mr. Responsibility, you know what I'm saying? We just had no idea Brian was so upset about his pop."

"Did Gloria try to contact Travis?"

He nodded. "Back in early November when the check didn't come."

"Brian tells me his dad's on the road a lot."

"Still a damn crummy thing to do, if you ask me," Larry said, "especially right before Christmas."

If the neglect was deliberate, much as I hated the thought I'd have to agree with Larry. To Brian I said, "Do you know if your dad carries your phone number in case he was in an accident?"

"Yeah, he does," Brian said. "Dad's got my name on a card in his wallet. And he told me I'd get money from insurance if anything ever happened, like the truck crashed or something, so I don't think he had a regular accident, but somebody could've hit him on the head, thrown him out of the truck. He could be laying someplace, hurt and—"

"Whoa, hoss," Larry said. "Talk about wild imaginations. You ask me, Delilah, I think old Travis is gonna come strolling in any day now all sheepish and loaded down with Christmas presents. But if it's gonna put Brian's mind at ease, well, I guess we ought to let you do some checking."

"Gloria agrees with this?"

"Of course, but this thing you got with Brian, that won't work. I don't know if I can afford your full rates. I mean, I wouldn't mind a discount. But I'm willing to pay for your services."

"I don't want you to pay," Brian said hotly. "It's *my* dad."

In addition, if Larry footed the bill, he'd be my client, not Brian. I could use the money, but I wasn't that desperate.

"That's nice of you, Larry," I said, "but it's not necessary. Brian and I will work it out."

"Hey, I know you run with some rich people and can afford it," Larry said. "But we're not looking for charity."

My office and its location do not exactly shriek success. *Ah, Christ,* I thought, realizing the newspaper must be his source of information. *Has everybody in the world seen that damned picture?*

"It's called pro bono work," I said evenly. "And you're right, I can afford it."

He didn't like it. He was a man who enjoyed calling the shots. He said, "Yeah, okay, have it your way, but Gloria expects to be kept in the loop about what's going on."

"Sure," I said. "I'll be glad to let Gloria know." I held out my hand. "Was that paperwork she gave you for me?"

He passed it over silently, a scant list of information including some addresses, Travis Hall's Social Security number, his last known address in Plano, Texas, and the fact that he drove a blue '89 Mustang but that she didn't know the plate number.

"Excuse us?" I asked politely and waited until he got up and went over to the door to assure Brian I'd get started as soon as I could, and I'd call him with any news.

"Thanks, Delilah." Brian hesitated and then leaned across the desk to whisper. "Please don't tell that asshole anything about my dad."

I said, "You're the boss," and offered my hand for a conspiratorial squeeze.

Glancing up, I caught a fleeting expression of rage and cunning on Larry's face as he watched our exchange. Until then I'd pretty much written him off as a self-centered bozo who enjoyed mind games and got off on verbal abuse and who was probably not shy about using some physical abuse as well.

But I was beginning to think I might have underestimated his malice, that petty tyrants could be dangerous to cross.

SEVEN

NOW THAT THE ROSE PARADE was over, the weather turned sullen and gray. By lunchtime there was a raw chill in the air that reminded me of Vermont and made Harry limp painfully as he came out of the utility room, waving the newspaper photo and bombarding me with questions as I returned from a quick trip to the deli.

Pleading work, I escaped upstairs to find there actually was some more coming in: a few skip traces and another nanny check. If I was going to give away freebies, I had to make some money, so these paying clients took priority over looking for Travis Hall.

After a quick lunch of corned beef on rye, Danny and I got busy. He did find time to pull a credit report on Travis Hall, which yielded even less information than Gloria had given me. Travis's only credit purchase had been the used 1989 Ford Mustang, the balance paid off two years before. The man had no credit cards, no ATM cards—damn little to leave computer tracks. I knew his car had Texas plates, for all the good that did me since I didn't have the number.

On Saturday I kept my nose to the grindstone. In the midst of the paying work, however, I took time to call the last place Gloria knew Travis had stayed, which turned out to be a transient motel in Plano, Texas.

A forwarding address?

"Lady, you got to be kidding," the manager said. "They don't tell me, and I don't ask."

Gloria had listed two of Travis's friends. I got an answering machine at one number, a message advising me the phone had been disconnected at the other.

I hoped the friend, a man named Joe Armstead, would call back and give us some help. Otherwise we would have to start contacting trucking companies. I had the sinking feeling that finding Brian's father might be a bigger job than I had anticipated.

The work was a great avoidance technique, providing a legitimate excuse not to talk to Nicki about lunch. I guess I was hoping Erik would let it drop.

Guess?

Of course that's what I was hoping. But he called me at the office Saturday afternoon with a pointed reminder.

"Sorry," I said. "I warned you I'd be busy."

"Come for dinner tomorrow night," he said. "You two can make plans then."

"Erik—"

"You promised, Delilah."

Hell.

"Seven o'clock," he said. "Should I send the car?"

ON SUNDAY the *Los Angeles Times* ran an editorial about the goodness of quiet, unassuming people like Ed Daley. After all those years and the risks of being a cop, he had unhesitatingly laid down his life to stop a madman and no matter that he was walking a mall beat for little more than minimum wage.

With even the *Times* conferring hero status on the man, and no calls from the police except for the one from Gary Hofer, you'd think my low-level anxiety would subside. Instead it built toward paranoia.

The dreams persisted. I damn near wrecked the van when a patrol car came barreling up behind me on the freeway, although it was not after me, as it turned out.

Once or twice over the weekend I sensed I was being followed, but I never verified my feelings.

Suspecting me of a whopper when I was a kid, my dad used to warn sternly, "Liars punish themselves."

Well, some certainly do.

Driving out to Erik's on Sunday evening, I considered making a clean breast of it, of going to the police with the complete and full story about what happened at the mall. But I know cops—I was one. Right now the incident had a nice, clean closure. Screw that up, and I would be dealing with some pissed-off people. Not to mention the fact that if you cover up one thing, they'd assume you were covering something else.

There was also another possibility. They might not believe me. Worse, I might be accused of trying to steal the glory from a real hero for my own selfish purposes.

Did I really need that kind of aggravation in my life?

Lord knows I already had plenty.

At the turnoff on Coast Highway I hesitated, tempted to just keep driving, go on down to Laguna, find someplace small and noisy for a beer and a burger. Instead, I made the turn and drove up a narrow asphalt road with the first drops of rain spattering the windshield and wind lashing the chaparral.

Things change. That's a law of life. Even the ground we think of as solid is constantly moving and re-forming. Relationships are always in flux. Nothing stays the same.

I know all that, but dammit, I was perfectly happy the way things were, content to have the fever without all the other symptoms of the virus. Why did Erik have to force the issue? Of course, Jack had, and our marriage had been wonderful.

No, no—there was no comparison. Jack and I had things

in common—our work, the way we looked at life. What did Erik and I have besides great sex?

By the time I passed the guard gate and pulled into the huge, brick-paved driveway, the storm had arrived in earnest, sweeping off the Pacific, which lay below, enormous and unseen.

It reminded me of the first time I came here with Charlie Colfax, the first time I met Erik. He'd come out himself with an umbrella to keep me dry. This time it was Vincent who hurried to the van and sheltered me into the house.

In the foyer, shedding my jacket, I could hear voices from what I suppose is the family room simply because it's casually huge, what had to be more than just two people.

Here, three large sofas form a U in front of the fireplace, which contained what looked like a whole oak tree blazing away. I suppose I should have been grateful that there was only one other couple there, sipping drinks with Erik and Nicki, considering the fact that the place is big enough to host most of the people who attended the New Year's Eve party at the Yacht Club.

Curious eyes turned my way, and I immediately felt like a fifth wheel rolling in, a cuckoo in a songbird's nest with my black jeans, an old yellow long-sleeved cotton sweat, and wind-ratted hair. At least I'd exchanged my running shoes for some black flats with only slightly run-over heels.

I froze, taking in the elegant silks and finely tailored wool. I guess Erik sensed I was ready to bolt, because he came quickly to lock a hand around my wrist and drag me over for introductions as Nicki struggled to keep from laughing out loud.

The couple was Hal and Virginia Weyland. The name sounded familiar, which meant they had to be important.

He was in land management—the current euphemism

for development. She made a career of charity boards and shopping. Over drinks I got to hear all about how a new commercial airport at the old El Toro base was going to revitalize the Orange County economy. During dinner I got the scoop on the new Bloomie's at Fashion Island.

The food, as usual, was wonderful: baked salmon, some kind of creamy potato dish, a salad that even Rita would have approved of that tasted like it had been picked out on the wild hillside, chocolate soufflé for dessert.

A bit hard to enjoy the meal, however, knowing I was being subjected to the Weylands' covert scrutiny and evaluation.

I suppose Erik thought we'd all have a nice, relaxing evening with his guests providing a buffer between me and his daughter. For a man who was so smart about most things, how could he be so dumb?

Back in the living room for after-dinner drinks, Virginia finally got around to saying, "Tell us about what you do, Delilah. It sounds very exciting."

I'd made a point of keeping my mouth shut, but by then I was feeling a little put upon and reckless. I gave Virginia a level look over my snifter of brandy. "Mostly I look for deadbeats and dig up dirt on people."

"Boring stuff, and all confidential, of course," Erik said with the kind of smile you give a naughty child who's acting up in company. "Virginia, you and Hal wanted to see my latest Edvard Munch. No, you and Nicki stay and talk, Delilah. We'll be right back."

When we were alone, Nicki asked, "Having fun yet?"

"Loads."

"You could leave."

"You think so? I got ten bucks that says your dad has Vincent stationed by the front door, ready to head me off."

She laughed, the first sign of any honest response I'd

had from her. For just an instant I could see what it would be like if we were friends.

"Course if the two of us made a break for it," I said, "we might stand a chance."

Her expression changed to a not-on-your-life smirk.

"Just a thought," I said sadly.

"This lunch thing…" She made it sound like a trip to the dentist. "Dad said you're busy, and I haven't connected with half my friends yet, so—"

"How about Wednesday? Come by my office. We can grab something quick in the neighborhood."

Erik and the Weylands returned from the art tour then. Mercifully, the couple left shortly afterward. Since our lunch date had screwed up Nicki's social calendar, she went off to make some calls.

That left Erik and me alone on the sofa in front of the fire. We sat in silence for a minute, listening to the rain lashing the window, and then he said, "Tonight was not one of my better ideas, was it?"

"Nope."

"But I got you and Nicki together."

"Yeah, you did that. Now I should go, too. Lots to do tomorrow."

I started to get up, but he wrapped his arms around my waist, holding me back, nuzzling my neck.

"It's pouring. And fair's fair, Delilah. I need a night in my own bed—with you in it."

The last thing I want to be accused of is unfairness.

I stayed.

MY IDEA of cuddling before sleep did not include listening to Erik talk about his daughter. But he seemed determined to soften my opinion of her.

He said, "She was the bravest little kid you ever saw,

you know, the one you see up on top of the swing set like a tightrope walker. I got her a pony when she was four, and she climbed right up, completely fearless. But nights—that was a different story. It started when she was two, screaming and crying and afraid of the dark. We kept trying over the years, but she would not sleep without a light. I think she just got worse after the divorce.''

Hearing the self-blame in his voice, I said, ''Lots of kids' parents get divorced.''

''Doesn't make it any easier for them. My poor baby—she still can't stand being in the dark.''

I thought of that terrified little girl and then my thoughts segued to Brian Hall. Worlds apart on the economic scale, they still had broken homes in common. And fathers they both loved. At least Nicki had hers. I only hoped she appreciated that fact.

IT WAS VERY EARLY and still raining when I slipped away the next morning. I went home for a shower and a change of clothes, and still had time to go by Mom's for breakfast. A couple of new faces among the staff, otherwise nothing ever changes at Mom's Kountry Kooking—which is the way the customers like it. The restaurant specializes in huge portions of plain food, fast service, and bright, clean surroundings. I'd moonlighted here on occasion when times were lean.

Jorge made me pancakes, bacon, and eggs, then took a break to come have coffee while I ate and to troll for the latest gossip about my love life.

I gave him a few tidbits to keep the party line humming, then went to the office, determined not to think about anything except work.

Travis Hall's friend did not return the call. New clients

continued to trickle in, so Danny and I barely made a start on calls to trucking firms.

Tuesday was a repeat of Monday. Then on Wednesday morning Gary Hofer phoned—just to make sure my stress levels stayed nicely elevated.

He said, "Got something that rang a bell, Delilah. Those two guys that bombed your office, was one of them named Sal Thomas Rizzo, aka Turk Rizzo?"

"Yes." I was suddenly overwhelmed with the memory of that shack down at Newport Pier, the stench of fish, the pain as a grinning, coked-up Rizzo drove a fishing lure into my earlobe. "Why do you ask?"

"He escaped," Gary said.

EIGHT

"Turk Rizzo escaped from a federal prison?" I asked incredulously.

"No details, but it looks that way."

"When?"

"December thirtieth. Sorry, would've told you sooner, but what with the holiday, I just picked up on it. No special reason for you to worry about this guy, is there?"

"Other than I helped put him in jail? I guess not. Listen, keep me posted, will you? And thanks for the call."

"Sure thing," Gary said, adding, "Delilah, why take chances? Move in with Erik. Great security up at his place, I'll bet."

I hung up with my earlobe throbbing and realized I'd been pressing the phone tightly against one of the little gold studs I wore after my free piercing job. The vague feelings I'd had of being followed—was it possible I wasn't being paranoid after all?

Turk Rizzo had not been particularly happy at being put away, but he never made any threats. Of course, he'd been sitting in jail, and there was nothing like a little time in stir to make a person fix the blame for his predicament on somebody else—in this case on me.

I had to call Erik. No, I was *not* moving in as Gary suggested. But it didn't hurt to take precautions and one of them was to stay away from Erik and Nicole. I picked up the phone, hesitated, and dropped it back in its cradle. If I told Erik, he would insist I move in, or he'd hire a squadron of bodyguards, or God knows what-all.

Unable to sit still, I got up and paced around my desk, telling myself to wait, hold on, think it over, and not do anything rash.

I'd been strung out since the shooting at the mall—wouldn't anybody be? And the fact was I'd never actually made any vehicle following me. Turk might not be the smartest guy I ever met, say, about one cartridge short of a full magnum load, but if he had any smarts at all he'd be hightailing it out of the country.

Of course, it was still better to keep some distance from the Lundstroms. I glanced at my watch. Maybe I could reach Nicki before she left and plead a work emergency.

Too late.

As I reached for the phone, I heard Danny speaking to someone and then Nicki answering. Hard to believe, but she was early.

Decision time. I could still come up with some lame excuse to send Nicki home. Only if I did, I had to ask myself if this was because Turk really was a threat, or if I was just looking for a reason to duck out on my lunch with Erik's daughter.

Bloody *hell*.

I grabbed my purse and went out to find her standing there, looking casually gorgeous in jeans and a blue turtle-neck under a distressed brown leather bomber jacket that was way too large for her, one I recognized as belonging to her dad. Her blond hair was charmingly tousled by the wind. The top was a silky knit, the same color as her eyes, Erik's eyes.

She gave my office a quick dismissive once-over. As I made introductions, the only thing her gaze lingered on was Danny. He returned the appraisal, and there was just enough spark between them to make me want to grab him by the scruff of the neck, haul him off someplace far away from Nicki Lundstrom, and keep him there until I talked some sense into him.

"So where are you two going?" Danny asked.

I was thinking Norm's, which was close by, had a noisy lunch crowd, and would guarantee that Nicki would not want to linger.

Nicki said, "We have a reservation at the Beach House in Laguna."

"I thought we were going to make it quick," I said.

"Dad's idea."

Figured.

"Well, I'll cancel the reservation," I said. "I really can't take the time to go all the way to Laguna Beach."

"Hey, it's no problem, Delilah," Danny said. "I've got things covered here."

"Gee, thanks," I said.

My scowl, of the looks-can-kill variety, only got me an innocent smile and a "Go, enjoy. Have a nice lunch."

Just on the off chance a client wandered in who needed to be impressed, I'd worn caramel-brown slacks in a light-weight wool, a cream-colored long-sleeved blouse, and a black knit blazer. Well, okay, I admit it. I didn't want to look like a slob next to Nicki. Also, being a Southern Cal-ifornian weather wimp, I had worn my ratty old parka over the blazer.

Now I could see it had started to rain again. Hard drops pelted the window as though there might even be a little ice mixed in. To heck with it. Impossible to compete with Nicki anyway. I grabbed the parka and took it along.

At the top of the stairs I could see Harry Polk, beginning a painful climb up. Beyond him, I had a view of the back parking lot and of Erik's Lamborghini parked in front of the door where the curb is painted red.

"I was comin' up to get you, Miz West," Harry said,

sounding relieved. "Mr. Kimura just come in, said he was gonna call the fire department."

"Who *is* this person?" Nicki asked, not bothering to lower her voice. "He kept telling me I had to give him the keys so he could move the car—like I would."

"Your dad always does," Harry said, looking hurt. "Don't he, Miz West?"

"He certainly does."

I hurried to tuck Harry's arm under mine and help him limp the couple of steps back down, then said, "Nicki, this is Harry Polk, who takes very good care of the building and all of us. Harry, I guess you already met Nicole Lundstrom."

"Well, not exactly," he said. "I just figured it must be her because of the car and because she looks so much like her pop." He gave her a stiff nod. "I didn't want that fine car towed away, Miss."

"Well, then, we'd better get moving so it won't be," she said, heading for the door.

Right on her heels, I said, "I'll drive. Take my space when I pull the van out."

"You're kidding, right?" She pushed the door open to a blast of cold, wind-driven rain, then strode out to get into the Lamborghini, so heedless of the weather you'd think it was mid-July.

Shoving my arms into my parka sleeves and swearing under my breath, I held the coat closed around me with the hood over my head, ran out, and climbed into the passenger seat.

I was still fumbling with the belt as Nicki zipped out of the parking lot and jockeyed the powerful car through sluggish lunch-hour traffic with careless skill. Even though she deserved a lambasting for the way she'd acted toward Harry, I kept my mouth shut, and I told myself this was a perfect example of what it would be like if I was ever stupid enough to become Nicki Lundstrom's stepmother.

Running a yellow light, she said, "Oh, this is going to be fun. You're actually mad at me over that old guy, aren't you?"

"That old guy nearly died once trying to save my life," I told her.

"Sorry," she said, sounding defensive rather than contrite. "How was I to know? I thought he was a homeless person getting out of the rain or something."

This was not good. Not good at all. I took a deep breath, counted to ten, to twenty. Then I was contemplating thirty as she went down the freeway ramp to the I-5, where—wonder of wonders—traffic was actually moving.

There, she jumped from lane to lane and exited the I-5 for the 55, the powerful car like an out-of-control rocket on the rain-slick pavement. I was gripping the bottom of the seat so hard I probably left permanent fingerprints embossed in the leather. For once I'd've been delighted to see a patrol car bearing down, light bar flashing.

She kept glancing over, daring me to be chicken enough to say something, so damned if I would give her the satisfaction.

Instead, stifling an urge to scream Slow down, I said, "If we were going to eat in Laguna, why come all the way to Santa Ana to pick me up? You should've called and had me meet you."

"Dad said it would just be a good excuse for you to beg off. Anyway, I like to drive."

"In the rain?"

"It wasn't raining when I left."

"Well, your dad must have a lot of confidence in you to let you take this car." Or a hell of a lot less judgment than I'd credited him with.

She flicked me a smile, and if she'd been a cat she'd've been picking feathers from her teeth. "Oh, Dad thinks I took the Jeep. How did he—Mr. Polk—how did he almost die?"

"He was stabbed."

"Do bad things always happen when you're around?"

I said, "Not always," but I was thinking about the mall again and a lot of other things that had happened over the last few years. I could deny it, but her observation was uncomfortably accurate.

Past John Wayne Airport we angled around on the short stretch of the 73 freeway, got off at MacArthur, and headed for the coast. The rain had slacked off by then—thank God for small favors. We splashed through small lakes that lay in the intersections, sending out roostertails of spray. Lush plantings of palm and hibiscus sagged under the weight of the water, the green colors dimmed under the thick dark clouds and the gray light.

"I read some of your publicity a few months ago," Nicki said. "Friends passed the clippings along."

So I was right. She had been checking up on me.

"Don't believe everything you read in the papers," I said.

"Oh, you mean the story wasn't true?" she asked with a touch of sarcasm. "You never shot anybody?"

"In self-defense—yes. I'm afraid that part's true."

"And the guy died."

"Not because of the wound. He committed suicide."

So, technically, I didn't kill anybody.

Not that time, anyway.

We were on Coast Highway in Corona del Mar now. Nicki maneuvered through the stop-and-go traffic in broody silence, forced to move slowly enough so I could quit worrying about dying in a pile of automobile rubble.

Gary's call was still in the back of my mind. Otherwise there would've been no reason to scan the sideview mirror. When I did, something looked familiar: a dark gray van, a big boxy Econoline with darkly tinted windows, two cars back. Hadn't it been on the '55? Yeah, sure, along with a thousand others just like it.

Come on, Delilah. Get a grip.

"I know why Dad's so hung up on you," Nicki said abruptly, her tone edged with venom.

"Yeah? What's my secret?"

"Most women throw themselves at him. But you, you come on like Miss Tough Shit, like you could care less. I know better. You're not fooling me. I see the way you look at him. But my dad's a smart man. He's going to see through you, too."

She accelerated through a final traffic light and hit the open stretch along the coast on the way to Laguna just as the heavens opened up again. A corner of my brain noted the van back there, right behind us, but I was busy swearing and holding on to the seat again. And noting that she'd used up any warm and fuzzy feelings I'd retained from her dad's story of her childhood phobias.

"Okay, that's it," I said. "I don't appreciate your trying to scare the crap out of me, and I especially don't like your remarks about my relationship with your father. If you intend to keep this up, you can turn around and take me back to my office."

"Sure. Fine by me."

She slammed on the brakes and cranked the wheel. Tires greased across the pavement, and the rear end fishtailed as we came around a full 360 degrees. It didn't make me feel any better that she executed the maneuver perfectly just when there was a break in oncoming traffic and that she steered expertly, so we were headed back the way we'd come.

"Are you crazy?" I roared. "Pull this car over, NOW!"

Delivered in the same tone used by marine drill instructors, high school gym teachers, and harassed, fed-up mothers, my bellow got instant results. She swerved over on to a broad graveled shoulder and slammed on the brakes.

I took a big breath, all prepared to yell at her some more. Maybe I'd order her from under the wheel and try to drive the damn car myself. Or call her damn father on my cell phone, have him get his butt down here. Hell, the house was practically straight up above. I could see the asphalt turnoff about three hundred yards away.

All that and a lot more was racing through my head as I turned to meet her furious glare. And saw that the gray van had made a U-turn, too, just down the road.

"Who do you think you are, ordering me around?" Nicki demanded furiously. "Just because you're screwing my father—"

"Oh *Jesus*," I said, staring back at the van that approached swiftly, fear like a big cold stone in my chest. "Nicki, get us out of here."

"What? First you want to stop and then—"

"*Move*, Nicki," I yelled as the van pulled in right beside us, just a couple of feet between us and a big sliding side door.

"No," she said indignantly. "There was plenty of room. I didn't do anything wrong. If he's got a problem—"

Maybe it really was just a pissed-off motorist, but these days even those sometimes come with guns to teach you a lesson. In any case, I said, "Don't argue, dammit. Just fucking *go*."

This time I got my urgency across. She worked the

clutch and gear shift, suddenly clumsy with fear, glancing from me to the van, her eyes saucer wide.

The Beretta was back in my purse, stowed there this morning along with my cell phone, the purse on the floor beneath my feet. I leaned down to grab for it. The seat belt caught me, held me, and I had to waste precious seconds fumbling for the release.

Metal grated on metal as gears clashed. The engine surged, freewheeling, bucked as Nicki dropped the transmission into first, then stalled and died.

I couldn't find the purse. It wasn't where it should have been, tucked under my feet. The U-turn and skid must have sent it sliding. And no more time to find it because the big van door was gliding open as Nicki frantically cranked the ignition.

She was also pumping the accelerator, flooding the engine—I could smell the gas—and through the Lamborghini's rain-smeared window I could see a man climbing out of the van, dressed in dark clothing, his head and face a flat, anonymous shimmer, something in his gloved hands.

I scrambled up, on my knees in the seat to get over the gearshift lever, then lunged across Nicki, trying to find a pin to shove down and lock the door, startling a scream from her.

"What's happening?" she cried. "What's happening?"

Cars whizzed past. Ordinarily if anything unusual was going on, people slowed and gawked. Not today. A few honked indignantly. The van must have been sticking out in the road—and also blocking the view, I realized, as the man swung the thing in his hand.

Tire iron, I thought as it smashed into the window. I used my body to shield Nicki, shoved her down as she bleated in wordless terror.

Popcorn pellets of glass stung my scalp and neck—the

mall all over again, the glass mixed with cold rain this time instead of lemonade, a smell of sea salt instead of citrus. Time slowed, stretching like taffy as I remembered the slide on my belly for the security guard's gun, the marvelous surge of power as I pulled the trigger.

I could do it again, dive for my purse, come up blasting.... I lived the whole fantasy even as I cringed and prepared to be the next target of the tire iron, my head and neck and shoulders exposed and vulnerable.

Through the wet curtain of my hair, I saw the man throw the tire iron back into the van, heard the clatter as it hit. Something else in his hand now, pointed at me. A remote control—no, that was crazy—and then I heard the sound, like the crackle of an oversized bug zapper, and saw a blue forked tongue flash out as he pressed the stun gun against my back and held it there.

High voltage slammed into my body. My heart stopped, stuttered erratically before it began to beat again. My body spasmed. I was dimly aware of the man trying to get the car door open and having trouble because the Lamborghini's doors pivot oddly.

Should've been able to take advantage of the time lag, but my arms and legs flailed, disconnected. I banged into the steering wheel, the door frame, all the hard, unyielding surfaces. And I think I hit Nicki, too, because she was screaming now in pain as well as terror.

Then he got the door open, seized me, and dragged me over to the van. As I was hauled roughly up a step and through the sliding door, I caught a glimpse of Nicki slipping from the car.

Run, oh God, Nicki, run.

But he had seen her, too. I heard a muttered curse, the only sound he'd made, then he dropped me on the bare metal floor and turned to go after her.

The bastard had me. Why take Nicki, too? Somehow, I launched myself at his back, clawing feebly.

He simply turned and shoved me away, back down in the van. And then he touched me with the stun gun again. This time the bolt hit me in the neck and seared a path straight for my nerve center, shutting me down.

But in those last seconds of consciousness, I saw Nicki stumble and fall, scramble up again in a last desperate attempt to escape. And I saw him catch her before she made it past the back of the van and into the road.

NINE

I KNOW A LITTLE something about stun guns, mostly from people trying to sell me one. The guns are advertised as effective, safe, and nonlethal. Rather than relying on pain for results, they are supposed to overwhelm the neuromuscular system.

A couple of sites on the Internet will sell you ones that generate up to 250,000 volts. However, as one seller confided, it's the amperage that really boosts the stopping power.

Was there a Web site telling you how to modify that amperage? Why not? There are directions for making everything else from Molotov cocktails to nuclear bombs. I just know that by no stretch of the imagination did the charge that put me down come from something that could be called a safe device.

I don't know how long I was unconscious. I remember only bits and pieces: a brief stop, my arms being wrenched back, something being wrapped around my wrists. The man was close enough at that point so I could see his face, except his whole head looked smoothly flat, shiny, and featureless.

Turk, it had to be Turk. But why was he wearing a nylon stocking?

Idiot.

I already knew what he looked like.

Then he was stuffing something in my mouth, yanking something dark and heavy down over my head, and after that for a time there were only isolated sensations: the oily metal smell of the uncarpeted floor, the throb of the engine vibrating up through the frame, the taste of cotton fibers.

Later, coming slowly awake, I hurt all over, the pain made worse as I skidded around with the motion of the van. The unmoving bulk of Nicki's body provided the only restraint. She lay beside me, so still I was sure she was dead. Erik's daughter had been murdered, and I had let it happen.

Fully conscious, all the typical questions of remorse raged in my head. Knowing that Turk Rizzo had escaped, why had I gone with Nicki for lunch? Why had I discounted the danger? Why hadn't I reacted sooner, used my cell phone to call for help? Gotten to my gun and shot the son of a bitch stone-cold dead?

I was good at that, having had some practice lately.

Rain drummed on the metal roof, the sound echoing in the cavernous vehicle, punctuated by sudden silences when I could hear the windshield wipers working, scraping against the glass. Even though I wore both the blazer and the parka, I was still so cold my teeth chattered. From shock, I suppose, or just because there was no heat in the van.

I wondered where he was taking me. Taking *us*—had to think positively. Had to pay attention. We were moving steadily—the freeway, then, and the silences had to be times we passed under the shelter of bridges. I strained for other identifying sounds, but there was nothing but the rain and the roar of traffic.

I had no way to know which freeway we were on or which direction we were going. Didn't even know how long we'd been driving. Not that it really mattered. But, somehow, not knowing bothered me.

At least I was conscious, even though I felt like I'd fallen out of a ten-story building—and never mind what the self-protection advocates say about stun guns. I was up against Nicki—our backs together, I realized. I touched her hands, cold but bound like mine.

Why tie her hands if she were dead?

Frantically, I searched for a pulse and found one: faint but steady. Tears came in a hot rush, a sob of relief muffled by the gag.

Cut it out, I told myself sternly.

Crying was a luxury I couldn't afford. With a gag in one's mouth, a person can choke on mucus and tears.

I shifted around and tried to check Nicki over. He had probably used the stun gun on her, too, but I was remembering the tire iron and the fact that I had been out cold when he put her in the van.

Immobilized myself, my range of motion was limited. All I could do was touch the outside of the jacket, the bottom of the hood that covered her head like mine. Her hair spilled over the jacket collar. At least the silky strands were not stiff with blood. I shifted back to feel for Nicki's hands again.

Just beneath the cuffs of her leather jacket, I touched the bonds and knew they were thin plastic strips. Some kind of Flex Cuff, not the kind cops use. Lighter weight, but just as effective. Probably cable ties, bought from the wide assortment available at your handy hardware store.

I didn't have a lot of hope that I could undo the ties on Nicki's wrists. These days cops swear by the plastic zips, especially those who tell about detainees handing them back their handcuffs or doing something much worse with the metal circlets.

Yanking against the ties just tightens them. That's the reason the things are so effective and once pulled through the tabs there's no pushing the strip backward, either.

Maybe, in time, I could gnaw through the plastic, but I couldn't even try that, hooded and gagged.

We had to get away. That much was a no-brainer. I'd had a taste of Turk's careless cruelty. God knows what he could do if he put his mind to it. As I said before, not the smartest of men, but the kind who could be endlessly inventive when it came to torturing a woman. I had the earrings to prove it.

Fun and games with me—and with Nicki as a bonus.

Two for one, what a deal.

Be easier to plan if I could think straight. This was hard to do with all the physical discomfort added to the fact that the voltage from the stun gun seemed to have short-circuited my brain—or was it amperage? About fifty percent of heat loss is through your head. With mine covered, now I was getting warm, much too warm, and dizzy with not enough oxygen coming through the fabric covering my face.

Which brought up the question again: Why the hood?

So he could take off the stocking, of course. Nylons are miserable to wear on your legs. Think how hot and uncomfortable they must be on your head. Anyway, he couldn't drive around like that. Even in L.A. somebody might think it a bit odd.

Still, why bother with a disguise in the first place? It made no sense, unless...

Unless our kidnapper wasn't Turk Rizzo.

Beside me, Nicki jerked awake. I grabbed onto her hand, nothing else I could do. I knew she'd be terrified when she woke up, and she was.

As she grasped the reality of the situation, I felt her stiffen, then thrash wildly and whimper in muffled terror. All I could do was squeeze her hand and press my body against hers as I tried to send the message that, for what it was worth, she was not alone.

WHEN YOU'RE HELPLESS, time has an elastic quality. Minutes stretch into hours while your mind fills with useless hope, numbing despair, and frantic speculation.

Every muscle burned. Every bone ached. My wrists were beginning to swell, and my fingers tingled with the loss of circulation. To make matters worse, I was miserably hot with sweat soaking my clothes and running down my face under the hood, stinging my eyes, light-headed from breathing my own carbon dioxide. And there was pressure building in my ears.

Would fate really saddle me with a cold on top of everything else? Oh, yeah, absolutely. It would be the ultimate thumbing of the old girl's nose.

Beside me Nicki lay very still. Maybe she'd passed out again. If she had, at least she would be spared the torture of this endless ride and the thoughts about where it would end.

Not just a grave in the desert. If this man had wanted us dead, he would've finished the job there on the road. Death might be the ultimate plan here, but first there was a score to settle.

Who carried a big enough grudge against me to do something like this? Turk was the first to come to mind. But the more I though about it, the more convinced I was that this man was not Turk.

There was the disguise, of course. But it was more than that. I remembered Turk distinctly. With his muscular shoulders and long arms he'd reminded me of a gorilla who lifted weights. The impression I had of this guy had been of wiry strength and speed.

My ears popped just then, equalizing the pressure in my

head. Not a cold coming on. We were gaining altitude. My surge of excitement quickly died. The realization didn't mean squat. The L.A. basin is ringed with mountains. We could be anywhere.

Surely Danny had sounded the alarm by now, worried when I was so late returning to the office because of rain and slick pavements, not because of Turk Rizzo's escape; I hadn't told Danny about that.

Come to think of it, the Lamborghini would probably be spotted first because it was parked so close to the entrance to Erik's estate. Staff frequently came and went. Erik might find the car himself, assuming a thief didn't get to it first— the car was sitting there with the keys still in the ignition.

Poor Erik. I could imagine his feelings seeing the Lamborghini with its shattered side window. But the sooner he realized what had happened, the sooner a search would be mounted. God knows Erik had the contacts and the resources to get past any official bullshit. He could also put together a small army to look for us—or rather, Charlie Colfax could.

What I really hoped was that one of those passing motorists on Coast Highway had seen enough to be suspicious, had reached for his cell phone, and called the cops. But with every passing mile, that hope faded. Anyway, such a report would probably just describe a big, anonymous van. How likely would it be for a driver, whizzing past in the rain, to have noted the license plate?

Face it, I told myself.

The chances of anybody tracking the Econoline were slim to nonexistent. Given that fact, I knew from experience that finding us would take time—might even be impossible.

While I struggled with my depressing thoughts, the van slowed and coasted to a stop. We were exiting the freeway.

Now time contracted as my heart hammered with dread. After a left turn, we drove slowly, made a couple more turns, and then the driver was braking to a stop and shutting off the engine. I felt motion beside me and knew Nicki was awake. A door slammed. A few seconds later the sliding door opened to a blast of rain-chilled air.

A surge of anger swept away my fear. As the silent man grabbed my bound wrists, I wanted to lash out with my feet, get in a good, solid kick, inflict some damage.

I couldn't do it. If I did, he might use the stun gun again or the tire iron. He might hurt or maim me in a dozen different ways. Even assuming I did cause some injury, then what? I couldn't make a run for it and leave Nicki there.

No, for Nicki's sake, I had to appear dazed and docile, to bide my time and hope that if I got the chance, I could take this man down.

I tried to keep that goal fixed in my mind as he dragged me from the van and then, with a hand clamped around my arm, forcemarched me through the wind-driven rain. But with every step hope leaked away, replaced by a terrible intuitive feeling that things were not about to get better, but much, much worse.

TEN

I DIDN'T HAVE TO fake my stumbling, halting gait. Dread unhinged my knees by the time Turk—or whoever he was—keyed a lock and shoved me through a doorway into a dark room where I caught a smell of old dust and disuse mixed with the odor of freshly sawed wood.

I had no idea what any of this meant, but it scared hell out of me all the same.

No dawdling—he pushed me along, and I bumped into a wall. A smaller space, I could tell that much. Then he stopped to fiddle with something. I heard a second door opening, and I discovered that the hood wasn't opaque after all. It had just seemed that way in the van on a dark, dreary afternoon rapidly turning into early night.

There was a light on in the room, and it blazed brightly enough so that when he hustled me forward I could see shapes through the thick cloth: a small place without furniture, just some unidentified things on the floor and the smell of wood even stronger. Maybe a storage room.

Or a prison cell.

I felt cold metal against the skin of my wrists—a knife blade. A tug as he cut the ties and my hands came free. At the same moment he gave me a rough shove. I took a header, facedown. My brain still wasn't sending out the proper signals, and I'd been cramped into one position for so long I was too clumsy and uncoordinated to break the fall. The side of my head bounced off the floor, and I really did see stars, brilliant bursts of blue and yellow light.

Dimly, I heard a door bang shut, and thought, *Dear God, Nicki...*

He'd lock me up and take her away. Or maybe there were two separate cells so he could keep us isolated. That way he could do whatever he damn well pleased to either of us without interference from the other. Back there in the van I hadn't even considered the chance that we would be kept apart. The prospect scared me more than I would have believed possible.

Then the door opened and closed again. I could make out the vague shape of somebody stumbling into the room, coming right at me. I couldn't get out of the way, so the person fell across my legs. Painful, but I was too relieved to care because I realized it was Nicki.

Then her hands grabbed my leg, one on my knee, the other on my ankle, and I knew that her zip ties had been cut, too.

She levered herself up, whimpering with fear and urgency, and I thought she was tearing off her hood. Adrenaline seemed to have taken care of whatever aftereffects she'd suffered from the stun gun.

"Oh, Jesus, oh, God," she cried in a litany of terror as she stumbled over and beat on the door. "Let me out! Let me out of here!"

All I could do was lie there and gather my strength, still mute, virtually blind, and helpless. My head hurt badly enough that I had to wonder about concussion. Finally I summoned enough energy to push up the hood and claw out the gag. The sudden assault of light turned up the pain in my head a notch and made me squint; my mouth felt swollen and raw.

"Nicki," I croaked. "Are you all right?"

Which was a fairly stupid question since she seemed in better shape than I was.

"No, I'm not all right," she cried, whirling on me. "Oh, God, he used this *thing* on me—"

"Stun gun," I said. "Me, too."

I was still flat on my back, all my energy spent, unsure if my limp-spaghetti muscles would support me.

She took off her father's leather jacket and threw it on the floor, heedless of the dirt we'd tracked in, sandy grayish soil, a clue if I ever saw one. But since my thoughts were too scrambled even to begin to decipher it, I began trying clumsily to retract my arms from my parka. Deal with the immediate problem of being too warm; worry about the rest in due time.

"This is all your fault," Nicki declared. "If you hadn't jumped on me, I'd have gotten the car started or grabbed the phone. What did you think you were doing?"

"I don't know. Protecting you?"

"Oh well, great job," she said. "Who is that guy? Why is he doing this?"

"I've no idea."

Well, I didn't, not at the moment, not if he wasn't Turk Rizzo.

"He's after you, isn't he? One of those people you shot, or pissed off, or—"

"Yes, he probably is," I said. "So you've got a right to be mad at me. You can be goddamn furious. But will you please save it for a few minutes and help me get up?"

She hesitated, and I thought for a second she was going to leave me lying there like a landed fish. Finally, she grabbed my arm and yanked. Somehow I came upright, then slumped there, willing myself not to topple over again, willing my head to stay attached. About the only good thing was the fact that my eyes were finally adjusted to the light.

"I should never have gone with you," she said. "I

should've stayed home." And repeating herself she declared, "This is all your fault."

How could I argue the point? Not only was my past peopled with nefarious characters, one of them had escaped from a federal prison. Worse, even though I'd known Turk was on the loose, I had gone with Nicki anyway.

The man who abducted us wasn't Turk. I was pretty sure of that. That didn't mean our kidnapper wasn't an accomplice, a cohort, sent to bring me here and netting Nicki in the process. He was probably going for Turk now, and when they got back...

Think, dammit.

"My dad's never going to forgive you for this," Nicki said, going on to list all the reasons why.

She was probably right, but Erik's forgiveness was a fairly low priority just then. First on my list was my desperate need to shed my knit jacket because I was still too warm. And after I'd done that, the second was to scan the small, dismal room for a weapon.

The place was about eight by ten feet. A sixty-watt bulb screwed into an overhead socket illuminated raw wood walls and the shiny heads of nails driven into the wood. No windows, one door. Some kind of vent in the ceiling. No electrical outlets.

Definitely not up to code. Where was a building inspector when you needed one?

Faded linoleum covered the floor, the pattern of blue flowers almost too dim to be seen and marked with drying footprints, the kidnapper's overlapping ours. I guessed a size 10 like about half the men in the country. Here and there I glimpsed the huge nails that had been driven at an angle to anchor the bottom layer of planks to the floor.

No help, unless I had a claw hammer and probably not even then.

Two rolled sleeping bags—useless. A Porta Potti—sturdy enough to be a possibility? A cardboard box of foodstuffs. A small cooler. Something there, maybe.

Even better, however, were the two gallons of water in plastic containers. I pictured them crashing down on Turk and his buddy's head. A shower as well as a concussion.

Because I was doing the inventory for something to be used as a weapon, at first I didn't catch the more sinister implication of the room's furnishings and supplies. Besides, Nicki was still haranguing me, my head was pounding, and, as I've said before, my thought processes were all screwed up.

Just about the time I was adding two and two and coming up with a very scary four, Nicki's anger was giving way to hysteria.

"Will you stop sitting there with that goofy look on your face?" she shouted. "You're supposed to know about things like this. *Do* something. Get us out of here!"

I could feel panic expanding in my chest. If I let myself, I could have joined her in a screaming fit. Instead, I kept my voice calm and even as I said, "He used that stun gun on me more than once, Nicki, and I banged my head when he threw me in here. As soon as I can, I'm going to go over this place inch by inch, see what I can find. Meanwhile, yelling won't help."

Maybe she felt sorry for me. Maybe she'd just exhausted her venom. She sank down on her dad's jacket, looking every bit as miserable as I felt. At least she kept her mouth shut.

This helped with the pain thundering in my head, but did nothing for the growing fear because I was remembering a kidnapping case Charlie Colfax had told me about, a little boy taken for ransom. Charlie had been brought in by the distraught father, who was afraid to go to the police.

The ransom was paid, and the boy was found alive. He had been kept in a crude box buried underground, supplied with packets of peanut butter crackers and Hi-C juice packs, a plastic pipe providing air from the surface.

While our accommodations were slightly better, the comparison was undeniable. Somebody had made plans and put some work into this. Turk did not strike me as a planner. If he was out for revenge, he'd want it up close and personal.

Now that she'd calmed down, Nicki had time to take stock of the room, too. I saw the realization quickly dawn. She was Erik's daughter, after all. Not surprising that she was fast on the uptake.

She said, "He's not coming back right away, is he?"

"I don't think so."

"But why?" she asked, still not ready to complete the connection. "It doesn't make any sense."

"It does if you were the one he was after, not me."

"Me? No, that's crazy. What reason would he have to…"

She trailed off, and I voiced what she already suspected was true. "The best reason in the world. Money."

The magic word brought relief and hope leaping up in her face. Well, I suppose you couldn't blame her. Money had been solving problems for her all her life.

"Well, then," she said. "It's no big deal. Dad'll pay. He'll do anything to get us out of here."

"Yes, I'm sure he will."

"Then maybe the kidnapper won't come back at all. I mean, he had that mask on, right? He didn't want us to see his face and identify him. So he won't come back and, and—hurt us, or anything. He'll ask for the money and then tell Dad where we are. It'll just take a little while, and this will be over."

She scrambled up and headed toward the box and the cooler, "Know what? I'm starved. And thirsty. It won't be Beach House food, but—"

"Wait," I said. "Hold it."

I got to my feet with considerably more difficulty than she had and staggered toward her. Ignoring me, she sat on her heels and flipped open the cooler.

"Gross." She made a face and held up a package of Slim Price hot dogs in one hand, some processed American cheese slices in the other.

Dropping these back into the cooler, she was digging into the box by the time I got to her.

"God," she said, taking out a loaf of white bread and a small can of Vienna sausage. "Do people really *eat* this stuff?" In went the sausages, out came a small jar of peanut butter. "Better than nothing, I guess."

My focus had shifted. Instead of potential weapons, I now saw elements of survival.

"Put it back," I said sharply.

"But I didn't have lunch."

"Neither did I. Listen, this may look like a lot of food, but we could be here for a while."

"That's ridiculous. Daddy won't argue. He'll give the guy whatever he wants. We'll be out of here right away."

"Maybe. But first the kidnapper may want to stall, to scare your dad as much as possible. It's a ploy kidnappers use, a damn successful one. And it's control and power. Believe me," I added grimly, "guys like that get off on power."

"You mean I may have to sit here—with *you*—in this, this *hole*—"

I don't know which she found more distasteful, the place or the company she had to share it with.

"I'm telling you it's a possibility and we'd better be prepared. Now, let's see what we've got here, and make some plans."

"Oh, yippee," she said. "I can hardly wait."

ELEVEN

I DID MY quick inventory while sitting down between the food box and the cooler. No point taking a chance of falling flat on my face. My headache had abated a little, but I was stiff and sore, and I would gladly have exchanged a couple of meals for a bottle of Advil. Still too warm, I unbuttoned the sleeves of my blouse and rolled them up above my elbows.

According to my watch it was 3:49, about four hours since I had heard Nicki's voice out in Danny's office. What time had we been taken from Erik's car? Considering Nicki's driving style, this might have happened as early as 12:30, certainly no later than 12:45.

I had no way of knowing if our kidnapper had zigzagged around on the freeways, killing time. If he'd come directly here, we could be a long way from Corona del Mar, north toward Fresno, east toward Barstow or Palm Springs.

Anywhere.

Putting this depressing thought aside, I focused on my calculations.

"We can get by on a pint of water a day," I said. This meant we would have a little more than a week's supply.

"I have to have my eight glasses," Nicki declared sullenly. "It's what I always drink."

I might have pointed out the limited amount of human waste the toilet would hold—another reason for limiting our intake of food and water—but I decided now was not the time.

On to the food. The white bread was so loaded with

preservatives I figured it would be around for an archae-
ological dig a few centuries from now. Two one-pound
loaves, forty-four slices including the heels. Ten hot dogs
in two packets of five each. Eight slices of cheese.

The higher math made my headache worse, but I figured
our activities would be limited, so we could survive on five
or six hundred calories a day. At that rate we'd have
enough food to go with our week's worth of water.

With only a small blue ice pack in the cooler, the hot
dogs were at the top of the spoilage list. We'd eat them
first. The cheese, with the taste and consistency of its plastic wrapper, would last longer.

"I don't care," Nicki said when she heard all this. "I
only eat *turkey* hot dogs. These things are loaded with fat."

In addition to the bread, two cans of sausages, and the
peanut butter, the box contained two rolls of toilet paper,
and, down at the bottom, a note. I held it by one corner to
remove the sheet, but Nicki snatched it away. So much for
preserving latent prints.

On twenty-pound copy paper a laser had printed in a
large font:

RULES OF THE ROAD

1. Behave and you'll be okay.
2. Act up and you get zapped.
3. Piss me off too much and I throw away the key.

"He wouldn't do that, would he?" Nicki asked, uncer-
tain fear replacing her surly obstinancy.

I thought he would do that and much worse, but I said,
"Charlie Colfax will be working on this for your dad. Do
you know Charlie?"

"I've met him, that's all."

"Well, I know him well, and Charlie won't give this guy a nickel unless he knows where we are and that we're all right."

Of course, I was pumping up Charlie's image just a little, but that was okay, considering the circumstances. I took the sheet of paper back from Nicki, still holding it by a corner, lifted the food box, and put the paper underneath.

"Leave this here and don't touch it anymore," I said. "Just in case the guy left fingerprints."

She nodded, looking subdued.

"Okay," I said. "Food."

Our host's thoughtfulness did not extend to utensils. I tore open one of the hot dog packets and used my fingers to dig out a frank that was slimy with gelatinous liquid. I wrapped a slice of bread around the meat and handed it to Nicki, but she refused to accept it.

"I lost my appetite," she said.

"Look, sweetie pie, forget your sensitive taste buds. You need to eat."

She shook her head.

"Nicki, this is a contest. No, it's a battle, the biggest one you'll probably ever be in. If we can keep ourselves well and sane until Erik finds us, we win. If we can't do that, we lose. I don't know about you, but I don't intend to let the asshole who dragged us out of the car and brought us here get the better of me."

I offered her the food again. She took it, grimaced, and nibbled off the top. Meanwhile, I fixed myself a weenie and bit off a big hunk. For about a second, with my stomach rumbling, it even tasted good.

She said, a little wistfully, "I've never in my life eaten a hot dog without ketchup."

"Me, either," I said. "Or mustard."

She managed another bite. "You know where you get

the best dogs in the world? From those sidewalk carts in New York.''

''Unh-uh,'' I said. ''Dodger Stadium.''

''No way. Have you ever *been* to New York?'' That old patronizing tone was back in her voice.

I shook my head, chewed my last bite, swallowed, licked my fingers. Some of the gooey bread was stuck to the roof of my mouth, and the frank had left an unpleasant aftertaste of nitrates and gelatin. I reached for one of the gallon jugs of Sparkletts. The label promised crystal fresh water, sodium free.

I said, ''We'll each have our own container.'' I tapped some small code numbers printed on the side. ''This looks about halfway. Try not to drink more than one fourth of that each day. *Sip* it,'' I cautioned as she tore off the plastic sealing tab, hefted the bottle, and chugalugged a couple of big swallows.

Reluctantly, she recapped the plastic jug—but not without a sour, mutinous glare in my direction.

I closed my eyes against a jab of pain in my right temple. Somehow I was going to have to put up with Erik's nasty, rebellious child and still stay on guard. I knew only a few things about our kidnapper. He was fairly intelligent, vicious, and determined, high-tech enough for laser printers and souped-up stun guns. It was the things I didn't know that scared the shit out of me.

I sent a silent plea for somebody—Charlie, the cops, whoever—to get moving and find us, and to make it quick.

SLEEPING WAS NOT in my immediate plans. I wanted to inspect the lock, then go over the room inch by inch looking for any weakness in the construction. But after the skimpy meal, Nicki spread out one of the bedrolls, announcing that she was going to take a nap because there was nothing else to do. I was so exhausted, I ached all over, and the old khaki bag looked so soft and tantalizing, I unrolled the other one.

Lying there, I could hear the faint sound of a fan running—up there, that vent in the ceiling, air being pumped in and out. Enough to replenish our oxygen, hopefully. Not enough to take away the smells. Already getting the slightest bit funky in here, both of us sweaty and no water to waste on bathing. Never mind. Had to take a look at that vent, somehow…

Sleep came suddenly, deep and dark and full of vivid nightmares. I started awake two hours later, my mouth dry and my heart pounding with no drowsy transition where I could deny what had happened.

Nicki was still asleep, only a few feet away. She lay with her knees drawn up, one arm over her head framing her face. Sweat plastered blond tendrils of hair against her cheek and left a half moon of underarm wetness on the silky fabric of the turtleneck. Delicate shadows smudged the area beneath her eyes along with tiny clumps of the mascara she used to darken the long, pale lashes.

Somewhere in that eighteen-year-old body was the little girl Erik had told me about, sweet and vulnerable, afraid of the dark. And, even without being able to see those blue, blue eyes, she looked so much like her father it made my heart contract.

No matter that she was a snooty, bratty pain in the ass, she was also his flesh and blood, and I knew then and there I'd do whatever was necessary to protect her.

Stifling a groan, ignoring the protest of sore muscles, I hauled myself up, used the toilet, then went to remove the cans of Vienna sausage from the box. I put one by the door, another near our bedrolls. Gripped hard and smashed into our masked friend's face, I thought they might do some real damage. Maybe give us precious seconds to escape—assuming he didn't get a chance to use the stun gun first.

That done, I began a systematic search of the room. The door opened outward, which meant the hinges were on the other side. No deadbolt, no keyed entry, no lock to pick. But something was holding the door in place, some kind of outside bolt, because it didn't budge.

The wood used in the walls looked to be two-by-sixes, rough and splintery. And solid. No give when I tried to push on them. The boards had been nailed in like paneling. Not a decor that would pack them in on the designer home tour but damned efficient at keeping us prisoners.

If I had a pry bar, I might get some of the boards loose, maybe find a window. But since my principal tools were fingernails and teeth, the prospects did not look good.

The ceiling and the floor were the most vulnerable spots in the room. What were the chances of finding a thick concrete slab beneath the linoleum and the subflooring? Quite good here in old shake-and-bake California. The ceiling was the best bet. And the vent—the vent went somewhere, perhaps to an attic. A *small* vent, only eight inches or so square. Nowhere near big enough to crawl through, but at least it provided an opening, maybe one that could be enlarged.

Yeah, right.

Anything I did to make that hole bigger was going to create some noise. And what would Mr. Kidnapper be doing while I banged away? And where was he, come to think of it? Was he out there in the house, going about his daily routine? Watching TV, stuffing his face, figuring out what he'd do with the ransom money?

I didn't think he was. Even with the thick walls, even if he'd laid on extra soundproofing, I thought there would be some faint transfer of noise, and there was nothing. Except for the whisper of the vent fan, the place was silent as a tomb.

I shuddered, sincerely regretting my choice of simile.

Anyway, all other considerations aside, *getting* to the vent would be the more immediate problem. I'm about five foot five. Even standing on the Porta Potti, I couldn't reach the ceiling. Was Nicki strong enough to boost me up there?

As though my thinking about her had called her from sleep, she bolted up with a wordless cry, her skin leached white in the harsh unshaded light. Wild confusion in her eyes was turning to bleak acceptance by the time I reached her, dropped down beside her, and grabbed her hands.

"It's okay," I said. "I'm right here."

She held on, squeezing hard for a second before she pulled away. "Just a bad dream." She hunched her shoulders and wrapped her arms around herself. "Only I guess it's not a dream, is it?"

"No, I'm afraid not."

I know, on some level, she understood that things were going to be pretty awful. It took the most basic of bodily functions to really bring home just how bad our situation was going to be.

"I have to go," she said with a stricken look at the portable toilet, and then, "How am I going to wash my hands?"

"You're not."

"Oh, *God*," she wailed.

I had to resist the impulse to give her a good smack. "Hey," I said, "Yoo-hoo. Wake-up call. This is Survival 101. You've got food, water, and a place out of the rain. Things could be a lot worse."

She glowered at me. "How?"

Didn't this girl ever go to horror movies? Read the papers? Study history? I was tempted to give her graphic details, but I said, "It could be summertime, or fall, with a Santa Ana blowing and a hundred degrees outside. This place would be a sauna."

I kept my back turned to give her some privacy, and, reluctantly, she finally used the potty. After she was finished, I wanted to offer something positive to think about, like trying to escape, so I told her why I'd left the sausage cans around the room, about my survey, and about my conclusion that we ought to investigate the vent.

She looked scared. "But remember what he said in his stupid rules? If he finds out, he might hurt us or go off and leave us here and never come back."

"Not if we get out first. Drag the toilet over here."

I had her position it under the vent, then I put the cooler on top of the lid, the bedrolls on top of that.

"Okay," I said. "You'll have to hang on to me."

She thought about it, her powerful drive to escape overcoming her fear and caution.

"I'm taller," she said.

She was, by a good two inches. She clambered up. I gripped her thighs to steady her. Even with the extra height, however, her fingers barely brushed the ceiling.

"Be careful of the light bulb," I cautioned, suddenly aware of how close she was, how easily the bulb could be broken.

Just then our makeshift tower began to teeter. Hastily, she jumped down, somehow avoiding the light and landing without mishap. Well, she was a skier, after all, used to shooshing or whatever they do on those icy slopes.

She looked up at the vent. "Now what?"

Face it, she weighed less, too. I said, "You can use me to stand on."

"Come on," she said. "Can you do that?"

"I can try."

"Okay, but I need some water first."

She picked up her bottle and took a couple of swallows—no, *sips*—and without a fight. She was just putting the cap back on when the light went out.

The blackness was sudden and complete, as dark as it gets. I stood there, stunned, listening to the water bottle crash on the floor, and then to Nicki as she began to shriek in mindless terror.

TWELVE

TO TELL THE TRUTH my immediate concern was for the Sparkletts, not for Nicki, so I made a dive in what I thought was the general direction of the bottle. I was off target, but I felt water on the floor, the precious fluid pouring out. Then I was bumping into Nicki, she was grabbing at me, and I was shoving her away and frantically searching for the plastic jug.

Hands in the water, I followed the source of the flow. Found the bottle, got it upright. Couldn't find the cap. Nicki was still clutching at me, shoving and screaming.

"Shut up, Nicki," I yelled. "Stand still and shut up, dammit!"

When her screams subsided to a terrified whimper, I said, "Now sit down, right where you. Stay there. Don't move."

"I didn't break the light," she babbled. "I didn't touch it. Turn it on, please turn it on, Delilah. I hate the dark."

"I know you do," I said. "I'd fix it if I could, but I can't."

"The floor's wet," she said. "Oh, God, I spilled the water."

"Not all of it. I've got the bottle. Feel around and see if you can find the cap."

I held the jug in one hand and began my own methodical search with the other. The weight told me at least half the liquid was gone.

"He's here, Delilah," Nicki said. "He heard us talking. He knew what we were doing, trying to get to the vent, so he turned off the light. He's punishing us, like he said he would. He's going to leave us here in the—in the—d-d-dark.''

I could hear the rising panic in her voice. I said, ''Not necessarily. Maybe the bulb burned out. We're all right, Nicki. We don't need light to live. Remember what I told you. It's a contest.''

''Can't let the asshole win,'' she whispered.

''Damn straight,'' I said.

Amazing what you can do by touch. After I found and replaced the cap, I used my knit jacket to sop up the water. Nicki's jeans and the bottom of one sleeping bag were damp. Everything else was, miraculously, dry. I put Nicki on the dry bag and made her sit there.

''Talk to me,'' I said, ''so I can keep a fix on you.''

''What about?'' she asked.

''Anything. Tell me about when you were little. Did you always live in Corona del Mar?''

''No. We moved there when I was five. What are you doing?''

''Housekeeping.''

Working carefully, I moved the food box, the cooler, and the water jugs into one corner, the Porta Potti into another, and I managed to do it with only two stubbed toes and one head-on collision with the splintery wall.

With a little prodding, Nicki told me about her early years when Erik and her mother were still married. They had lived in an old house in Villa Park where Nicki had a fairy tale room upstairs with a gabled roof and a built-in window seat.

''Everybody had horses,'' Nicki said. ''I had a pony named Taffy. Mom didn't like it. She was always worried I'd fall off and break my neck. Daddy used to tell her there were some things in life worth the risk. Delilah?''

"Right here."

My fingertips brushed her hair, and I sank down beside her on the sleeping bag I had placed up against the wall next to hers. We had been a long time in the darkness now, plenty of time for my eyes to adapt, and I still couldn't see a thing.

I explained to her how I'd positioned everything, how she could get back and forth by feeling her way along the wall.

I had found our jackets and brought them over. I rolled mine up, gave it to her, and said, "Pillow."

"I won't be able to sleep."

"You might. I think we're both exhausted."

"I can't sleep in the dark." That note of hysteria rose in her voice again. "I have to have a night-light on."

I knew the feeling, having battled a few boogeymen of my own of late.

"Just hang on to my hand, Nicki. We'll talk for a while. You'll be okay."

She laced her fingers through mine without hesitation. We didn't talk much, however. We were both as tired as I thought. She told me a few more things about her childhood: moving to the house where Erik lived now, how her mother called it "Casa Magnifica" and came to hate it, how much she missed her old room and how she was sure Taffy missed the old place because his eyes were so sad.

I had a few quiet minutes before I trailed her into sleep. I'd made myself a pillow, too—of Erik's leather jacket. I breathed in his scent from the lining, the smell bringing both great comfort and the enormous fear that despite my confident assurances to Nicki, I would die in this place and never see him again.

IT WAS A LONG, terrible night. I slept fitfully, and every time Nicki cried out I was startled awake. Mostly I was able to talk her through her fears. Once she huddled against me, trembling and inconsolable for what seemed like an hour.

After my brave words about doing battle, I was beginning to think the darkness was the one thing that would break us. There was a feeling of being adrift, without moorings or bearings. I'd had a taste of being blind and helpless back in the van, but that was nothing compared to this.

I slept again and then was wide awake. I heard Nicki turn over restlessly.

"What time is it?" she asked.

"Don't know."

I couldn't read my watch, but I was hungry and thirsty, and I needed to used the toilet. Still, dragging myself over to the corner I'd designated as the bathroom, fumbling around in the dark—just the thought was overwhelming.

And then the light came on.

We both bolted up and sat, blinking like owls, stunned to silence for a moment. Nicki began an excited speculation. A faulty bulb—maybe it was okay now. Or would it go out again?

When I could finally squint at my watch, I saw it was a little after eight. Eight o'clock in the morning? It had to be. And what time had it been last night when the light went out?

"A timer," I yelped. "Nicki, the cheap bastard's got the light set for twelve hours off and twelve hours on."

"So the light'll be on for a while?"

"I'd bet money."

"The bulb could still burn out."

"Could, but let's not anticipate the worst, okay? Now,

I don't know about you, but I could sure use one of those wonderful hot dogs.''

Breakfast. Toilet.

I'd have given a lot for a toothbrush, a shower stall. Some air freshener would have been nice, too.

My knit jacket was still sopping wet. A two-day supply of water gone. I opened the Sparkletts container and carefully wrung as much liquid as possible back into the bottle. Then, holding the wet lump of jacket, I decided I couldn't let the water go to waste.

I said, ''Spit bath.''

''What's that?'' Nicki asked.

''You'll see.''

I took off my blouse and my slacks and used the jacket to sponge off my body, taking care to use only one side of the garment. Nothing had ever felt so good.

I offered the makeshift washcloth to Nicki. ''This side's yours.''

She hesitated. I was beginning to wonder about this modesty of hers, when she said, ''Don't tell Dad,'' and peeled off the turtleneck.

Come to think of it I'd never seen her in anything without a high neck. Now I understood why. A small blue butterfly was tattooed on the upper swell of her left breast.

As body mutilation goes these days, the tattoo was nothing. But I figured she was probably right to keep it hidden from her father.

''He'd have a fit, wouldn't he?'' Nicki asked.

''Oh, yeah,'' I agreed, although I speculated briefly on Erik's reaction if he saw the butterfly on my body. ''It's beautiful.''

''You like it?''

''Yes, but I bet it hurt having it done.''

''A lot,'' she said with a touch of pride. ''Guys love it.''

"Nicki," I said hesitantly, "I hope you're not—I mean, I hope you're careful."

"Oh, give me some credit," she said with a scornful look that also told me to mind my own business.

While she skinned out of her jeans and scrubbed herself with the wet jacket, I rolled up the sleeping bags and tidied the small space. Her bath completed, both of us air-dried and dressed, she sat down on her bedroll, glumly silent again, our camaraderie over. I wanted to sit down myself. Actually, I wanted to unroll the sleeping bag and take a nap.

Although I really hoped the claims that stun guns leave no permanent damage were true, I now knew the side effects caused by muscle spasms and flopping around were being downplayed. I was stiff, sore, and bruised, and my head hurt. Hunger, broken sleep, and low-level panic contributed to the headache, of course.

Still, even with all that, the fatigue worried me the most. It weighed me down, like a stone around my neck.

Concerned about my knees and other joints, I'd given up running. Instead I walked and worked out at Ultimate Fitness, taking advantage of a freebie from Rita. Well, *usually* I walked and worked out. How long had it been since my last session?

I wasn't sure. Sometime before Christmas.

I'd been focusing on escape, but I understood criminal behavior well enough to know how unpredictable these people are. Our abductor—call him Turk for want of a better name—might be fantasizing about having two women at his mercy. A little alcohol, a little crack cocaine, and his well-laid plans could be abandoned.

And for all my reassurances to Nicki, I could imagine a situation where he got his hands on a ransom without an exchange, in which case why take a chance and leave us alive?

I needed to be ready, we needed to be ready, for those worst-case scenarios. Instead I was out of shape going into our internment and rapidly getting softer.

"Come on, Nicki," I said. "We can't just sit around. We need some exercise."

"I'm tired," she whined.

"All in your head," I said briskly. "Up. Move. We have to stay on our toes, Nicki. Whatever happens we have to be prepared."

She didn't like it, but she followed my example as I paced and did a few jumping jacks and sit-ups with my muscles screaming protests.

Resting, she said, "What happened to the great escape plan?"

"Still on. Give me a minute, and we'll go for the vent."

"What exactly am I supposed to do?"

"Take a good look. Pull on the edges. See if the hole can be enlarged."

Under the vent, I got on my knees, bracing myself with my arms, psyching myself up. Lot of good it did. As soon as she put her weight on my shoulders, I crumpled like an empty milk carton.

"Oh, *shit*," she said. "This is stupid. This is totally *nuts*."

From my vantage point on the floor, pain radiating down my arms, I was looking up at the ceiling vent and thinking she was probably right, but I was also thinking that if I could stack up a climbing tower, jump from it, and grab on to the edge of the vent, I just might pull a hunk of ceiling loose.

Of course, I could also miss and break the light bulb, or the light socket might come down with the ceiling.

Just the chance of going back into blackness, of *staying* there with no hope of the light coming back on—no, thanks. Not worth the risk.

"I don't know why I listened to you," Nicki raged. "We're never going to get out of here. And I think you're full of shit about us being kidnapped, too. It's what I said in the beginning. Somebody's getting back at you. He left some food and water so you'd suffer longer, that's all."

This almost made sense, especially if the guy had any idea what kind of torture he was putting me through by leaving me here with Erik's daughter.

"It's true," she insisted stubbornly, "and you know it."

"I don't think so, but I'm not going to waste my energy arguing."

While she lay on her bedroll and sulked, I dragged myself up and went over the room again inch by inch. Nothing new, except this time I paid close attention to the door— or rather to the wood butting up to the frame. One piece just below the knob was especially rough, a hasty cut that had left a ragged edge.

First lunch—the hot dogs and an added piece of cheese—and a little water. Then I took one of the Vienna sausage cans and used it to dig at the wood next to the door frame.

Nicki just muttered, "Waste of time," and went to sleep on her bedroll.

She was probably right. The stuff inside the cans was loaded with fat and nitrates but rounded edges protected both consumer and wood from harm. As a tool, the can was practically useless.

She was probably right about why we were here, too. Logic be damned, this could be an act of pure vengeance directed at me, with Nicki an innocent bystander.

While I worked, I thought about every person who had

a grudge against me, both real and imagined: cripples on disability I'd photographed line dancing, loving husbands cheating on their wives and vice versa, the ones I'd put in jail.

I even remembered the family of the man I'd shot in the mall, George Mendel's lookalike brother Albert and the anger on his face as he said, "Georgie was a good man, and he didn't deserve to die like a dog."

Could Albert Mendel have found out about me somehow and decided to revenge Georgie's death?

Meantime, where was Erik? And where the bloody hell was Charlie Colfax?

I kept digging at the wood, my emotions swinging from hope to rage to despair. I tried to think positively, I really did. But how could I be optimistic when down inside I knew things were bound to get a lot worse?

THIRTEEN

DARKNESS AGAIN, Thursday night.

"I'll never be able to sleep, Delilah," Nicki said miserably.

"Then we'll talk for a while. Tell me about when you lived in Corona del Mar."

"No, I want to know about when you were little. Did your folks stay together?"

"My mother died when I was five," I said. "My father never remarried."

"I'm sorry. My mom and I don't always get along, but I can't imagine her not being around. At least you have your dad."

"No, he's gone, too. He died when I was a freshman in college."

"God, you're an *orphan?*"

"I guess I am."

"And your husband died.... How did you stand it?"

"You do, Nicki. You'd be surprised how much you can survive."

"My folks' divorce was bad enough. What I always wonder—do you think they split up because of me? I mean, that's typical, isn't it? The shrinks always say it's not true, but sometimes I bet it is."

"I suppose in some cases, it's possible. But why do you think that?"

"Because they were always fighting about me. Like the pony and, I don't know, everything."

"Sometimes people argue about one thing when they're

really mad about something else. You're going to screw up plenty of times in your life, Nicki. You'll have lots to blame yourself for. Don't take the blame for the divorce, too.''

"If I have a life. If we don't starve to death. I want to finish school, Delilah. I want to get a job and fall in love—really love somebody and not just screw around. Maybe get married someday. I don't want to die in this awful place.''

I held her hand, and I kept telling her that all those good things were going to happen, that we were going to get out of this. She cried anyway, until she went to sleep.

How could I convince her when I couldn't convince myself?

FRIDAY MORNING.

I was lightheaded with hunger, but I had to force myself to choke down the last of the hot dogs. The thirst was worse, a constant ache in my throat that a sip of water didn't cure.

"If I was home I'd be having waffles,'' Nicki said. "Maple syrup. Fresh orange juice.''

"Coffee,'' I said.

I was in the full throes of caffeine withdrawal in addition to everything else. My headache had settled into a dull throbbing behind my eyes.

"What is Daddy *doing?*'' We sat on the sleeping bags. Nicki ate with small desperate bites while tears ran down her face. "Didn't he call the police? The FBI? Why can't they find us?''

"I've looked for people, Nicki. It's not an easy job.''

"But there were other cars on the road. Didn't the drivers see something?''

"Maybe, but I'm afraid the van was blocking the view.''

And it wasn't as though the media would be broadcasting the story, asking for witnesses to come forward. Kidnappers have a real aversion to publicity. And they usually threaten dire consequences if contact is made with the police, so bringing in the authorities would have to be done carefully.

I explained this to Nicki, but it was not something she wanted to hear.

"Admit it," she said. "You don't think they'll ever find us, do you?"

"They might," I said. "But I don't think we should count on it."

I got up and reached down a hand, but she ignored it. She got up by herself and followed as I walked around the room. The place seemed to have shrunk during the night, the walls pressing in.

To take my mind off a growing sense of claustrophobia, I said, "Nicki, did you notice anything unusual the past week?"

"Like what?"

"A car? A person? Somebody staring at you when you were out, that sort of thing."

"I don't know. Sometimes people look at you. Maybe you'd think it was strange. You're used to dealing with creepy people."

"Everybody reacts to being watched, Nicki. I'm sure even you have had the experience. My question is: Did you have it lately?"

"No." She plopped back down on her bedroll, uncapped her water bottle, and gave me a defiant glare as she took a big swallow.

"Sixteen ounces, Nicki. The day's just begun."

"I don't care. I'm *thirsty*."

But she recapped the bottle and put it aside.

"What about back in New York?" I asked. "Any guys hanging around, somebody who won't take no for an answer?"

"You mean like stalking me? No. Are you really any good at this detective thing?"

My headache geared up a notch. "Not lately."

Accomplishing nothing with my brilliant questioning, I decided to concentrate on breaking us out of our prison. I got the sausage can and went back to work on the wood beside the door, trying not to despair over how little progress I'd made the day before.

All that time, nothing to do but that monotonous work, wouldn't you think my mind would've been cranking away? Coming up with theories, stitching together bits and pieces and finding a pattern? At the very least sorting through some personal stuff and making some life-altering decisions. Instead, my thoughts hopped and skipped around, never staying with anything long enough to accomplish much.

Having cheese for lunch was the high spot of the day. Afternoon was a long, slow slog. What had I said to Nicki about staying sane?

By four o'clock I decided the ersatz paneling only looked like cheap pine. Instead, the planks must be some new kind of hardwood, impregnated with steel. My hands were swollen from gripping the can, my knuckles scraped and sore from contact with the unyielding wood. I went to join Nicki, who was sitting on the bedrolls.

"It's not going to work, is it?" she said.

I was sick and tired of providing all the optimism. I was just as depressed as she was, and I wanted to say that nothing would probably work, that we just might die here.

Instead I mumbled, "Takes time," and lay back on the bedroll.

After a while, Nicki said, "I'll bet Mom's in California."

It hadn't occurred to me, but of course Nicki's mother would have come.

"She was on a cruise," Nicki said. "But Dad would call the ship. She's going to be so mad at him for letting this happen to me."

"For God's sake," I said, "how can she blame Erik? Short of a twenty-four-hour bodyguard, I don't think your dad could've prevented this."

"You don't have any kids. How would you know how mothers feel?"

Touché.

Actually, there had been times of late when I had felt the ticking of my biological clock. However, this forced togetherness with Nicki was making me think along other lines, like how I now empathized with species that eat their young.

I closed my eyes and wished for a stiff drink, or at least solitary confinement. Since neither was a possibility, I went to sleep instead.

FRIDAY NIGHT.

Having napped in the afternoon, as soon as the lights went out I was wide awake. So was Nicki. At least she hadn't freaked out tonight. She had moved her bedroll close enough so our shoulders touched, and she was off on a stream-of-consciousness monologue that mostly centered around the battle royal she envisioned going on between her parents.

"Do they always fight?" I asked.

"Always," she said with a something like pride in her voice. "Aunt Deirdre says she's never seen two people as much in love as Mom and Dad were. Aunt Deirdre is

Mom's best friend. She was the maid of honor at Mom and Dad's wedding. She says you never get over a love like that, so the sparks still fly when they're together.''

"Yeah, what does she know?" I muttered under my breath.

"I think that's why it didn't work out with Claudia," Nicki said.

Claudia was Erik's second wife. He'd married her eighteen months after his divorce from Margaret, and the marriage had lasted less than a year. I know these things, having once put together a complete dossier on the man. We hadn't talked about any of this during the past year. I'd steered away from the subject of ex-wives and dead husbands.

Now I felt sorry for Nicki, because what I was getting from her conversation was that she'd never really given up on the hope that her parents would get back together, and nothing could be further from the truth—could it?

"What about your husband, Delilah—what was his name?"

"Jack."

"Don't you still think about him?"

Jack... How could I ever have imagined that I'd forgotten him? His memory was suddenly fresh and whole, and the loss as painful as it had ever been.

"Enough talking," I said harshly, moving away from her. "Go to sleep now."

"Delilah?" she said, a little shaken by my reaction. "Are you all right? I didn't mean to upset you."

"Yes, you did, Nicki."

"I'm sorry." She put her hand on my shoulder and for the first time I thought she sounded genuinely contrite as she whispered, "I really am sorry, Delilah. Don't be mad. Please."

I gave her hand a noncommittal pat. Let her worry a little. If you asked me, this young woman was short on empathy, and took far too much delight in needling people. Or maybe I was just too thin-skinned and cranky—understandable under the circumstances.

I relented enough to say, "Forget it, Nicki. Just go to sleep."

I didn't sleep, however. I just lay there in the blackness, mourning Jack, berating myself for my recklessness in getting involved with Erik Lundstrom and for those few moments of weakness when I considered a future with him, and then telling myself how stupid it was to be thinking about the future when I wasn't even sure there would be one.

SOMETIME in the middle of the night, she shook me awake, terrified. "What is it, Delilah? What's that sound?"

I listened. A faraway rushing of wind and pounding of water on the roof. "Rain. Just rain."

The sound was a connection to the real world, proving we were not totally isolated; a comfort, lulling me back to sleep.

FOURTEEN

SATURDAY MORNING.

The storm system had brought colder temperatures. We could see our breath in the small room, and we shivered in our jackets.

I finger-combed my hair, but Nicki let hers tangle around her face. She looked gaunt and miserable, refusing to get out of the sleeping bag, sitting with it up around her legs.

"I feel awful," she complained. "My head hurts. My back hurts from sleeping on the floor."

"We'll eat something. You'll feel better."

"Peanut butter."

"Sorry, it's cheese today."

"I'm not going to eat the damned cheese. I'm sick of it. If I want some peanut butter, I'm going to have it. You're not in charge here. You can't tell me what to do. You're just trying to make this as miserable as possible because you hate me."

So much for her remorse the night before.

"I don't hate you, Nicki."

"Yes, you do. Well, I don't care. I hate you, too."

"Fine, Nicki. Hate me. Yell at me. Swear at me, if it makes you feel any better. But keep one thing in mind. I'm not going to let you do anything to jeopardize our survival. We're going to ration the food and the water. You're going to exercise if I have to drag you around the room, kicking and screaming. Now, come on, up and at 'em."

After some token foot dragging, she did what I told her,

but she didn't like it. I pushed myself to eat, to walk, to do a few sit-ups, then I took one of the Vienna sausage cans I'd placed by the door and went back to work on the wood next to the frame.

It made me sick to see how little I'd accomplished so far. I thought about all the prison escapes I'd heard about, tunnels dug with teaspoons, years of patience and persistence. Yeah, well, prison inmates get three squares a day, all the water they want, and some portion of fresh air and sunshine. Easy for them.

After some stomping around, Nicki came to sit, hunched inside Erik's leather jacket, and watched me work.

"Delilah," she said abruptly, "do you really love my dad?"

The $64,000 question. And after my soul searching, I still wasn't ready with an answer.

"Oh, Nicki," I said, "it's not that simple."

"Seems to me it ought to be."

She sat silently for a minute. I hoped for peace and quiet, or at least a change of subject, but no such luck.

She said, "My dad has lots of women, you know. They come and go. So if you think you're special—"

"Nicki, please. I really don't want to discuss this."

"I'm thinking about you, too, Delilah. You're an okay person, sometimes. I mean, I don't think we'll ever be best friends or anything, but I'd hate to see you get hurt. And I think you will. You're just—well—*wrong* for my dad. You don't fit in."

I couldn't tell if she was being genuinely concerned for once or just manipulative. In any case, her observations were right on the money.

"You really ought to think about it," she urged.

"Oh, I will," I said dryly. "Thanks for the input."

I KEPT WORKING, chipping away a splinter at a time. By noon I felt as though I'd been digging ditches. After a lunch break—more plastic cheese—I said, "Your turn to work for a while, Nicki."

"Me?" She sounded like what she was: somebody who'd been catered to and waited on her entire life. "I can't do that."

"We're not building a rocket or doing brain surgery. Here." I slapped a can in her hand. "Go for it."

She glowered at me, then made a few savage scrapes. Good. Put her anger to some use. She did, for maybe five minutes. Then the can slipped, and her knuckles skated across the jagged wood, driving a sliver into her skin.

She howled in pain and threw the can down.

I grabbed her wrist. "Stand still. Let me see."

"Oh, ow, what are you doing?"

Enough of the sliver protruded to grab. I yanked and was rewarded with another wail and a horrified look at the blood oozing out. I used a couple of squares of toilet paper to stanch the flow.

"Okay, you're relieved from duty," I said, picking up the can she'd dropped.

"Oh, will you cut out the heroine act?" she snarled. "And quit fucking around with that goddamn thing, acting like there's a chance, because there isn't any way to get out of here."

"Maybe not, but we have to try."

"Why? *Why?* Why do we have to do stupid exercises and save our food and act like we have some hope? I'm sick of it. I'm thirsty. I'm starving. This place is gross and it stinks and we stink and I can't do it anymore. I can't *be* here. I can't, I can't—"

She began beating at the door. This caused her hand to

bleed some more. Little droplets flew up to spatter the raw wood.

"Stop it, Nicki," I said.

I seized her arm and dragged her away. She twisted and struggled but I held on.

"Nicki, listen to me. *Listen.* You ski down mountains that would scare the shit out me. You drive that sports car like one of the Unser brothers. You're tough, girl. You can do this."

"Can't—"

She tried to wrench free, but I wouldn't let go.

"Yes, you can," I said. "You think about Charlie Colfax breaking down that door, okay? Think about your dad coming in right behind him. How he'll grab you and hold you so tight and take you home to your mom."

"Is he coming?" She stopped struggling. Tears brimmed on her lashes. "Is he really coming?"

"Yes," I said fiercely, wanting to believe it as much as she did. "Keep that picture in your mind because it's going to happen." Easing my grip on her arm, I reached out to cup her cheek with one hand and smoothed back her tangled hair with the other. "Okay?"

"Okay," she whispered.

LIGHTS OUT, Saturday night.

"I hate the dark, Delilah. I've always hated it. But— what I think now—it wasn't that dark back then that frightened me. It was *this* dark—this *blackness.* I think I always knew it was coming. I was always waiting for it."

"Oh, come on," I said. "I don't believe in ESP, precognition, whatever it's called. You were a little girl, and little girls get scared."

"But they get over it. I never did. So maybe, somehow, I knew I was going to wind up here."

"No, no, stop. Don't you see what's happening? You're fixing up your memories. People do that. Witnesses do it all the time. We're not fulfilling your psychic vision, Nicki. We're the victims of some penny-ante, piss-ant lowlife who's out to make a big score."

"I guess so. I'm just so afraid, Delilah. I want my dad. I want to go home...."

She trailed off into sobs and huddled against me.

"Shh," I said. "It'll be okay."

I kept murmuring other reassurances, trying to sound as if I meant them. Her forehead, pressed against my cheek, felt warm, maybe even feverish. Oh, God, what if she was getting sick?

It was okay to lie to Nicki, but not to myself. I didn't know for sure we'd been snatched for ransom. Maybe we had been left here to rot. Even if my suppositions were right, shit happens. The kidnapper could get knifed in a bar, shot by his wife or girlfriend, get his van mangled by a semi on the freeway. Where did that leave us? Here in this room with three, maybe four days of supplies left.

We had to get out of here before hunger or illness sapped our strength completely. I'd made some progress digging at the wood next to the door frame. I'd work harder tomorrow, make Nicki help me. If that didn't start showing results and soon, I would have to risk losing the light and tackle the ceiling.

Nicki had finally cried herself to sleep. I eased her back on her makeshift pillow and pulled the sleeping bag up over her shoulders.

Definitely colder tonight. I put on Erik's jacket, wrapping it tightly around me, both for comfort and for warmth, and lay back down.

Had to rest, conserve my energy. Practice what I'd been preaching to Nicki, think good thoughts. Erik's arms closing around me that day in the lobby of the hotel in Vermont, our bodies together later in bed...

I was drifting off on sweet memory toward sleep when the light blazed on.

All my thinking, all my planning, and there I was, stupefied by sleep and surprise in the critical moments when the door opened and he came in the room.

Squinting, trying to get my legs out of the sleeping bag, I saw only his shape and the motion of him coming at me. the slick head under the stocking, then the blue flicker of the stun gun and that hideous bug-zapping sound as the bolt hit. Nicki started screaming. My muscles contracted, my back arched, my head banged against the floor.

The room began to distort, to slide away. Some little corner of my brain was still thinking happy thoughts as the man seized my wrists and dragged me toward the door. *Erik's paid the ransom. First me in the van, then Nicki.*

I was dimly aware that Nicki wasn't waiting her turn. She was up and charging the man—Turk, whoever. A real tiger, she kicked and beat at him, connecting at least once from the way he yelped.

All that time she was calling, "Delilah, come back! Don't leave me," until he used the stun gun.

I saw her fall as he dragged me out. He slammed the door, and dropped a wide wooden bar across it. I *think* he used the stun gun again on me for good measure. I lost some time, however, and really don't remember. Maybe I was zip-tied, maybe he put on the hood. But maybe neither of those things happened, and I could have picked up clues to our whereabouts. I'll never know.

When I opened my eyes, sensory details overwhelmed me, but two things I knew instantly: I was outside, sitting on cold pavement, and I was alone.

FIFTEEN

I FELT LIKE I'd been beaten with a baseball bat. I was shaking with cold. A gust of wind lifted my hair, chill and fresh and wonderful. However, the breeze didn't blow away the stench from the dumpster I leaned against. The thing smelled almost as bad as our prison room.

It was night, but there was plenty of light to see that I was in back of a building, and that this building was a lone structure in front of a strip mall. Lots of parking spaces, all empty. Late. The shops closed. In the distance I could hear the hum of traffic, my brain immediately concluding *freeway.*

I staggered up, hugging Erik's jacket around me, calling, "Nicki," my voice a strange croak.

After a few moments of false hope and fruitless searching, I knew she wasn't there. By then I'd fumbled my way around to a door, saw the cheery double arches rising out front, and smelled the signature aroma of french fries and onions. A couple of lone cars sat near the entrance, and the door was unlocked.

Even disoriented and hurting, my stomach growled as I pushed inside. There were no customers. Just a couple of people cleaning up. A young guy was wiping tables, a skinny kid Nicki's age with his hair in a ponytail, trying to hide his bad skin with a ginger-colored mustache and a goatee. A young Hispanic woman was behind the counter, cleaning the pop machines.

The young guy saw me first. I was close enough to see from his name tag that his name was Doug and to read the disgust on his face. No wonder, considering what I must look like.

"We're closin'," he said.

He raised his voice as though I was hard of hearing as well as dirty. The young woman just stared at me, but I thought there was a hint of sympathy in her dark eyes.

Ignoring them both, I mumbled, "Phone."

I spotted one in the back near the rest rooms. I had to hang on to chairs to stay upright until I reached it. I listened for the dial tone, punched 0, and when the operator answered, said, "Collect call," and gave her Erik's private number.

He answered on the third ring. "Erik Lundstrom."

So much tension in his voice, and just the sound of it flooded me with giddy relief, guilt, a dozen emotions.

"Erik? It's me."

"Delilah? Oh, God. Are you all right? Is Nicki—? Where are you?"

"I'm in a McDonald's. I don't know—" I turned to ask Doug, "Where is this place?"

"Fuck, you are totally wasted," he said, shaking his head, then named the off ramp.

"Off what?"

"The Riverside Freeway."

I repeated the location to Erik. "Please come and get me. I'm hurt."

"Nicki?"

"She's alive, Eric, but she's not here. I'm sorry. I woke up, and she wasn't with me."

"Where is she?" Charlie Colfax demanded. Of course, he'd be listening in. Expecting the kidnapper to call, he'd have a recorder going and a tap in place.

"I don't know. I wish to God I did, but I don't. Erik, please hurry. I'm not—not doing real well."

"I'll call the paramedics," Erik began.

"No," Charlie said sharply. "We can get there almost as quick if we stop wasting time. We'll bring somebody, Delilah. I'll explain later."

"We're on our way, darling," Erik said. "Hang on."

It took three tries to get the phone back on the hook. Then I made my way carefully, like a very old person, up to the front, where I collapsed into a chair.

"*Hey,*" Doug said loudly. "Don't sit there. I told you we're closin'. Get outta here. You're stinkin' up the place."

Lots of appropriately nasty responses came to mind, but I restrained myself. "Listen, my boyfriend's coming. I'd like to wait here out of the cold. I need some water. Food would be nice. Coffee would be better. Help me out and he'll make it worth your while."

"Yeah, sure," Doug said scornfully. "Prince Charming, and I suppose he'll be in a white limo."

"Not tonight. Probably a helicopter."

"Fucked up and dee-lusion*al*," he said to the young woman. "I'm callin' the cops."

"Oh, come on," she said. "We're going to throw the stuff out anyway. A few minutes, what can it hurt?"

Alicia—according to her name tag—brought me a couple of small, cold hamburgers, a cup of water, and some old, oily coffee.

"You okay, lady?" She scrutinized me with a worried look. "Maybe we *should* call the police. They'll take you to a hospital, get you some help."

"Thank you, but I really do have somebody coming."

I was trembling from the smell of the food. I needed to wash my hands, but I wasn't sure I could make it back and forth to the bathroom, and I was too damned hungry to care enough to try. First I gulped the water, then I tore into the burgers, wolfing them down.

Sipping the coffee, savoring the warmth, I asked Alicia if she'd noticed a van earlier. She kept shaking her head right through my description.

"Are you sure?" I asked. "It's important."

"Sorry," she said. "We were kind of busy. There's a movie theater across the freeway. People come over after their shows. Doug?"

But Doug just gave me a contemptuous sneer. "Gotta stop smokin' that bad dope, lady. Finish up, willya? I'm not hangin' around past quittin' time."

Just then the noisy thrumming of rotor blades shook the window. As the chopper settled in the parking lot, Doug's contempt turned to openmouthed astonishment.

Erik was out of the helicopter before it barely touched down and racing inside. Charlie was right behind him with another man who carried a medical bag. Three long strides from the front door and Erik scooped me up and held me so tightly I gasped.

"Sorry—sorry, darling." He eased his grip a little, touched my face as though he couldn't quite believe it was really me. "Oh, God, I was so afraid—"

"Let me take a look, sir," the man with Charlie said as he took a stethoscope from the bag.

He had to work around Erik, however, to do the quick exam because Erik and I weren't about to let go of each other.

"What did he do to you?" Erik asked.

"Stun gun."

"Nicki, too?" Erik's face looked ashen at the thought I nodded.

"Looks like she can travel," Charlie said. "Let's go."

"Wait," I said. "Erik, this young woman went out of her way for me. Could you—"

"Of course," he said.

In retrospect I think this was a big mistake. There was the money he left on the table. I saw several fifties in the pile. But mostly it was the power in those beautiful blues when he thanked her. I knew it well, and from the dazzled look on Alicia's face I knew she was ruined for the Dougs of the world for all time.

THEY TOOK ME to a private clinic. Charlie had a suitcase with him packed with high-tech communication devices. Any calls to Erik's personal phone line would be patched through.

It was too noisy in the helicopter for explanations. Not that it mattered. Even though I wasn't tracking all that well, one thing was clear: Erik and Charlie hadn't called in either the local police or the feds.

As soon as we landed, two attendants whisked me to a large private room. Not exactly first-class, more like a good-quality motel, but it did have its own bath and shower. No staff were invited in. Erik and the medic, an EMT, I suppose, helped me up on a hospital bed. Erik had to move away when the medic began checking my vitals again.

Charlie planted himself right in front of me and fired questions. He had a team arriving at the McDonald's where the kidnapper had dumped me, and he needed as much information as I could provide.

"I asked the two counter people," I said. "They didn't see anything."

"Well, we'll ask them again," Charlie said brusquely.

Short and squat, Charlie's a fireplug of a man who dresses in a suit, white shirt, and tie no matter what the occasion and looks like he ought to be wearing one of those hats you see in old gangster movies. He has the relentless energy of a bulldozer and about as much tact.

"Who took you?" he demanded. "One guy? More?"

"I only saw one man."

"What kind of vehicle was the guy driving?"

"Ford Econoline van."

The medic moved aside with a frown. "I think a doctor ought to check her out."

"In a minute," Charlie snapped.

Erik sat next to me and put his arm around me. "Delilah?"

"It's okay," I said, leaning against him.

"What color was the van?" Charlie asked. "Year? Did you get the plate?"

"It was older, I don't know what year. Dark gray. Tinted windows. I didn't see the plate."

"Shit," he muttered. "The guy—describe him."

"Five ten or eleven. Maybe a hundred sixty-five pounds."

"Eyes?"

I shook my head.

"Well, try to remember details. I got a sketch artist standing by."

"M-m-mask," I managed to say as the room started to whirl around. I would have slid off the bed and hit the floor if Erik hadn't been holding me.

"Enough!" Erik thundered at Charlie. "Get a doctor in here, *now!*"

One came on the double with attendant nurses—one male and one female. Charlie's EMT vanished, never to be seen again. Erik and Charlie were asked to leave. Charlie did, saying he had to call his people and pass along the van description. Erik was used to giving orders, not taking them. Besides, he was paying the bills. He stayed.

The doctor's name tag looked remarkably like Doug's back at McDonald's. The tag said he was Dr. Miltown. From his military brush cut and no-nonsense expression I decided pharmaceutical jokes would not be well received.

After a thorough once-over Dr. Miltown said I was suffering from dehydration and exhaustion, but otherwise was doing as well as could be expected for somebody who had been subjected to repeated electrical shocks. He said a complete cardiac evaluation might not be a bad idea.

"How long?" I demanded.

"A day or two, depending on the tests."

"No, no way." I've spent far too much time in hospitals these past few years to agree voluntarily to stay in another one, so I declared, "I know about stun guns, and they don't do permanent damage," even though I had my doubts.

"How important is this, doctor?" Erik asked. "Can it wait?"

"I suppose so," he said reluctantly.

"Then I can go home?" I asked.

"Absolutely not." He turned to Erik. "I want her here at least tonight for observation and so we can get some fluids in her."

A curt nod and he was heading for the door, while one of the nurses was pushing over a stand and hanging a bag of glucose solution for an IV.

"I'm getting out of here," I declared. "I'll drink lots of water. I have to help find Nicki."

But Erik had moved over to stand right in front of me and put his hands on my shoulders. "I want you to do what the doctor says. Charlie's looking for Nicki."

"I'm not staying here."

"Yes," Erik said with gentle firmness. "You are."

Hell.

"Okay," I said, "but can I at least have a shower?"

"Out of the question," the male nurse said. "You almost passed out before. We can't risk you falling and hurting yourself. I'll have an aide come in and clean you up."

Ultimatums came to mind. Noisy tantrums and last-ditch stands, all of which required more energy than I possessed just then. So, I admit it. Even I will resort to that age-old tactic of a desperate "Please?" delivered with appropriate amounts of helpless female appeal.

Erik knew exactly what I was doing, but he capitulated all the same.

"Bring some extra towels," he said. "I'll see to it she doesn't fall."

WE HAD SHOWERED together before, but for pleasure and usually in larger and more luxurious baths. Still, nothing could have been more wonderful than that small, crowded stall with hot water streaming down and the smell of Dial soap, just leaning against Erik while he scrubbed my body with a plain old cotton washcloth.

And for a moment while I clung to him, all I could think of was how easy it would be to let this man take care of me for the rest of my life.

Out of the shower and toweling dry, I thought of Nicki and me giving ourselves a spit bath with my wet jacket.

The memory brought a fresh jab of pain, and then I was remembering how she had flown at the kidnapper. She'd gotten in a few licks before he used the stun gun. I'd seen her fall. Had she hurt her head? God, she might already have been getting sick. She'd seemed feverish to me earlier.

Think. There's got to be something to help find her.

Erik dressed quickly in his same clothes. Mine were in

a big paper bag to be kept and analyzed for forensic evidence, leaving me with one of those wonderful gowns that expose your behind.

After I was in the hospital bed, Erik left to check in with Charlie, promising he'd be right back. The female nurse began putting in an IV.

The male nurse was drawing up something from a vial into a hypodermic. "Mild sedative."

"No," I said. "No sedatives."

"The doctor wants you to rest."

"I can rest later." I still had one arm free and I balled up a fist, ready to deck him if he came near me with the needle. *"Erik!"*

The man was used to dealing with unreasonable people. When Erik and Charlie burst in, he explained patiently that the doctor had prescribed sleep.

"Nothing doing," Charlie said. "I've still got questions."

"Delilah, I'm worried about you," Erik said, clearly torn. "I want to know about Nicki, but if you're not up to this—"

"Listen," I said, "I'm not sure if I can remember anything, but I have to try. She may be hurt or sick, and she's alone, Erik. She's all alone in the dark."

He nodded and slumped down in a chair, too far away for me to touch him. All this time he'd been concentrating on me, making sure I was all right. Now his guard was down, and I could see just how hard Nicki's kidnapping had hit him.

And suddenly I understood how it would be if anything happened to Nicki: his devastation a barrier as real, as deep as any physical chasm, him on one side and me on the other, and the gulf so wide I might never get across.

SIXTEEN

"ERIK?" Charlie said. "You don't have to be here for this."

"Yes, I do," Erik said. In the unforgiving hospital light, his face looked raw with pain and etched with every one of his fifty years.

"Anything on the van yet?" I asked Charlie.

"Nothing," Charlie said. "Not much open in the area. We'll hit everything that is. Be nice to give 'em something to work with. Now what was this about a mask?"

"The guy wore a stocking," I said. "I never got a look at his face. And if you're running down prints from Erik's car, forget it. The slimeball was wearing gloves."

"And you didn't see any landmarks, either, I suppose?"

"No. He put hoods over our heads. Ziptied our hands."

"This place he took you, tell me about that."

"A house, I'm pretty sure. I didn't see anything, but it seemed like a quiet area. Not much traffic. I'd estimate three hours before we arrived. Freeways, I think, but no way to tell if that was a direct route or if we drove around."

"Christ. So we're talking maybe a one-hundred-fifty-mile radius. How about distinctive sounds—trains? Jets?"

I shook my head. "Only thing I can tell you is we gained some altitude. I could feel it in my ears."

"Oh, that really helps a lot," Charlie said sarcastically. "That really narrows it right down."

"Sorry, it was all I could get, considering the circumstances. Now I have a question: Why are you going this alone, Charlie?''

''Erik's decision. Guy left a note in the car. Short and straight to the point.''

I made a guess. ''Rules of the Road?''

''Yeah, how did you—?''

''He left us one, laying down parameters. Tell me what yours said.''

''Basically just don't call the cops or you'll be sorry.''

''One: Call the cops or the FBI and she's dead.'' The way Erik recited it I knew the note was burned into his memory. ''Two: Get two million in bearer bonds right now or she's dead. Three: Pay up when I ask and do it damn quick or you'll never even see her body.''

He stood, brought his chair over, and placed it on the right side of my bed, then sat close enough to lean over and put his head against my damp hair and hold my free hand. ''The bastard called just once, a few hours after we found the car and the note. All he said was: *Get my message? Well, it goes double for the girlfriend.*''

It hit me suddenly that the kidnapper must have prepared the note ahead of time. ''So he was after Nicki,'' I said. Which left me off the hook, didn't it?

''You have reason to think he wasn't?'' Charlie asked sharply.

I should've told him about Turk right then, of course. I was just too tired to deal with the questions the subject would generate, and anyway, I'd been right. Turk hadn't grabbed me, snatching up Nicki as a bonus. She was the target.

I said, ''I didn't know what was going on, Charlie. Naturally, I did some speculating.''

''You must've known something at some point. Like when the guy forced you off the road. You had a gun in your purse, for Christ's sake. You had a cell phone. Why the hell didn't you use them?"

If I wasn't up to talking about Turk, I sure wasn't going to go into the whole fight with Nicki that had kept me too distracted to notice the van. Instead I told him what he wanted to hear. "I just screwed up, Charlie. That's what you're thinking, and you're right."

"I don't believe that for a minute," Erik said with a pointed look at Charlie to back off.

"How do you think the kidnapper got your private number?" I asked Erik.

"He called the office. Charlie thought he might. I had them give it to anybody who mentioned Nicki. This place he took you, Delilah—how bad was it?"

"Bad," I admitted.

I described the dismal room and the supplies our abductor had left.

"Ah, Jesus," Erik said. "I know it was awful for both of you—but Nicki..."

I hesitated, thinking about his terrified child, knowing he deserved the truth.

"I want it straight," he said. "Tell me."

"She was scared, of course," I said. "But she's a brave girl, Erik, and strong—underneath."

The way he looked at me I knew he didn't believe a word of it, but maybe he appreciated the intention of the lie.

"You said she might be hurt or sick."

"She fought him when he took me away," I admitted, already regretting my earlier outburst of truth. "And she seemed a little warm to me. It may be nothing. She'll be all right."

He'd do whatever he could to find her. What purpose did it serve to add to the burden of worry he was carrying?

"I just wish we knew what kind of mind game this bastard's playing," Erik said. "Why let you go and not Nicki?"

That was the question we were all asking, of course. Charlie posed it a dozen different ways until I was so tired all I could do was nod or shake my head.

The nurse came back to remove the IV and firmly stated that the hospital was not going to be responsible for my health if the menfolk didn't go away and let me get some rest.

I must've looked downright panicked, because Erik said, "Don't worry. I'm not going anywhere."

Charlie figured that meant he was staying, too, I guess, until Erik finally said, "I'm sure they've got a room you can use, Charlie. Get some sleep so we can go at this fresh tomorrow."

"I got to check in with my people." Charlie fussed some more, positioning the communications suitcase next to the bed. "I've got my beeper. If he calls—"

"Don't worry. I'll let you know."

Then we were alone at last, with polite orders from Erik to the nursing staff not to disturb us. The bed was actually wide enough that Erik undressed and slipped in beside me.

We were both exhausted. Still, skin to skin, the most basic needs take over. Life must reaffirm itself after a brush with death. The mind seeks forgetfulness, the heart offers comfort. And if I didn't whisper the answer to Nicki's $64,000 question, at least just then I knew what the answer was.

I KNOW SEX is supposed to be nature's sleeping aid, but this time it didn't work. Every time I drifted off, I'd be back in that prison room hearing Nicki cry. I think, somehow, Erik could hear her, too.

We talked in brief snatches. At one point he said, "My poor baby, always so afraid of the dark. It was the one bad thing, growing up. Otherwise, she was such a happy little girl. Margaret and I saw to that. Whatever problems we had, we made sure they didn't affect Nicki."

I could have told him otherwise, but what was the point in hurting him?

"Where is Margaret?" I asked. "Nicki said she was on a cruise. Didn't you call her?"

"No. I probably should have, but I just couldn't deal with it. She'll be back in New York in a couple of days. Maybe by then we'll have good news."

I was disgusted with myself for being so pathetically happy because Margaret had not been around, fighting with him, igniting all those sparks Nicki described. And I couldn't help wondering what would happen when Margaret did arrive. In her shoes I knew that if I found out he'd delayed even a second in telling me about my child's plight, I'd be coming after him with teeth and claws.

Not wanting to pursue that line of thought any further, I changed the subject and asked if he'd called Danny or Rita. He had. He told them the truth about what had happened but asked that they keep it in confidence. Charlie was to provide an agent to give Danny any help he needed with the caseload at the office.

Work... I realized I'd given my office little thought. Most of the stuff was routine, even the trace on Brian Hall's missing father. Danny might let that slide, however, and concentrate on the paying customers.

"Delilah?" Erik said. "I was the one who found the car. I was...running errands. Decided I'd join you and Nicki for lunch. So I was driving south on PCH and the car was sitting there, the windshield smashed. My first thought was an accident, but when I got to it, there was the note and both your purses.''

"What time was that?"

"Just before one o'clock.'' His arms tightened around me. "God, if only I'd been there ten minutes sooner, five minutes…''

I couldn't convince him he wasn't to blame. Nobody could. All I could do was hold him and wait for the night to end.

WHEN DAWN finally came, we skipped the hospital food and choppered back to Erik's place. I had been too disoriented to know where Charlie had taken me the night before. Now as I looked down at the megalopolis that Orange County has become, I guessed Yorba Linda.

This far inland, the sky was a clear, crisp blue. The sun just cleared the mountains to the east, promising a bright, warm day. On this early Sunday morning, the network of freeways below was as empty as I had ever seen it, flowing fast and free.

Fog still drifted into the coastal canyons, but Erik's isolated hilltop was in the clear. Casa Magnifica, Margaret Lundstrom had called it. From the air I could see just how huge the house really was and how easily a person could get lost in it.

I was wearing green scrubs and a windbreaker borrowed from one of the men—the pilot, I think—for the trip from the hospital. Erik's leather jacket had been placed in the bag with my clothes and smelled almost as bad. Charlie had taken the bag when we left. I knew what could happen to clothing subjected to forensic tests. I didn't care about my outfit. I'd never wear it again, but I hoped the jacket wouldn't be destroyed.

As soon as we got inside the house, I headed for a long,

steamy shower—alone this time. Then I dressed in some of Nicki's sweats, a soft navy blue and expensive, and the three of us gathered for breakfast.

Erik wore khaki slacks and an old forest green L. L. Bean pullover. Charlie was in a gray suit, white shirt, and a tie with the smallest of red accents in the textured charcoal pattern. The guy probably wore a necktie with his pajamas.

The phone in Erik's study had been set up for monitoring. Charlie put somebody in there while we ate, on the unlikely chance we wouldn't hear the phone ring. He had other people in the house, too, although they stayed out of the way, using Erik's office for a control center.

We sat in the small breakfast room right off the kitchen. Tall ferns dripped water on the Mexican tiled patio outside the sliding glass doors. Beneath swiftly retreating fog the ocean sparkled with the brilliant morning sunlight.

Erik picked at melon and toast. Charlie shoveled in eggs, sausage, and blueberry muffins like the fuel they were. I ate like a person who'd been on a starvation diet of cheap hot dogs for three days, every wonderful mouthful ingested with an equal portion of guilt.

Without me there to bug her, maybe Nicki was having her peanut butter. I hoped to God she was. I hoped she was up to eating anything. Alone, she had food and water for six, maybe seven days, if she was careful. Surely we'd have her back long before then. The kidnapper had to be getting antsy for his ransom. Two million in bearer bonds that could be cashed without questions. He wouldn't even have to fence off cash that he feared was marked.

At least I hoped to God this was true because Charlie's investigators had turned up nothing in the area where I had been left the night before. Even money had not refreshed any memories. We hoped it bought silence, however. Now was not the time for the media to come nosing around.

I asked about the rest of the investigation. How about disgruntled employees from the household staff and Erik's business? Any security people at Charlie's firm in doubt? Charlie waved off my questions with an irritated glare that said: *What am I, an idiot?*

"We have to be sure we're clear about one thing, Erik," Charlie said. "When the guy calls about the ransom—"

"Maybe he won't call," I said. "He likes to write notes. Maybe there will be another one."

"Could be," Charlie said, although he hated to admit I might have some worthwhile input. "In any case, you have to think of it as a negotiation. You need to get something, too. The best thing is to make him let you talk to Nicki."

"And what if he won't negotiate?" Erik asked.

"You insist. You have to have some assurance that Nicki's still—that she's okay." Charlie couldn't bring himself to voice the grim truth that Nicki could be dead.

"I'll try," Erik said, pushing aside his uneaten food. "But my daughter's the first priority here."

"Of course," Charlie said. He looked at his watch. "The sketch artist will be here in a few minutes."

"I don't think it'll do any good," I said.

"It might give us something, maybe jog your memory. And speaking of that, I'm going to call a hypnotist. I have a good man who's done amazing things with people."

"I don't think so," I said.

"Why not?" Erik asked.

"For the same reason courts don't allow statements taken under hypnosis," I said, although that wasn't the whole truth. Just the thought of being under somebody's control made me queasy.

"But it's worth a shot if he can help you remember something, isn't it?" Erik insisted.

"You have to see something before you can recall it," I said. "Anyway, I don't think I'd be a good subject."

Charlie gave me a look that said he knew I was afraid of just the opposite, of sinking instantly into a trance and spilling the secrets, big and small, I'd been hiding.

"I'd like you to do it," Erik said. "At least to try."

"I'll think about it," I said, then changed the subject, asking if my purse had been rescued from the Lamborghini.

Charlie produced the brown leather bag, avoiding my eyes as he handed it over. In the bathroom a quick look told me everything was there, including my mini-automatic, but I could tell Charlie had searched it. Well, I would have done the same. Still, I wondered what he'd thought when he saw that compact container of birth control pills in my purse, pills I'd missed taking these last few days—as though I needed one more thing to worry about.

I'd known Charlie for a long time. We'd even been friends, sort of, until he introduced me to Erik. Once, briefly, I had wondered if he was jealous of our relationship because of some hidden lust for me. Now I think he sees the situation as a betrayal of trust on my part, a failure of judgment on his own. At any rate the man was not going to cut me any slack, that much was obvious.

We were trying to keep Erik's line clear, so I sat on the bed in Erik's room and used my cell phone to call Danny and Rita and reassure them that I was all right.

"You don't sound all right," Rita said. "Is it Nicki?"

"She's still missing."

"Dear God," Rita said, her voice full of sad horror.

If anybody knew what it was like to lose a child, Rita did. Her only son had died years ago.

"I can't go into details right now," I said. "I just wanted you to know that I'll be here at Erik's for a while."

"Call me," she said. "And tell Erik he has my prayers."

Danny was happy to hear from me, but sickened by the news of Nicki. He said not to worry about anything. He'd been getting along fine and hadn't needed any help from Charlie's people. Somehow this didn't surprise me.

"I'm pretty much caught up," he said. "I think I can make some calls about Mr. Hall. Okay?"

"Yes, go ahead."

"Brian called and came by a couple of times. I told him you had to go out of town on a case."

I promised Danny I would let him know as soon as we found Nicki and went out to the family room, where the sketch artist had arrived with her drawing pad and array of charcoal pencils.

With her slender, boyish figure clad in jeans and a black T-shirt, Marcy Tobin looked scarcely older than Nicki until you noted the fine lines at the corners of her eyes and the silver strands in the thick dark hair worn in a long braid down her back.

Erik held out his hand, captured mine, and drew me down beside him on one of the sofas. Charlie beetled a sullen scowl at me. Well, to hell with Charlie. I sat there with my fingers laced through Erik's while Marcy moved next to me and went to work.

She was as good as advertised. Still, what she came up with was a picture of a smooth, stocking-covered head that looked both eerily familiar and a little like the aliens described in UFO abduction stories, only without the big, insectile eyes. The sketch lay on the table after she left, a sinister reminder of who we were dealing with as we sat our vigil.

There were two phones on the big coffee table so that Charlie and Erik could pick up at the same time, along with all kinds of other high-tech equipment, including a caller-ID box. The instruments stayed maddeningly silent. Only three calls that morning, so I had plenty of time to stare at the sketch and think of Nicki in that dreary claustrophobic room.

Since few people have Erik's private number, the first two calls were friends with dinner invitations that Erik gracefully declined. When the phone rang a third time, the two men picked up, Erik listened, said, "Yes, she's right here," and handed the phone to me.

"Delilah? Hey, it's Gary. Pretty closemouth at your office, but I figured you'd be there."

Right away I got a sinking feeling in my stomach because I knew it was a good bet that Gary Hofer had called with something about Turk and because I could see that Charlie was still listening the way he did on all the calls and that the tape recorder was going.

"Yeah, listen, Gary," I said. "I don't want to tie up Erik's line, so let me get back to you—"

"No, no, hey, I won't keep you," he said. "Just wanted you to know I checked in at work and found out Turk Rizzo was picked up yesterday in Trenton, New Jersey. Not exactly a big jail break, as it turns out. There was some paperwork snafu, and they turned him loose. So guess you didn't have to worry after all. Course if you want to hang out with Erik for a while, you don't have to tell him, not right away."

Yeah, right.

Gary had barely hung up before Charlie was rewinding the tape and hitting the play button so Erik didn't miss a word.

SEVENTEEN

"TURK RIZZO," my ex-friend Charlie said in the dead silence that followed his playing of the tape. "Isn't that the guy who bombed your office awhile back?"

I marked the gloating on his face and in his voice, but all I was really concerned about was Erik's growing look of dismay as the meaning of Gary's words sunk in. He got up abruptly and went to stand in front of the huge windows, turning his back and leaving me to face Charlie alone.

"If Rizzo was picked up," Charlie said, "that must mean he was out loose. Yet all this time we're brainstorming, trying to come up with something, anything, to find Nicki and you never once *mention* the guy? Jesus!"

"Why cloud the investigation? I knew it wasn't him."

"The hell you did," Charlie snarled. "You didn't know for sure until we told you what was in the note. Guess this explains why you didn't want to work with a hypnotist."

Erik still hadn't said a thing. With his back turned, I couldn't read his face, but his body language spoke volumes, none of it good. I wanted to tell Charlie in specific detail where to put his accusations, but it was more important to explain what I'd done so Erik could hear.

"The note just verified what I already knew," I said. "I don't have to be hypnotized to remember Turk. The man's got a very distinctive body build, and"—I picked up Marcy Tobin's sketch—"believe me, mask or not, this is not Turk Rizzo." I put down the sketch. "Anyway, what's the point of this discussion? You heard Gary. Turk was picked up in Trenton, New Jersey—*yesterday*. That means he could not have been the man who dropped me off at McDonald's, so he was not the man who kidnapped me and Nicki in the first place."

"Maybe not," Charlie conceded. "But he could have some connection—a friend, a cellmate."

"Oh, duh," I said. "Gee, wonder why I didn't think of that."

Ignoring my sarcasm, Charlie said, "Turk tells him all about you. Maybe he reads the society page, spots your picture with Erik and Nicki, and sees dollar signs."

He had a point, but I was feeling too defensive and angry to concede it. "And maybe pigs can fly," I snapped. "Look, Turk Rizzo swims with the bottom feeders, the kind who can barely string two sentences together. The guy who took us plans things. He's got some smarts."

"Maybe, but I'm going to let *you* decide all that? I don't think so." To Erik, Charlie said, "I'm going to follow up on this right away. Get somebody in Trenton to interview Rizzo."

"Do it," Erik said, his voice cold and tight with anger.

"I'll make the calls from your office." On his way out the door, Charlie couldn't resist one last zinger in my direction. "Got any other little secrets you're hiding?"

Immediately I thought about the mall shooting, but no way was I going to tell Charlie about that. Anyway, it could not possibly be connected to the kidnapping…could it?

I covered my moment of doubt with a glare and said, "None I'd share with you."

"I'll bet," Charlie said with a slight smirk, went out, and left Erik and me alone.

Three or four seconds dragged by before I burst out, "Okay, come on. Your turn. Have at it."

Finally, Erik turned to give me a look full of wounded anger and sad insight. "Save your bluster for Charlie. You're not telling us everything. You never do."

I sank back into the soft leather couch. "Oh, great, you think I'm a liar, too."

Which of course I was, but it still hurt to hear that Erik knew it.

"And a really good one," Erik said. "You know just what to leave out and when to change the subject. Most of the time I don't care. It's a defensive thing with you, and usually harmless."

He came back to sit on one of the sofas, kitty-corner from me. Close enough to touch me, but he made no attempt to do so.

He said, "This is different, Delilah. My daughter's life's at stake. So I'm asking for a straight answer now. Is there something you're keeping from me?"

I could have equivocated some more. God knows equivocation was called for. But there was a war going on in my head. I still had all my original reasons for keeping my mouth shut. Now there were more. Tell Erik about killing George Mendel and Charlie would know. I had no doubt that, sooner or later, Charlie would turn me in to the cops.

Worse, he'd sidetrack the search for Nicki to look for some nonexistent connection because he *wanted* this to be my fault.

So I flat out lied and said, "No. I've told you everything."

Even as I said it I was thinking of another favorite line of my father's when he was trying to change his little girl's prevaricating ways: *Liars dig a hole, young lady, and then they have to stand in it.* Well, it had taken me thirty years, but now I fully understood my dad's warning.

"All right," Erik said. "But if you remember anything—if anything comes up that's even remotely connected, you have to promise me—"

The two phones rang then, startling us both, abnormally loud because Charlie had turned up the ringers, taking no chance that we would miss a call. Erik tensed, waiting two rings, then three until Charlie scurried in. They picked up the phones together.

I knew from the look on Erik's face that it was the kidnapper. He said, his tone glacial and clipped, "Yes, I'm listening," and he flipped a switch to put the call on the speaker so I could hear it, too.

Like I said, the kidnapper had some smarts. He'd masked his face. Now he made sure nobody would identify him with a voice print by using a filter.

The mechanically altered voice said, "How's the girlfriend? Hope she's up and around 'cause here's how it's gonna be. Today. Four p.m. Foothill exit on I-Fifteen. You'll see an old field. Used to grow grapes, or something. Dirt road up the middle. Half a mile up there's a big rock covered with graffiti. Delilah brings the bearer bonds."

There was no number on the caller-ID display. The number had been blocked. Charlie gestured for Erik to stretch the conversation. He had contacts at the phone company and hoped to trace the call. He also mouthed *Nicki,* to remind Erik of their earlier conversation.

Nodding, Erik said, "No, Delilah's recovering. She's not up to doing that. I'll bring them myself. And I want to talk to my daughter. I want—"

"You'll shut the fuck up and do what you're told. Shit!" The man slammed down the phone.

"Wait," Erik cried, then turned to us in panic as the dial tone hummed. "What did I do?"

I reached over and depressed the disconnect button.

"He's afraid we're running a trace, so he got scared. He'll call back."

Charlie gave a grudging nod. Erik's hand shook so badly he could barely get the phone back in the cradle.

"I hope you're right," he said, "because if you're not, if I screwed it up—oh, Jesus—"

The phones rang again and Erik snatched his up. The speaker was still on. As soon as Erik said hello, the filtered voice said, "Lundstrom? I want the bonds in a backpack. She stands by the rock and waits. Alone. She can wear a jacket, but soon as she sees me coming, I want it off so I can tell she's not hiding something—like maybe a sawed-off shotgun. Got it?"

"What about Nicki? How do I know she's alive?"

"You don't. You'll get her back when I get the bonds, so listen up, shithead. Here's the deal. You put a bug in the backpack, you put dye or shit like that—if I see anybody besides the girlfriend, *anybody*—I go back and finish off your sniveling little bitch of a daughter and I do it slow. Four o'clock. Don't be late."

THE ARGUMENT didn't last long, mostly because Charlie had too much to do and too little time to do it in.

Charlie's first point was that the kidnapper had given us nothing, that maybe we shouldn't do what he demanded, that Erik should wait and insist on speaking to Nicki. I knew Charlie's fear was well-founded. The money was our only advantage.

Erik was having none of it. "Didn't you hear him? He'll kill her. I don't care about the damn money."

"All right," Charlie said. "But you better be prepared. He may be back for more."

"We'll deal with that if it happens," Erik said. "You just be sure your people are ready."

"They are," Charlie declared.

"I don't know, Erik," I said. "Charlie's got a big staff, but there's no way he can cover every possibility. Are you sure you don't want to call in the police, or the FBI?"

"At this late date?" Charlie said. "Christ, Delilah, how long do you think it would take to get them up to speed? What if there's a media leak? Of course, if Erik wants to—"

"No," Erik said. "Not if you can handle it."

"I can," Charlie said, then threw out his other bone of contention. "One thing we need to be clear on. We are not gonna let *her* carry the ransom." His contemptuous look told me his concern had nothing to do with my safety. "No way. It's not gonna happen."

"I don't like it either." Erik's arm tightened around me.

Differences be damned. After the brutal phone call I'd gone to hold him while we waited to hear the results of the trace: a phone someplace in Anaheim, nothing more specific than that.

"You heard the guy," I said. "What choice do we have?"

"I'll find somebody who looks like Delilah," Charlie said to Erik as though I wasn't there. "The guy'll be in a hurry. He won't notice."

"All right," Erik said.

"Wait a minute," I began.

"I'm not going to argue about this," Erik said. "If anything happened to you—"

I pulled away and barely restrained myself from yelling, "*Listen,* both of you. Everything the man says and does tells us he's a control freak. Did you hear what he said? *He's not bringing Nicki.* Maybe he'll be so delighted to have the bonds, he won't care who delivers them. But are you really willing to bet Nicki's life that he won't do exactly what he says if we cross him?''

Charlie didn't like it, but I was adamant, and Erik reluctantly backed me up. One of Charlie's people brought in a map, spread it out on the big square coffee table in front of the sofas, and pinpointed the location: Foothill Boulevard, old Route 66, where I-15 turns northeast and heads up toward Cajon Pass and on to Las Vegas.

"Well, okay," Charlie exulted. "Piece of cake. We can set up some tag teams here and here."

He stabbed the map at obvious intersections. Not that many roads out there on the edge of the basin, so surveillance looked easy enough.

"My people are the best," Charlie said. "We'll follow the guy after he makes the pickup. Hell, we'll follow any suspicious vehicles, in case he's got a scout."

"You're sure about this?" Erik asked.

"We'll have four cars on a team. He'll never know we're behind him."

At this point our best hope was that the kidnapper would lead us to Nicki. But while nobody said it, there still remained the question that would haunt every moment during that long afternoon along with that enigmatic face in the sketch: What if he never went back to the place where he was holding her?

Another skin-crawling possibility had also occurred to me: Maybe the guy planned to grab me again along with the money. And if he did, it did not necessarily mean he'd take me to join Nicki—unless we were destined to share a common grave.

Next to me, Erik felt my shiver. "What?" he said.

I shook my head, unwilling to share my gruesome thoughts. Charlie was on his cell phone, barking orders. His people were running around. Vincent and Ben, Erik's houseman, brought in food—sandwiches, fruit, and soft drinks—reminding us it was lunchtime.

I remembered the two had been in and out all morning, hovering, keeping a coffee urn filled. It gave me a jolt to realize how they had stopped being people and become part of the background.

I had a sudden, urgent longing for my own small place without a servant in sight. I knew I'd never make it to the front door, however, because in the act of biting into a chicken on sourdough all the physical stuff caught up with me. Stress, trauma, and exhaustion hit me like an avalanche of boulders. Even the thought of chewing was too much.

"Delilah?" Erik said with concern as I put my plate and glass on the coffee table, and keeled over on the sofa.

"Tired," I mumbled. "Need some rest for later."

"Oh, fucking terrific," Charlie muttered. "I'm telling you, Erik, we can't count on her."

"That's it," Erik snapped. "Back off and leave her alone, Charlie."

Well, hooray and about damn time, I thought as I slid off into sleep.

I dimly realized that strong arms were scooping me up and carrying me away. Erik playing Prince Charming again. The silly fool would hurt his back. Silly but sweet...

"Erik, I..."

"It's Vincent, ma'am."

I opened my eyes to see I was in Erik's room, in Erik's bed, but it was the big chauffeur tucking a blanket around my shoulders.

"Sorry, I thought..."

"He'll probably come in later," Vincent said. "He has to think about Miss Nicki now. Go to sleep, Ms. West. You need your rest."

I slept for an hour, soundly and deeply. Even so, I knew that Erik never came into the room.

EIGHTEEN

ERIK AWAKENED ME about one-thirty and insisted that I eat a bowl of soup and drink some coffee. Then I stood in my bra—Nicki's borrowed sports bra—with the sweat top off while Charlie, impersonal and businesslike for once, taped a communications device about the size of a cigarette pack to the small of my back. A flesh-colored wire went up my neck, through my hair, and connected to a tiny plug in my left ear. A voice-activated mike the size of a peanut was attached to the knit band of Nicki's sweatshirt after it was pulled carefully over my head.

While this was going on, Erik stood at the windows, his face turned away, staring blindly at the fog that was moving back in and swallowing the sun.

When Charlie finished, I excused myself and went to the bathroom, where I took out a roll of adhesive tape from the medicine cabinet and considered how I would use it to make sure I had my little Beretta close at hand.

My ankle, just above the sweatpants cuff? Too easy to find, the first place he'd look. I settled on a spot right next to the communications device in the small of my back. Not trusting the elastic waistband of the sweatpants to hold the clip-on holster, I secured the holster with tape. A backup piece would have been nice, but I didn't have one handy, and I wasn't about to ask Charlie, who had been perfectly willing to let me go unarmed. With the Beretta in place, next I raided the cabinet for Tylenol and four leftover capsules of ampicillin, stuffing the pills in my pockets.

Be prepared, my new motto—me who had gotten kicked out of Girl Scouts for breaking one of their silly rules.

While I was conked out, Charlie and his people had been frantically busy. With two Sig-Alerts in progress on the main routes east—an overturned oil tanker on I-10, a collision involving five cars and a bus on 91—just putting together surveillance teams and getting them into position had been a nightmare.

It was two-thirty when Erik, Charlie, and I got a look at the chaos from the helicopter—long lines of cars clogging every road running eastward. We flew over it all to a parking lot behind a small complex of light industrial buildings in Fontana where some of Charlie's people waited in two vehicles. One was a Jeep Wrangler, the other a white van with lettering on the sides that said it was part of a local cable TV fleet.

In the van speeding along side streets, Charlie briefed me for the tenth time, urging me to keep my eyes open, to talk to the guy, to try to come up with anything that might help—just in case. He didn't specify in case of what, not being one to admit the possibility of failure.

We reached Foothill Boulevard at the I-15 exit a few minutes after 3 p.m. with the Jeep behind us. The bright day had been dimmed out here by a faint yellow pall, smog from L.A. backing up against the ring of mountains that loomed all around. I could smell the combination of auto exhaust and ozone. Above the chemical haze, long streamers of wispy clouds flew like pennants from the high peaks.

The field designated for the ransom pickup was easy to spot: a square mile of old stumps that had once been a vineyard. At one time this area had produced lots of grapes, enough to support several wineries. Most of the industry was gone now, finished off by the combined assault of development and foul air.

In this field a small billboard announced: COMING SOON—WORLD'S LARGEST AUTO MALL! So the bulldozers would be arriving to rip up the roots of the old vines. For now, the field looked dry and dead except for the green of wild winter grass and a few tenacious curls of vine at the bases of the stumps.

Massive power lines marched along one edge of the field with a gravel service road running alongside. Just as the kidnapper had described, a dirt track ran through the middle of the old vineyard, the big graffiti-covered rock visible from the road. Maybe the rock had been too big and too much trouble to remove.

It was easy to see why the kidnapper had picked the spot. Visibility was good for more than a mile in all directions. The freeway was close by for a fast escape. He'd also chosen daylight instead of night so we couldn't mine the field with our people, watching and waiting.

We drove past slowly and went on up toward Baseline Road, which was about a mile north. Right away it became apparent that unless ground squirrels and coyotes were now watching cable TV, the command post van was a big mistake. The thing stuck out like a sore thumb. Charlie swore steadily and had to agree with the judgment that had been made by a team during a preliminary sweep: the van would have to be parked about a quarter of a mile west on Baseline, where a clump of trees offered the only cover.

Charlie had some high-powered scopes and the tracking devices, but there was a lot less than I'd expected. All of Erik's money could not buy the time needed to assemble an arsenal of high-tech surveillance equipment, and even if we had the time, much of that kind of equipment was available only to civil authorities.

At this point, however, we were committed. It didn't do any good for me to keep second-guessing the situation. So,

with the van in position, all I could do was sit on one of
the bench seats and wait while Charlie once again checked
with the surveillance teams.

Erik sat across from me, holding the knapsack with the
bearer bonds inside. Regardless of the kidnapper's warning, there was a state-of-the-art tracking device in the bag.
One of the padded straps had been carefully opened up,
the tiny device installed, the strap resewn. With the memory of the kidnapper's threats still ringing in his head, Erik
had vetoed a second tracking device, which could have
been installed in an envelope containing the bonds, as being too easy to spot.

I was still wearing Nicki's sweats and carrying one of
her ski jackets—the same one she wore when I met her
for the first time in the lodge in Vermont, white with turquoise trim. There was already a chill in the late afternoon
air, and, besides that, the jacket would be easy to see out
there in the vineyard, both for the kidnapper and for Charlie's people, who would be watching.

I know it cost Erik something to see me in his daughter's
clothes, but his face had hardened into stony resolve, the
blue eyes dark and hard as frozen pond water.

At twenty minutes to four he and I got into the back of
the Jeep. One of the operatives drove. Dirk? I'd given up
trying to remember names. Erik and I sat with our bodies
touching, but he was gripping the knapsack with both
hands, holding it tightly against him. When we got out at
the lone rock where I was to wait, I had to take the bag
from him.

"I should never have allowed you to do this," he said.

"It'll be all right," I said, a promise neither of us believed.

"Mr. Lundstrom," the driver said, reminding him of
time passing.

Our good-bye was wordless, Erik's embrace quick and hard, his kiss just a brush of his cold lips across mine.

The knapsack still retained the warmth of his body. I hugged it against me as the Jeep drove away. I'm not a great believer in the power of prayer, but I said one anyway, ready to make a bargain with God—or whoever was out there granting requests.

Let him have a change of heart and bring Nicki along and I swear I'll never tell another lie.

At least let him take me to her, so I can take care of her.

My life for hers—okay? Is that a deal?

I got a cold blast of wind down from the mountains, needle sharp against my skin. Not necessarily a reply, maybe just a reminder that there was snow and ice on the tops of the mountains where Old Baldy rose more than ten thousand feet.

I moved over to shelter against the rock. Up close, the huge slab of granite was about the size of a Volkswagen, the surface covered with spiky writing that had a strange, almost ancient quality to it. I wondered if a few hundred millennia from now some archaeologist would spend his life trying to decipher the thing.

A piece had broken off at the bottom, providing a small ledge. I propped the knapsack beside me against the rock and sat with the twin lumps of the communication device and the Beretta keeping me from leaning back and getting too comfortable.

Now, wait—I really had been sincere in offering my life for Nicki's. I just hadn't mentioned in my prayer that I would kill the SOB who took us if I had to.

Too nervous to sit there, I got up and stood, shifting my weight from one foot to the other, and noted that much smaller rocks protruded from the soil out in the field. I knew that water had brought them here, down from the highest peaks of the San Gabriels—millions of gallons of water, proof of ancient floods of Biblical proportion. The land was still cut with old lines of run-off. And here and there among the old stumps I glimpsed tracks left by weekend invasions of dirt bikers who seemed to consider any unfenced field an open invitation.

Charlie's voice crackled in my ear, demanding a check-in.

"Four-oh-five," he said. "You see anything?"

"Nothing," I said. "He's probably stuck in traffic."

The minutes crawled past. A couple of cars came up the gravel service road bordering the vineyard, but never even slowed.

At four-thirty the western sky began to turn a dusky red as the sun sank in the haze. Darkness swiftly followed.

"Where the fucking hell is he?" Charlie growled. "Goddammit, son of a bitch."

"Amen," I said.

I began to walk around in tight circles, trying to stay out of the wind. I turned up the collar of Nicki's insulated jacket, stuffed my hands in the pockets, paced, and waited. In the deepening darkness the lights of L.A. created a vast, muted glow to the west. A fingernail of moon came and went in clouds that had thickened to lie like crumpled and torn tissue paper overhead.

Unable to contain my worry, I said, "Charlie, is this going to work? Do you have a night scope? Can you see out here?"

"You do your job and let me worry about mine," he snapped, not answering my question and making me even more apprehensive.

Although it wasn't much consolation, I figured the kidnapper was as jittery as we were. Unless he was back there in the smash-up on the Riverside Freeway. Maybe trapped in the sea of cars dammed up behind the oil spill on I-10. I didn't think he was, however. I thought he was nearby, waiting. That this was all planned, a deliberate ploy to bring us here in daylight, then to leave us waiting until darkness fell. All I could hope was that he was nervous enough to make a mistake.

"Time," I kept asking.

5:49.

5:53.

6:05.

"Heads up," Charlie growled in my ear. "Tan Honda, turning on the service road."

Just because the kidnapper had used a van to grab Nicki and me didn't mean he would use it now. Any vehicle was suspect. My stomach churned as I stood there, straining toward the faint headlights approaching beside the power lines. Slowing? No, the car kept going, taking the short cut to Baseline, no doubt.

I swore softly, but I wouldn't say what I was thinking for fear Erik was listening in: *What if this was just another one of the bastard's power trips?*

As more seconds ticked past a feeling began growing that something was definitely wrong, some detail overlooked, that disaster was going to hit like one of those flash floods down the mountainside. My skin crawled with the strength of the premonition, but I could just imagine Charlie's reaction to a burst of female intuition, so I kept my mouth shut.

"Van on the freeway exit," Charlie barked. "Gray Econoline. Coming your way."

"Got it," I said. "He's turning on the dirt road. Gotta be him."

And my heart did a sudden leap. If the kidnapper was

driving the van, he might bring Nicki after all. Hell, if I
hadn't been such a pessimist, I might even have believed
it.

But cynicism is part and parcel of my business. As the
van wallowed toward me, I knew things would never be
that smooth, life did not operate that way, and ridicule be
damned, I said, "Charlie, I don't like this. Charlie?"

But Charlie was elsewhere, spitting orders to tag teams
maybe, and the van was fast approaching in a swirl of dust.
I pulled the zipper down and peeled off the jacket as the
kidnapper had directed. Held it out away from me and
lifted my arms so there was no mistake: I was unarmed.

Except for the Beretta, of course.

Then two things occurred to me at once: The sound of
the van's engine was too loud, and the glass in the side
windows was wrong.

As the van pulled up and stopped, I could see the two
young guys inside even before they rolled down the window, and I was remembering the kidnapper's van had
darkly tinted glass as the driver shouted, "Hey, baby,
woo—take it all off."

A bray of drunken laughter and the other one leaned
across to add, "Your boyfriend said to tell you he's on his
way."

Then they both laughed and pulled away. A beer can
came flying out the window. I had to duck to keep from
getting hit.

Charlie was yelling in my ear, something like "We're
on it, we're on it," and never listening to me screaming,
"It's not him. It's not him, you moron!"

And then I realized the engine noise was still loud even
though the van was leaving and getting louder because it
wasn't coming from the van at all.

A motorcycle with no lights was roaring up, coming
right at me.

NINETEEN

HE HIT THE HEADLIGHT on the motorcycle at the last minute, just long enough so he could locate the knapsack. This time there was no stocking mask. Instead he wore a big, smooth black moon-man helmet. The headlight went off as he braked, and the back tire skidded around, spewing rocky soil, just missing me as I stumbled back hard against the granite boulder, dropping the jacket.

I felt the heat of the exhaust and the end of the handlebar brushed my sleeve as he reached down and snagged the knapsack. Then he juiced the hand throttle and was gone, roaring off into the night. The moon came out just long enough so I could see him, dodging and weaving through the old stumps.

"Charlie! Goddammit, Charlie," I yelled, but I knew the mike was useless.

The surge of adrenaline, nature's pain medication, was wearing off. I could feel the ache caused by my body slam against the rock. Worse, something sharp was poking me in the small of my back. I lifted the sweatshirt and peeled off the tape. In the sporadic moonlight I could see the Beretta in its holster had survived just fine, but the communication device was now just so many pieces of broken plastic adhering to the sticky side of the tape.

"Bloody hell!" I cried. Charlie and his goddamn high-tech stuff, better to be using string and tin cans.

How come nobody had noticed that the van went one way and the tracking device was going in a different direction? Why wasn't somebody watching me—wasn't that the plan? For all Charlie's confidence, I'd bet money he didn't have a night scope available and that he hadn't seen a damn thing out here. Even so, didn't they wonder about that flash of headlight from the motorcycle? Not to mention the fact that I wasn't checking in.

The Jeep was supposed to be dispatched for me right after the ransom was picked up, but I knew I was low on the priority list. Everybody would be busy getting the teams in place to tail the Econoline. I'd be lucky if they didn't leave me standing here all night.

I grabbed up Nicki's jacket, stuffed my arms in the sleeves, and began to run—with the Beretta in my hand just in case the kidnapper planned a return visit. Never mind that the spot where the command post van was parked was up on Baseline, more than a mile away once I got to the gravel road.

I didn't dare cut through the old vineyard. The moonlight was dim and unreliable. I could fall and probably would. I had no idea how the kidnapper had gotten through the stumps without a spill, but I could hear the receding drone of the motorcycle's engine and knew he must still be upright and speeding away.

I'd been right about my physical condition back there with Nicki in our prison room. I was totally out of shape. My muscles felt like old bubble gum, and my breath soon became a saw in my chest. I doubt I'd gone a quarter of a mile before I saw headlights approaching. I didn't pocket the Beretta until I knew for sure it was Charlie's Jeep.

There was only the driver in the vehicle, the same fellow who had dropped me off. "Sorry," he said, "things got a little hectic—"

"Not him," I wheezed as I climbed in. "Get Charlie."

"I don't think he has time right now."

"Tell him!" I bellowed. "A motorcycle—not a van. Off road. Get the chopper out here. Hurry!"

Erik's small chopper was meant to ferry businessmen around L.A., not to locate fleeing criminals with infrared detectors, but I thought it was our only chance to spot the motorcycle.

To his credit, the driver was a quick study. Well, Charlie hires the best. Dirk, Deke—whatever the hell his name was—got on the phone, peeling us around and rocketing back up the gravel road as he passed on the bad news.

Back at the command post van, Charlie was swearing and shouting orders that were relayed by a calmer person at the communications console. I got the gist: a receiver had malfunctioned. Now that it was fixed, the tracking device had been located—out there in the middle of the old vineyard, the knapsack empty without a doubt. And I knew Charlie had not brought a night scope, because nobody had seen the kidnapper.

Slumped on one of the bench seats, Erik had the look of somebody blindsided by some terrible natural disaster: fire, flood, earthquake. I might have gone directly to him, but Charlie seized my arm.

"I knew you'd do it," he snarled. "I knew you'd screw everything up. You were wired, for Chrissake! All you had to do was open your mouth, but you couldn't even do that while we wasted time on a wild goose chase."

That did it. Using my last ounce of energy, I balled up a fist, hauled back, and punched him squarely in the nose.

This got me a satisfying yelp and a squirt of blood as Charlie staggered back and almost fell, but to tell you the truth, judging from the pain shooting up my hand to my shoulder, I think it hurt me worse than it hurt him. I did make my point, however. He sat down to nurse his schnozz and left me alone for a minute.

Later, I would understand how much better it would have been if I'd marked the depth of the hatred and humiliation in his eyes. Just then I ignored him and turned to the communication person, who was trying to hide a smile and readily agreed to have the surveillance team stop the gray van.

Through the windshield I could see the helicopter beginning to sweep a searchlight across the abandoned vineyard. Erik just sat, stone still and silent, and didn't even comment on my altercation with Charlie. I sank down next to Erik, sucked my tingling knuckles, and tried to think positive thoughts as we drove off to join the team, who now had the drunken teenagers in tow. But the reports coming back from the helicopter didn't surprise me a bit.

The man on the motorcycle had vanished.

SEEN UP CLOSE in a lighted parking lot, it was obvious that the van was not the one the kidnapper had driven. In addition to the absence of darkly tinted glass, there were dents and dings on the panel behind the sliding door, and some rust in the front wheel well.

The Econoline was in front of an all-night liquor store down in Rancho Cucamunga, stopped by one of the surveillance vehicles. Nobody in the store was showing the slightest bit of curiosity about what was going on outside. Experience had probably taught them to mind their own business.

The teenagers were being questioned when we arrived. Well, one was, leaning against the van. The other sat on the curb and puked in the gutter. The two had headed like homing pigeons back to the liquor store, where, it turns out, the kidnapper had approached them as they had kicked back in the parking lot, finishing off a couple of six-packs and passing a joint.

Charlie's agents reported that, after some initial bluster, the two had folded quickly, giving up ID's and even offering the fifty dollars the kidnapper had given them. The one answering questions was Jason, the one barfing up his beer was Tony.

"Man, this is fucked," Jason moaned. He eyed Erik, Charlie, and me nervously as we joined the crowd. He was even sorrier looking than I remembered with greasy blond hair stringing down over his eyes and a line of pimples edging his jaw. "Dude said he was like playin' a joke on his girlfriend. Said she'd been givin' him some lip, and he dumped her out there. Said he wanted to shake her up, scare the bitch a little. Sorry, ma'am." He gave me a humble little hound-dog look.

"Forget it," I said. "Just tell us what he looks like."

But Jason was shaking his head. "He was like on this motorcycle, wearing this helmet and all. Had the visor open, but I didn't really see the dude. What's he done anyway?"

"Never mind." Charlie had that stuffed-up sound of somebody whose nasal passages are swollen and completely blocked. "You sure you don't know this guy from somewhere? Maybe seen him around? Or recognize the bike?"

"No, no way. I'm telling you—listen, man, I don't feel so good...."

Jason bolted over to join Tony, and questioning had to be put on hold.

"This is a waste of time," Erik said, the first words he'd uttered since I'd gotten back to the command post.

"Maybe not," Charlie said. "We'll go over it again. You never know. And we'll run the money he gave the kids for prints."

"The guy on the motorcycle was wearing gloves," I said.

Charlie shot me a malevolent look that said the last thing he wanted was input from me. "So maybe he handled the money *before* he put on the goddamn gloves. We'll talk to the people in the liquor store, Erik. They could know something."

"All right," Erik said. "You stay and do it. But get the chopper here. I'm going home. Delilah?"

He strode off back to Charlie's van, assuming I'd follow. My instincts were to do just what Charlie was doing and squeeze everybody who was anywhere near this parking lot in the past couple of hours. I also felt the smallest spark of resentment at being ordered around like the hired help. Still, knowing how much pain Erik was in, it was easy to forgive him. Anyway, I thought he was right. In the end this was all a waste of time.

In the helicopter, Erik sat as remote and unmoving as that big rock where I'd waited with the ransom. At the house, he brushed past Ben and went straight to the bar in the family room. There he poured an inch of scotch into a tumbler, drank it down like medicine, and refilled the glass.

I waved away an anxious Ben and went to join Erik at the bar.

"I'll have one of those, too," I said, even though scotch is not my alcohol of choice.

We took the drinks over and sat down in front of the fireplace, where a pile of oak logs blazed away. One thing about having servants, you always come home to a fire when you need one, even though the flames were not guaranteed to thaw the chill in your bones.

"He has the bonds, Erik. He'll release Nicki now. He'll take her someplace and leave her like he did me."

I carefully left out words like probably and maybe and pray God.

Moisture sizzled up out of a log, hissing and cracking. Orange flame reflected on Erik's stony face. He leaned forward like he had a big weight on his back, sipped scotch, and said, "I think I'm a damn good businessman, Delilah. I can sweet-talk banks, play hardball with unions, just roll right over the competition. But this, the most important deal in my life, and nothing works. I am just so completely goddamn helpless...."

"I know." I linked an arm through his and leaned my head against his shoulder. "I'm sorry, love. All we can do now is wait."

Ben brought in snacks: raw vegetables, an assortment of cheese and crackers. I nibbled, but Erik only drank, steadily and sparingly, and stared at the silent phone.

Charlie showed up about eleven-thirty to confirm what we already knew. The investigation out at the liquor store was a bust. Nobody knew anything. Even offers of money failed to refresh any memories.

As for the bills given to Jason and Tony by the kidnapper, only the teenagers' prints were found. Everything else was too smudged to be read.

The three vehicles that had been in the vineyard area had been tailed and stopped on one pretext or another. None was connected to the kidnapping.

At some point I went to the bathroom and put back the Tylenol and the ampicillin. Returned the Beretta to my purse. So much for my preparations.

None of us had any thought of going to bed. Ben and Vincent brought blankets and pillows. We each took a couch and stretched out there for another night of broken sleep.

And during all that time the phone never rang.

YOU HAD TO WONDER what kind of favors were called in to get a federal prisoner alone for a private talk. Well, Charlie accomplished it, and finally, first thing the next morning, got a report back from the operative in New Jersey.

Turk Rizzo remembered me, all right. "Foxy bitch," he'd recalled. "Looked a lot better when I fixed her up a little."

The first thing he'd done, however, after his escape was to rob a convenience store and spend the money on some crystal meth, so his short-term memory was pretty foggy. He could barely remember how he slipped out of custody, let alone whether my name had been a topic of discussion in the jailhouse.

Even Charlie had to admit that the Rizzo connection was a dead end, although he was not giving up on his theory that the kidnapper was somebody from my past. Tenacity is Charlie Colfax's biggest asset.

Frankly, he scared hell out of me.

His nose was puffed up, he was sporting a shiner, and he was definitely not a candidate for president of the Delilah West fan club. If he could find any way to blame me for what had happened to Nicki, he would, if nothing else than to downplay his own mistakes.

At this point I doubted Erik would be paying much attention to his putdowns. Anyway, I wanted to shower and change, and I couldn't stand the thought of rummaging through Nicki's closet and wearing something else of hers. I desperately needed to be in my own clothes, in my own space at least for a while.

Erik said he understood, he'd have Vincent drive me home. Yes, of course, he'd call the minute they heard anything.

At my apartment building, Vincent jumped out to open

my door, saying he'd wait, but I could see my van, parked in a corner, and knew Danny must've brought it over.

"That's okay," I said. "You go on back. I can drive myself. And, Vincent? If something happens—something bad—and Erik forgets, call me, will you?"

"If I can," he said, reminding me of where his loyalties lay.

Upstairs in the shower, letting the hot water beat down on me, I had to admit that it wasn't the likelihood of Erik's forgetting to call that bothered me. I thought Erik was drawing away, and I couldn't lay all the blame on Charlie.

Not that I blamed Erik either. Logical explanations and excuses be damned. Human feeling is based on the most basic truths, and the truth was that I was free and Nicki was imprisoned. I was alive, and Erik's only child could very well be dead.

All those times I'd told myself I had to break off the relationship with Erik, and now it seemed that fate, in the cruelest of turns, might accomplish what I could never quite bring myself to do.

TWENTY

I WAS PACKING a suitcase, preparing to go back and rejoin the vigil, when the phone rang. I snatched it up, hope dying quickly at the bleakness in Erik's voice as he said hello.

"Have you heard?" I asked.

"No," he said. "Nothing."

"You will."

"We can't assume anything at this point. Charlie's questioning the staff here and his security people, still checking personnel files at the office. He wants names from you. Anybody you even suspect may have a grudge. Can you have Danny go through your files and work with him from here?"

I probably could have, but there was a remoteness in Erik's voice, and the suggestion sounded like something he was expected to say, like he didn't really care one way or the other.

My reaction was immediate, and almost as quickly regretted, but he didn't argue when I said, "No, I think I'd better do this at my office."

After I hung up, I backed up and sat down on the bed, feeling sucker-punched. I'd just been telling myself what fate was up to, but, dammit, did I have to be right all the time?

ONCE IN A GREAT WHILE, Harry nods off for a minute down in his utility room lair, allowing me to sneak in unnoticed. Not today. When I arrived, he was mopping the hall, and stopped immediately to hobble over and intercept me at the bottom of the stairs.

"Miz West, hey," he said. "Ain't you a sight for sore eyes? Danny went to the Hall of Records for a while. You want I should get the bus and go over there and let him know you're here?"

"No, no, that's okay," I said, brushing past. "Thanks anyway."

Harry has a hard time taking a hint. He stood, looking up at me, and kept on talking. "Brian's sure gonna be glad you're back. I told him he should stop worryin' about his dad, if you're lookin' for him—"

"Brian?" I stopped to stare at Harry. The last I'd heard, he considered Brian Hall just another juvenile delinquent with a spray can.

"Yeah, he's come by once or twice. Not such a bad kid when you get to know him. He's been showin' me how to work that Game Boy gizmo of his, but it's a little hard with my arthritis. So we been playin' checkers instead. I know Danny said you been off on a real important case, but I hope you're gonna have some time to look for Mr. Hall. That boy sure misses his pop."

"I know he does. I'll get busy as quick as I can."

"Good, good. Knew you would." Harry beamed me a smile I didn't deserve as I fled to my office and called after me, "Anything I can do to help, why, you give me a holler."

Harry might be too preoccupied with his newfound young friend to ask many questions. Danny was going to be a lot more persistent, and to tell the truth I was just as glad my assistant was out. I wasn't anxious to explain about Turk Rizzo and why I had not been forthcoming about his escape. Just *thinking* about the whole fiasco made my head hurt.

Since Turk and friend had turned most of my paper records into so much confetti with their bomb blast, a limited number of files remained to be pulled. The rest of the information had to be dredged up from memory.

My resulting list of names and last known addresses, some of them in places like San Quentin and Soledad, was a hell of a lot longer that I expected. I had no idea so many people had reason to do me harm. Still, I couldn't help but think if the kidnapper was somebody with a grudge, it was just as likely to be against Erik.

I mess with people's freedom. Erik messes with their bank accounts.

I was preparing to fax off the list to Charlie when the phone rang.

"Delilah?" Rita said, sounding surprised. "I was calling Danny to see if he'd heard anything. What are you doing there? Is Nicki—is she—?"

"There's nothing yet," I said. "Erik paid the ransom, but the kidnapper still hasn't released her. I came in to check out a few things."

"You think it's somebody who's after *you*," she said, making one of her gigantic intuitive leaps.

"No, I don't," I said. "We're just trying to cover all the bases."

"Uh-huh," she said. "Sure. You have some idea who it is?"

"Well, it's not Turk Rizzo," I said, and instantly regretted the slip. "All right, if you must know, he escaped from prison, but he couldn't have had anything to do with the kidnapping. They caught him on Saturday in New Jersey—*Saturday,* when the kidnapper was dropping me off."

"Oh my God," she said. "You didn't tell Erik."

"No."

"But he found out."

"Yes."

"Is that why you're not with him?"

"No, not really. Things just got—complicated. I'm not even sure he wants me around right now. He's focused on Nicki. I understand that."

"You listen to me," Rita said, "when a thing like this happens, you're just a big ball of pain. You're inside yourself, and you don't know what you want. Remember when you lost Jack? It was bad, but I'm here to tell you that losing your only child is worse. And knowing you may lose her and not being able to stop it happening, that's got to be a living hell. Erik needs you now, even if he seems to pushing you away."

"Okay," I said. "You're right."

"Then what are you waiting for? You can work out all the other stuff later."

"Rita?" I took a big breath. "I think I might—that maybe I love him."

"Oh, kiddo," she said. "Everybody knows that. Now for goodness' sake go and tell Erik."

WELL, okay, I didn't do what Rita said instantly. But I think I would have done it.

I was hanging up the phone and reaching for my purse, hesitating a little maybe because this was a very big step. And then the door to the outer office opened.

When Danny's away, I keep my door open in case anybody comes by, and since there's been some petty theft in the building recently, I've moved my desk so I have a direct view of either client or thief stopping by. The person who walked in was Charlie Colfax, soon to be in a class all his own.

He headed straight through to my office and dropped down in a chair across from me without a word of greeting.

I stared at him, feeling as though the air had been sucked from the room, thinking that Nicki was dead and he had come to break the news.

"I was in the neighborhood," he said. "Thought I'd pick up that list from you."

"Why aren't you with Erik?" I asked, somehow not relieved that he hadn't delivered bad news.

"My people are there," he said. "They'll call the second anything happens."

His eye had puffed up some more and the bruise had turned a nasty yellow. His gray silk tie had just a trace of the same color. You'd think he might have chosen the tie as a joke unless you knew he had absolutely no sense of humor.

"I was just going to fax this to you," I said, passing over the list of names.

He took it, gave it a quick scan. "What about the cases you're working on now?"

"What about them?"

"They're not here."

"Come on," I said. "Do I have to remind you about confidentiality?"

"About what I expected." He made a show of deliberately ripping my list in half. "This is shit, Delilah. I wouldn't waste my time. The name I want would not be on any list you gave me."

There was a shine in his eyes that made me feel cold inside. I had no idea what was coming but was sure it would be bad.

He leaned forward and said, "Do you know where Erik was the day you and Nicki disappeared?"

"I want you to leave," I said. "Right now."

"No, you'll want to hear this. He was up at Cartier's at South Coast Plaza. He told me you wouldn't let him buy you a Christmas present, but that your birthday was coming so he wanted to get you something special.''

''Oh, *Jesus*,'' I said faintly, understanding now the errand Erik was on the day Nicki and I were kidnapped.

''He didn't tell me what he bought,'' Charlie went on, ''but I made it a point to find out. A diamond, coupla carats, a little flashy but tasteful. So you see, you had him hooked, Delilah. He was going to pop the big question. All you had to do was wait.''

I was back there with Erik, coming home from that shopping trip, delighted with himself and making plans and never thinking that I might not want an engagement ring, that I might say no, because men like Erik don't think that way, then finding the Lamborghini with the window smashed and the note and both our purses in the car....

Caught up in the scene, it took a second for the import of Charlie's last remark to sink in.

''Just a minute,'' I said. ''What do you mean, *all I had to do was wait?*''

''I hear Nicki didn't like you. I don't know. Maybe you started sweating the program. Maybe you thought Erik was gonna dump you, your business going down the tubes without him feeding you clients, and you saw yourself back waiting tables. I mean, if you think about it, it's a pretty slick plan. I gotta hand you that. You get taken with Nicki, and then the kidnapper lets you go. Poor Delilah, all beat up—but, of course, just enough to make it look good.''

''You son of a *bitch*,'' I said, so full of rage I could barely get the words out.

''Then guess what?'' he plowed on, not missing a beat. ''*You* have to deliver the ransom. *And* the guy gets away with it, imagine that.''

I was up and swinging, aiming another punch at his

puffy nose, but this time he saw it coming. Out of his chair, he grabbed my wrist and clamped down hard.

"You can blindside me once," he said softly. "But never again, trust me."

"You vindictive *snake*." I jerked my arm away. "I'm going straight to Erik and tell him every foul thing you've said."

"Go ahead. But are you so sure he'll believe you? And say he does, it won't keep me from taking your life apart. Fact is, it'll just make me come after you harder. I'm going to burn you down, Delilah, one way or the other. I hope to God I find enough evidence to put you in the middle of Nicki's kidnapping so I can see you in jail where you belong. If not, at the very least I'm going to shitcan your little business here, and you'll be on the street."

I got one look at his venom-filled face before he turned and stalked out, but it was enough. There was not a doubt in my mind that he meant every word he had said.

TWENTY-ONE

I WAS SHAKING so badly my knees gave way, and I had to sit down. Even the thought that somebody could suspect me of such a thing, even *Charlie,* filled me with alternating waves of horror and rage. Could he really believe that nasty scenario he'd concocted?

And never mind about Charlie. Would Erik believe it?

Come on, stop it, I told myself. *Get a grip.*

I had no doubt Charlie would keep his promise, and that I would pay dearly for that moment out on Baseline Road. Charlie was a man who would not forget humiliation and he sure as hell would never forgive.

And yes, he could make my life miserable. If he dug enough, he might even connect me with the shooting at the mall. But after all I'd shot the man in self-defense. Ed Daley, the mall security guard who was credited with the kill, was being crowned a hero.

Once the kidnapper was found, we'd know the whole story. Charlie's accusations would be seen for the back-stabbing attacks they were. And surely Nicki would confirm that I was as much a victim as she was, no matter how much she preferred that I not be with her dad.

But what if the kidnapper took the money and vanished? What if Nicki died? What if Charlie decided not only to tell Erik his blatantly absurd suspicions, but to plant a few signposts pointing to me?

Maybe this was rampant paranoia, but just then I knew that sometimes the big lies are the ones that are believed and that I had to make sure Erik heard everything from me and right away.

I jumped up and charged from the office. Running down the stairs, I remembered I hadn't locked the door. I yelled for Harry, asking him to please lock up, then ran on out to the van, ignoring his bewildered questions about what was going on.

Driving south was a nightmare. Every traffic light was red on the surface streets. Every slowpoke in Orange County was out blocking the freeway. I had lots of time to think about what I would say to Erik and how Charlie could undercut me.

I'd tell Erik the whole story about that day in the mall. He wouldn't like knowing I'd killed George Mendel. He might be sickened by the whole thing, but surely he would understand.

"No wonder she lied," Charlie would say. *"Jesus, she just blows some guy away and goes about her business because she didn't want a little publicity? Seems to me she didn't want you to know because you might start having some doubts. I mean, if she could do something like that, what else is she capable of?"*

I'd tell Erik the shooting at the mall was the only thing I was keeping from him. Well, the only major thing. There might be a few minor lies here and there, but nothing important, nothing I wouldn't confess to as soon as I remembered what they were.

"You got to ask yourself," Charlie would say, *"if she keeps something like that from you, what else is she hiding?"*

Most important of all, I'd tell Erik I loved him. Yes, there, I'd said it to myself and I'd say it to him. Once I'd told him, once he understood I'd never do anything to hurt him or Nicki, he would never believe any of Charlie's vicious slander.

"Good timing, don't you think?" Charlie would say. "Stringing you along, not one peep about this undying love of hers until she knows I'm on to her."

God! Big mistake trying to punch him out in my office. I should've shot the bastard and had Harry take him out and bury him—with a stake through his heart as an added precaution.

I spent the next few minutes giving myself a stern talking-to. Wasn't I selling Erik short here, imagining he would believe Charlie? I might have thought differently in the beginning, but I'd come to see Erik as a decent, caring man. God knows he'd taken care of me, even when I'd made it known loud and clear that I didn't want his help.

Rita was right. Even Gary Hofer was right. Erik had gone out and bought a ring. He wanted to marry me, for God's sake. So what I had to do was tell Erik everything and trust to his good sense and the bond between us.

That was my decision as I drove up the asphalt road to the guard gate at the entry to Erik's estate. The man on duty was a stranger, which, I suppose, should have been my first clue that things were about to go wrong.

"Sorry," he said. "No visitors."

"I'm on the list," I said. "Delilah West."

"Not today," he said politely.

"This is ridiculous. Call the house."

"I have my orders, Ms. West."

"I'm sure you do, but they're not from Erik Lundstrom."

And no point yelling at the guy who was only doing his job. I dug in my purse and took out my cell phone.

"Excuse me," the guard said. "Move your van before you make your call. I'm expecting somebody."

Somebody who *was* on Charlie's list, I supposed. I put the van in reverse, backed up just past the gate and over a ways, out of the road. Then I punched in the main number at the house. Charlie answered, just as I figured he would, probably alerted as soon as I turned off PCH.

"Tell your man to let me in, Charlie," I said without preamble.

"It's not a good time, Delilah."

"You're damn right it isn't. Not for you, anyway. Now let me in or I'll call Erik on the private line."

"You can do that. I don't think it's a good idea, though. You'd have to explain why. Get into this whole thing. Do you really think Erik needs that right now? I mean he's got Nicki to worry about and besides that, Nicki's mother's on her way."

"Margaret's on a cruise."

"She was. She called as soon as her plane landed at Kennedy, right after he spoke to you this morning. She didn't even go home, just got on the next flight to L.A. Erik sent the limo. She'll be here any time now. He's going to have his hands full."

I heard Erik's voice in the background, muffled, but Charlie hadn't quite clamped his hand over the receiver fast enough. "Charlie, I know he's there. Put him on the damned phone. Right now."

A few more muffled exchanges and Erik said, "Delilah? Charlie told you about Margaret."

"Yes, she must be terribly upset."

Having finally gotten to him, I found I couldn't just blurt out everything. I couldn't even say, *I'm sitting a quarter of a mile down the road, and Charlie won't let me through the gate.* This would be hard enough. We needed to be face-to-face.

"Margaret's devastated," Erik said. "And angry. And completely unreasonable the way she always is."

"Erik, I want to be there. I know it'll be awkward, but I don't care. I was with Nicki. Margaret may want to ask questions."

"No, Delilah. Believe me, that's not a good idea. Wait—"

I could hear Charlie's voice rumbling, but couldn't make out what he was saying.

"Erik—" I began.

"Charlie needs to talk to you again," Erik said. "Here he is. I'll call you later."

"Erik, I have to see you," I said but it was Charlie who answered.

"Like I told you," Charlie said softly, "he's got a full plate." Then his tone returned to normal pitch, telling me Erik must have left the room. "You can come on up if you want, Delilah, but I just talked to Vincent and he's about through Corona del Mar. You can probably see the limo turning off pretty soon. You really think now's the time?"

"No, probably not. That doesn't mean I won't talk to Erik, it just means I'll do it later."

"Well, when you do, there's something else you ought to keep in mind. If you throw this at him and there's the slightest chance he sides with you, he'll fire me. Or else I'll quit. Either way he's going to *have* to go the cops. And cops won't let the money go, you know that. They'll concentrate on recovering the ransom, Delilah, not on Nicki. To make matters worse, Erik'll have nobody on this thing that's been in from the beginning, which could delay the search. Maybe it'll be a critical delay. You really want that?"

"No," I said, hoping I didn't sound as defeated as I felt. "I don't want that."

"Okay, then. Go on home. Think about it."

The phone clicked, denying me even the satisfaction of hanging up on him. At least he hadn't made any accusations about me yet. No, and he wouldn't, I realized, not without something to back up his ridiculous charges. But he would be spreading his poison, a drop at a time, and not a damn thing I could do about it.

I swung the van around and headed back down the winding road. It occurred to me that Charlie might have been lying, that Margaret's plane hadn't even landed yet, but Erik's limo was waiting to make the turn as I rolled to a stop on PCH, coming in as I was going out. I couldn't see who was in back through the darkly tinted windows, but of course it had to be Margaret.

I drove a short distance and found a place to get off the road. Sat there, feeling as though I'd been thrown into one of those wood-chipping machines, chewed up and spit out, as helpless as I'd felt in a long, long time.

What the bloody hell did I do now?

Only one thing I could do. Find Nicki. Find out who kidnapped her and me. Spike Charlie's guns and do it quickly.

I thought about that list I'd put together for Charlie, imagining everybody on it in a stocking mask. Charlie was right about one thing. None of those people probably had anything to do with any of this. There was one name, however, I had not put on the list.

A wild card.

Somebody I had to check out myself: Albert Mendel, George Mendel's brother.

IF DANNY WAS BACK in the office, I thought he could probably find Albert Mendel fairly fast. Just about anything about anybody can be accessed over the Web these days. But, of course, by asking Danny, I'd be opening a great big can of worms.

No, I had to do this myself.

Fortunately, Albert Mendel wasn't all that hard to find. I have a couple of phone books in the van, two of the many required now to cover the whole area. Mendel was in the one for north Orange County, with an address in Placentia. When I called the number that was published, however, I found it had been changed and was no longer listed. Of course, he could have moved. There was only one way to find out. I headed north.

I'd seen Albert Mendel only briefly in the video clip right after the shooting, and that was a close-up. If I saw him walking, moving around, would I really recognize him as the man who kidnapped Nicki and me? And if I thought there was any possibility that Albert Mendel was that man, did I want to face him alone?

Well, I planned on surveillance, not confrontation, and, anyway, how could I tell anybody where I was going without explaining why?

I might have been an emotional wreck, but the body still functions, and I'd had only coffee that morning. Hunger pains forced a quick stop at Del Taco. After that I found the address easily enough: an older two-story stucco house on a tree-lined street with enough cars parked along the curb so I could sit in my van and not look conspicuous. I ate my taco, sipped a little Coke, and settled in to wait with the Beretta close at hand and the .38 waiting in the glove box.

Stakeouts are, by their nature, boring as hell and hard on the kidneys. Worse, they provide lots of brooding time, and God knows I had plenty to brood about, starting with the day after Christmas when I took Isabel shopping at the mall and ending up at Erik's gate today, being refused admittance.

Were Erik and Margaret fighting, rearguing all the old grievances, slashing and hurting as only people who have loved each other know how to do? Or were they beyond that, comforting each other and remembering how that love had created a child who might be lost to them forever?

Sitting there with sunshine spilling on beds of bright purple pansies in the Mendel's front yard, I was suddenly back in that prison cell with Nicki, hearing her confide that she had always known she would end up in that desolate room in the dark. I had quickly put a stop to her depressing discussion of ESP, so she'd never voiced the rest of her fears. I knew them all the same. She was afraid she would die there.

Never mind Charlie and his threats. Never mind my petty little pangs of jealousy and my fear that I'd dragged my feet and maybe lost Erik. All that mattered was Nicki.

How much longer could she survive, abandoned and alone? She ought to have some of the food and maybe two quarts of water left. If she'd been careful; if she hadn't spilled the water again or binged on the food; if, regardless of what I told Erik, she was still alive.

I pushed aside that last grisly thought, and tried to think of what I could do next if Mendel was not the kidnapper. I'd gone over our capture so often and come up with nothing useful. And nothing came to mind this time, either, because just then a Ford Taurus cruised past.

I got only a glimpse of the driver as the car drove by, then I ducked down because he was looking back at me. But I had enough time to recognize Albert Mendel.

Inching up, I watched as he braked, turned into his driveway, and got out of the car. Short and thickset, he looked so much like his brother, it made the hair on my arms stand up.

He took a couple of bags of groceries from the trunk of the car and headed for the house, so I had a good opportunity to observe the way he moved on his short, stumpy legs. By no stretch of the imagination was this the man who had dragged me from the Lamborghini and thrown me in that gray van.

Now what? Go in and talk to him? Maybe there was another sibling, cousin, or crazy friend out to revenge Georgie's death and pick up a couple of million bucks along the way. Of course, there still remained the small problem of connecting that person to me.

Albert was in the house about two minutes while I sat there and tried to decide what to do next. Then the front door banged open and somebody hurried out—not Albert, an older woman, plump and determined, who made a beeline straight to my van. I could have made a run for it, but I thought she would probably have walked right in front of the van to stop me.

There was no mistaking the resemblance to her two sons. Anyway, I remembered Mrs. Mendel from the same news broadcast featuring Albert. Then, she had been distraught and tearful; now she was hopping mad as she came up to my open window and demanded, "Who are you? What are you doing out here?"

"Charline Colfax," I said and named the sleaziest tabloid show on television. "I want to do a follow-up, ask Albert a few questions—"

"You people never give up, do you?" Then she took great delight in telling me why I was wasting my time.

There was no need for Albert to kidnap Nicki. He was making his money the old-fashioned way by signing with a top-notch agent, highjacking his brother's fifteen minutes of blood-stained fame, and getting himself a book deal.

I ACHED with exhaustion, but I couldn't go home. At the office maybe I would think of something, or at least I'd have work as a distraction. At my apartment I thought I just might go crazy.

I managed to avoid Harry, but had barely sat down at my desk when Danny charged in.

"Anything?" he asked.

"Nothing good," I said.

"Poor Mr. Lundstrom. I'm surprised you're not with him."

"I'd like to be," I said. "But Nicki's mother is there. I need to stay busy, Danny. Catch me up on things around here."

For the next hour we went over the cases that had been pending when I went for my ill-fated lunch. Most of them were wrapped up and reports ready to be sent, waiting for my review and signature. A couple more routine things had come in, plus one from an old lady down in Leisure World who was becoming a regular client—which explained Danny's trip to the Hall of Records.

A confirmed conspiracy nut with plenty of money to fund her hobby, the old gal was constantly putting together lists of holding companies she wanted traced, hinting darkly of links between organized crime and every assassination in the past fifty years. The scary part was that some of them even made a weird kind of sense.

Of course I had no brainstorms about Nicki, and I started drooping while Danny told me about this latest project, putting an elbow on my desk and propping my chin on my hand.

"You have any time to spend on Travis Hall?" I asked with a yawn.

"Some," Danny said. "I called that friend of his again, Armstead, but never reached him. And I've started checking trucking firms, but no luck so far."

"Harry said Brian came by a couple of times."

"So I heard. I only saw him once. I wondered if I ought to chase him away. But I know his mom works, and I guess playing checkers with Harry can't be any worse than hanging out at malls...."

Danny's voice kind of faded away. I laid my head down on the open file folders and simply drifted off. The next thing I knew he was shaking me awake.

"The phone," I said groggily. "Did Erik—?"

"Nobody called," Danny said. "Come on. I'll drive you home."

I slept in the van and roused just enough to let Danny walk me upstairs to my apartment. I said only, "Bring the phone," when I lay down on the couch and barely remembered that he did before he let himself out.

At first sleep was smooth and seamless, but the dreams came soon enough. I was six years old, astride a pony, riding on a wild hilltop on a glorious sun-struck day. The pony's mane and tail flew like honey-colored flags in the wind. The margin of the hill yawned, but I was okay. I could see the edge just fine. I could tell exactly how far I could go.

Then the ground at the rim began to crumble under the pony's feet. The little horse was screaming, I was screaming, and still I could hear my father's voice saying sternly, "Liars dig a hole and then they have to stand in it," as we fell into the darkness.

TWENTY-TWO

I SLEPT FOR THREE HOURS and woke with the dream hanging around me like smoke. Danny had left the portable phone right beside the couch as I had asked. Surely I would have heard it ring. I stumbled over to check the answering machine anyway.

No messages.

Margaret Lundstrom had to have been at Erik's for at least eight hours. What had Nicki told me? *Aunt Deirdre says she's never seen two people as much in love.... She says you never get over a love like that....*

No, no. I was not going to do that to myself.

Worry about Charlie. He was the bigger threat. Think about Nicki.

Worry and thought both required fuel. First fatigue had caught up with me and now hunger. My refrigerator looked as though it was being used to grow biological specimens, and there was nothing in my freezer that didn't contain the words *fat free* or *low-cal* on the packaging.

I went to the bathroom, washed the sleep crusts from my eyes, yanked a brush through my hair, and went to find a nice anonymous Denny's. There I devoured meat loaf, mashed potatoes, and lemon meringue pie. Thought about Nicki with every bite, imagined every man who came through the door with a stocking over his head, and convinced myself Charlie was too smart for a frontal attack. Sabotage was more his style.

Much as I hated to credit Charlie with any useful suggestion, what about his idea of seeing a hypnotist? I'd been right to shy away from Charlie's choice, as it turned out, somebody he could've fed his own slanted, hand-picked questions. But there was no reason I couldn't find a hypnotist of my own choosing. I even had one in mind, but it was long past office hours. I would have to wait until morning.

All the while, during the drive and the meal, I kept checking to make sure I had enough signal strength on my cell phone to receive a call. When I got back home, I checked the answering machine.

Nothing.

I tried to call Rita, but got the machine and hung up without leaving a message. I prowled the apartment, remembered I hadn't picked up my mail for days, went down to get it, came back and sorted it, tossed ninety-nine percent into recycling, prowled around some more.

And the twin worms of doubt kept chewing away. I had no trouble at all picturing Erik's stricken face as he listened to Charlie's lies, or he and Margaret together, holding and comforting each other all night long over the terrible thing that had happened to their child because of course she would stay there....

Stop it, I told myself fiercely.

I really was going to go crazy if I hung around here. After my nap, I couldn't even escape into sleep.

But what could I do? Go out, drive around. Lot of good that would do, unless...

I called Danny, apologizing for the late hour.

"No problem," he said. "I was just surfing the Net. What's up?"

When I explained what I had in mind, he said he'd come right over.

DANNY DROVE. I lay on the floor of my van with a sweatshirt over my head as a substitute for the hood. Using the turnoff for Erik's place as a starting point, we were on the road for hours, trying every possible freeway route.

By 3 a.m. I knew it was hopeless. There was no way I could duplicate that ride in the kidnapper's van. In cleverly plotted movies, strange sounds might turn into clues to point the way, but everything I had heard had been modified with terror and pain and further muddled by the rain pounding down on the Econoline's roof.

Giving up, I climbed into the passenger's seat and said, "It's a bust. Might as well go home."

"You'll come up with something else," Danny said.

"I don't think so," I said bleakly. "Not this time."

"Delilah, what is it? Are you all right?"

"No, Danny, I'm not. I won't be until we find Nicki."

SINCE IT WAS SO LATE Danny bunked on my couch. Next morning while I got dressed, he took the van and made a quick trip home for a shower and a change of clothes. I'm sure he was barely out the door before he found a phone and called Rita, and seconds later Rita called me.

"Danny didn't waste any time," I said.

"He's worried about you. What's wrong?"

"Everything."

"You didn't see Erik," she said.

"No."

"What happened?"

I took a shaky breath and closed my eyes. The conversation with Charlie and everything that took place afterward were like an obstruction in my throat that I couldn't force out.

I said, "I don't think I can talk about it. Not right now."

"Is it really that bad?"

"Yes," I said. "It is, or it may be."

"Well, whatever happened, I told you before and I'll say it again: Talk to Erik."

"I wish I could. But Margaret's there, Nicki's mother. I can't just barge in."

"And you still don't know anything about Nicki?"

"No. I'm sure Erik would call if he heard. I have to find her, Rita. I have to."

"Oh, kiddo," she said with growing alarm. "I've never heard you sound so desperate. I'm coming over there."

"No, Rita, it wouldn't do any good. I'm going to work, stay busy, try to think."

"And talk to Erik."

"I hope so."

WHEN DANNY CAME BACK to pick me up, he had brought his bicycle, along with two Egg McMuffins, orange juice, and coffee, which we ate on the way to the office. He kept shooting me apprehensive glances until I let him off the hook.

"It's okay," I said. "I forgive you."

"Sorry," he said sheepishly. "You won't talk to me. I thought maybe Rita could help."

"Well, she can't, so please, no networking, okay? I don't want to hear from anybody else."

At the office, I plunged into the stacks of mail that had been piling up. That done, I dispatched Danny to the Hall of Records to finish up the work for our conspiracy nut. Then I put in a call to Alice Carew, who teaches psychology at Cal State Fullerton and uses hypnotherapy in her private practice. Her secretary promised to give her the message that I urgently needed an appointment.

After I tied up a few loose ends on some other cases, I began to slog through the list of trucking companies, taking up where Danny had left off, looking for some record of employment for Travis Hall.

If I didn't manage to forget my immediate problems, at least I buried them for an hour or so, still listening for the phone to ring.

I'd had enough of unexpected visitors, didn't want another, but about ten o'clock I got one anyway. I'd never seen the woman who walked into my outer office before, never even seen a picture, but I knew who she was. Before, I had been struck by how much Nicki looked like her father. Now I could see the resemblance to her mother, too.

Maybe it was the cheekbones, the kind that can make a career in modeling possible, or the arrogant assurance in that slender, well-toned body. In any case there was no mistaking that Margaret Lundstrom had come to call.

It was amazing the flood of conflicting emotions I felt. This woman had shared Erik's bed, borne him a child, loved him all those years—maybe still loved him. *You're just wrong for my dad,* Nicki had said. Now, seeing her mother, I knew she was probably right.

Margaret wore skinny knit slacks tucked into brown suede boots and a long knit top, both in a light apricot color that set off the tan acquired from cruising the Caribbean. Artful streaks in the brown hair might have been bleached by the sun at the same time or maybe they were just the work of a skillful hairdresser.

Seeing her raw, ravaged face I suspected that dressing well was a reflex. Most likely her wardrobe consisted of nothing but beautiful clothes.

She was also humming with unfocused rage as she crossed the outer office in long, graceful strides and paused in my doorway, her green eyes glittering. "Charles Colfax thinks you're hiding something that could help find Nicki. Are you?"

God, it was starting. Of course, Charlie wouldn't be content to just malign me to Erik. And, come to think of it, Margaret didn't know me. She was a perfect target for his slanderous campaign.

"I don't care what Charlie told you," I said, getting to my feet so I could look her straight in the eye. "I've been racking my brain to think of anything, *anything*, that would help find Nicki. I'm the one person who really knows how dire the situation is, Mrs. Lundstrom. We were together for three days in that terrible place. I held her when she cried—when the light went out and we were in the dark."

Seeing the sudden anguish on her face, I broke off and said quickly, "I'm sorry. That was thoughtless. Please, I didn't mean to—"

"No, it's all right." She sat down in one of the client chairs abruptly, as though her legs wouldn't support her.

"Can I get you something? Water or—"

She shook her head, then fumbled in her purse for cigarettes and a slim silver lighter. "Do you mind?"

I did, but I sat back down behind my desk, opened a drawer, dug out an ashtray, and passed it to her.

"I've tried to quit for twenty years," she said. "One of the many things Erik and I used to fight about—*still* fight about. I'm so furious with him for not calling me immediately." She took a long drag on the cigarette and blew out a cloud of smoke. "He keeps saying he's done everything he can, but why didn't he bring in the police or the FBI? Why doesn't he do it now?"

"It's a judgment call," I said, and one, despite some reservations, I agreed with. "The police have other agendas. Erik only has one: finding Nicki."

"Well, he hasn't found her, has he?" She took another drag of the cigarette, then stubbed it out. "The two of them—Erik and Colfax—they keep trying to smooth things over, to make it easier, but dammit, it's not easy, and I have a right to know. So tell me—would you, please?"

Even though I felt sorry for her, maybe I didn't have the same kind of protective feeling I did with Erik. Maybe there was some kind of strange bond forming between the two of us. Anyway, I told her everything.

Well, almost everything.

I left out her daughter's tactless personal remarks, and I edited out all the things Nicki had confided about her childhood, things I was sure she wouldn't want her parents to hear.

Margaret listened, unflinching, and when I finished she looked years older and as if she were on the verge of some catastrophic illness.

"No wonder Erik tried to play things down." She took out the cigarettes and the lighter, held them as though she had no idea what their purpose was, then put them back in her purse. "He says she's alive, that we'll get her back, but I'm not sure he believes it. And Colfax—I can tell he thinks Nicki's dead."

"Well, I don't think so."

"Why?" Margaret asked. "I don't want false hope. I want the truth."

"I could be wrong about this, okay? But my take is that we're dealing with a guy who's having a lot of fun putting us all through hell. But torturing us—and Nicki—that's one thing. Murder is something else. If I was in his shoes, I'd be thinking that Erik's a rich, powerful man, that he'd come after me if I killed his daughter, and eventually he'd track me down. So I'd get my kicks and then I'd let her go."

I didn't add that those kicks might include more than locking Nicki away. Margaret might be strong, but I didn't think she was ready to hear that.

"Nicki has food and four days of water," I said. "She'll be okay."

"If she rationed things the way you told her. I just don't know, Delilah. She's not prepared to endure something like this. Best schools, best doctors, best of everything, but she's not prepared for this."

"Maybe you gave her what she needs to survive without knowing it," I said. "She's stubborn. And the most important thing: She wants to live, Margaret. She told me that."

"I pray you're right." She stood up, shouldering her purse as though it weighed fifty pounds. "I can't stay at Erik's. I hated that damn place when he built it, and I still hate it. I'll be at the Ritz in Dana Point until we know...something."

She held out her hands across my desk and gripped mine briefly. "Thank God you were with her. I'm sorry if that sounds selfish."

"I understand," I said. "Margaret? I'd be there in her place, if I could."

"Yes, I think you would. That man, Colfax—Vincent told me you punched him in the nose," she said with the faintest glimmer of a smile.

"I'm afraid I did."

"He probably deserved it. If you think of anything you can do to find Nicki, if you need anything—money, extra help—just ask."

I said I would and hoped it wasn't an empty promise. And even though she had an instinctive dislike for Charlie, I wondered what her reaction would be when she heard his whole nasty tale about me.

And I wondered something else, too. It must have been more than an hour now since Margaret left Erik's place. Why hadn't he called?

I remembered being in the hospital on Saturday night, seeing Erik and thinking about the kind of chasm grief could put between us.

Me and Nicki, both with our premonitions. I had told her I didn't believe in ESP, any of that stuff, and I didn't. Now it seemed that fate in the form of a vengeful Charlie Colfax just might make a believer of me.

TWENTY-THREE

I CLEANED OUT the ashtray, opened a window to air out my office, and went back to waiting for the phone to ring.

Of course, at any time I could have reached Erik by calling the private number, which I knew he'd pick up instantly. But Charlie would pick it up, too, and he'd hear every word I said. The thought made my skin crawl. There was also an element of desperation in making the call, and I wouldn't give Charlie the satisfaction of hearing it in my voice.

Damn the man. He'd taken a terrible situation and made it intolerable. Worse, as I would soon discover, he had clouded my mind with his threats just when I needed a clear head.

Stymied and frustrated, I did what I always do in such situations. I went back to work, doggedly calling trucking companies until my stomach began to growl. Only eleven-fifteen, but late enough for a trip to Subway, early enough to beat the lunch crowd. I bought a couple of sandwiches for Danny and me, chips, cookies, pop, and a large coffee.

When I returned, bearing two bags of food, Harry came barreling out of the utility room to intercept me. Brian Hall was right behind him.

"Miz West," Harry said. "There you are. Brian came by right after you left. Told you she'd be back quick," he said to the boy. "Don't worry about the game, we can finish 'er up later. I know you want to catch up on what Delilah's doing to find your dad."

"Yeah, I sure do." Brian sounded like his old cynical

self, and the look he shot me before he bounded up the stairs ahead of me said he might be asking for his ten dollars back so he could look for another detective.

In my office, he slouched on his spine in one of the client chairs while I went around my desk to sit across from him.

"Isn't it a school day?" I asked.

"Early dismissal."

I raised an eyebrow.

"Teachers' meeting," he said.

"Hungry?" I took the lid off my coffee and took a sip.

"Harry had doughnuts." He looked at me from beneath the bowl-cut hair that had grown out enough to hang over his eyebrows. "I thought we had a deal. You said you'd find my dad."

"I'm working on it when I can, Brian. I'm sorry, but something else came up."

"Larry said you were probably off with your boyfriend, Hawaii or someplace."

"Well, Larry's not even close," I said. "You want to know what we've done so far?"

He wasn't quite ready to forgive me the delay, but his longing for news about his father overrode his hostility. I moved the food over to the top of the file cabinet, opened the file, and while I had my coffee I began showing him the credit report and the notations of the calls we'd made.

We had just gotten started on the list of trucking companies when the door opened in the outer office, and Larry Vogel came in.

Brian got a glimpse of his mother's boyfriend, slouched lower in his seat, and muttered, "Oh, shit."

Larry had a crutch under his right arm, and he made his way awkwardly across the outer office and into mine. "Sorry to barge in on you, Delilah, but I've been looking all over for this one.'' He stopped behind Brian's chair and put his left hand on the boy's shoulder, digging in his fingers hard enough so Brian winced. "Jesus, Bry, your mom's worried sick. They called from school, said you took off. She can't leave work, so she called me.''

I looked at Brian. "Early dismissal, huh?''

Busted, he offered no excuse.

Larry said, "Do you mind if I call Gloria?''

"No, I'm sorry she was worried. Brian, pull up the other chair.''

The suggestion let him move away from Larry as he dragged over my second client chair.

"Did you have an accident?'' I asked.

"Nah,'' Larry said. "Knee's acting up—all this rain. Car wreck when I was in high school.''

He sat with a grimace and reached for my phone. He also scanned the open file folder that contained the information on Travis Hall as he punched in Gloria's number. There was not a whole lot for him to see, but I closed the file anyway.

After a short conversation with Brian's mother, Larry hung up and said, "You go wait in the truck, Bry. I need to have a word with Delilah.''

"We were talking about Dad,'' Brian said. "I already missed math class. What's the big deal if I'm here a little longer?''

"Listen, hoss, I got business I need to attend to. Instead, I'm out limping around looking for you. So I'm not in the best of moods, know what I mean? Just get on down and don't mess with me.''

Brian wanted to argue, but he did what he was told. Larry shook his head as the boy left, and turned to me with a wry smile. "That kid. Drives poor Glo nuts.''

"What is your business?'' I asked. "You never said.''

"You never asked. Used electronic gear. Mostly parts. You want a few transistors? Maybe a stepper motor?" He shrugged. "It pays the rent. How about you? I take it you haven't found Travis yet—I mean, I heard you were taking a little trip so you didn't have a whole lot of time."

"No," I said, "but I'm working on it."

"Well, look," he said. "You're a busy woman. I know you're trying to be a nice person, but Gloria and me talked, and we just don't feel right about this pro bono stuff. And besides that, finding his dad has become like an obsession with Brian, you know? Now he's ditching school—it's not good for the kid no matter how you slice it."

"You mean you want me to stop looking for Travis?"

"It's the best thing, Delilah."

"I agree that Brian's got to stop playing hooky," I said. "But I made a promise to find his dad. Until Brian tells me to stop, I'll keep on trying."

Irritation and anger flashed in his eyes, but he did a good job of covering it as he got up and balanced himself on the crutch. "Well, you do that. Just going to be a lot harder on the boy, getting his hopes up."

As he hobbled out the door, I had to wonder if his concern for Brian was really genuine, or if he had another reason for wanting me to stop looking for Travis Hall. Either way, I thought for the second time that it wouldn't hurt to do some checking up on Larry, if nothing else than to see what kind of guy was hanging around Brian.

And, once again, those plans went straight out of my head as the phone rang. I snatched it up, hoping to hear Erik's voice, but it was Alice Carew's secretary. Ms. Carew was in class until late afternoon. She could fit me in at five-thirty if that was convenient. I said that I would be there and quickly broke the connection as call waiting beeped.

"Yes, hello?"

"Uh—I'm trying to reach, let's see, West Investigations."

"You have. This is Delilah West. How can I help you?"

"I'm Joe Armstead," he said. "Somebody called me from there, said you're looking for Travis Hall. What's that all about?"

There was wariness in his voice, so I explained that Travis's son hadn't heard from his father since late October, that the boy was worried, especially since there had been no word from Travis during the holidays, and that I was trying to track down Travis to make sure he was okay.

"Huh," he said. "It is damned odd, Travis not showing up for Christmas. Not like him at all."

"Have you heard from him lately, Mr. Armstead?"

"No, it's been awhile. And it's kind of strange, now that I think about it. He called from this truck stop out on I-Fifteen, had to be—wait, I'm looking at the calendar—first week in November."

Travis was scheduled to take out a load the following morning, but something had come up, and he wanted Joe to fill in for him.

"I'd just got back from Chattanooga," Armstead said. "I really needed a day off. But Trav said he'd owe me a big one, that he had something to do that couldn't wait. Well, I wasn't happy about it, but I did the run. Never heard another word from Travis. Not thank you, kiss my ass, or nothing. Kind of ticked me off, to tell the truth. Jesus, I hope nothing bad happened to him."

"You have reason to think it might?"

"No, but it's kind of weird. That's just about the time you say he dropped out of sight, isn't it?"

"Sounds like it," I agreed. "You know anybody else I could call? Friends? Girlfriend?"

"No. After he split up with Gloria, he moved around a lot. Last I heard he was living in Texas. We had a beer now and then when he was in town, but he mostly talked about Brian. Really loved his kid."

"What about the truck stop he called from? Do you know where it is?"

Armstead did and gave me the location, up near Cajon Pass on the way to Victorville and Barstow. He wasn't sure, but he thought Travis was staying at a motel there.

"When you find Trav, tell him to call me, will you?" Armstead asked.

I promised I would, but I have not had a lot of experience with happy endings, and the way things were going, that was not about to change. No, I was growing more and more afraid that Joe Armstead might never get that phone call and sheepish apology from his friend.

I WORKED my way east through light traffic to pick up I-15, then north and east toward Barstow. Temperatures hovered in the high sixties, but wispy cirrus clouds trailed high above the San Gabriels, harbingers of a new winter storm, according to weather reports on the radio.

Danny still hadn't returned from the Hall of Records by the time I had finished my sandwich, so I left him a note. To hell with waiting for the phone to ring. I was bound to be more successful at getting information about Travis Hall in person. Even if going to the truck stop turned into a wild goose chase, it was better to be in motion, and there was at least the *possibility* that I might accomplish something.

I figured three hours, tops, to go up to Cajon Pass and back. I would be driving against rush hour traffic on the return trip, so even with a few delays I should be able to make my appointment with Alice Carew.

The problem was that cell phone reception would be poor once I started up the grade into the mountains. Did I really want to be out of touch completely? I pulled over into the slow lane, torn, debating, and just then the phone rang. I snatched it up and heard Erik's voice at last.

"Nicki?" I asked as soon as we said hello.

"Nothing." There was a world of misery in the word. "I just thought I'd check in with you. Danny said you went out to do an interview. Did you think of something?"

"About Nicki? No. Another case. Trying to stay busy. Wait a second," I said. "I'm going to pull off the freeway, so I don't lose the signal."

I took an exit and parked along a ramp. It was only after I'd braked to a stop that I realized I had taken the exit leading to Foothill Boulevard. Turn left over the freeway and there was the old vineyard where the kidnapper had snatched up the ransom and vanished.

"Ah, Jesus," I whispered.

"Delilah? What is it?"

"Nothing," I said, not wanting to remind him of what had happened here. "Traffic. Margaret came to see me this morning."

"Oh, God, I'm sorry, Delilah. I had no idea she'd pull something like that."

"No, it was okay. I think she just wanted to talk about Nicki. Erik, is Charlie there?"

"He's in the other room. If you need to speak to him—"

"No," I said quickly. "I just wondered. Erik, listen, this interview can wait. I have to see you. To be there. I don't care if you plan to sit by the phone, or get drunk, or whatever—I want to do it with you."

"Well, then come, of course." There was a touch of puzzled wonder in his voice. "Last night—it was just dealing with Margaret and worrying about Nicki—Christ, I don't know what I'm doing half the time, but if I made you feel like I didn't want you with me—darling, you must know that's not true.''

I felt a little dizzy with relief. If Charlie had started his campaign against me, Erik hadn't paid any attention.

"I'm turning around," I said. "I'm coming straight there."

"Here? No, wait, I'm not at home. I'm at the office with Charlie. We're going over all the personnel files again. It's going to take awhile—four or five hours at least. You can come here if you want, but are you sure you don't want to go ahead with your interview?"

All set to break the land speed record going to Corona del Mar, it took a second to regroup. Did I really want to be at Erik's office, where it would be impossible to escape from Charlie? I didn't think so. And there was no point in sitting around that big empty house, waiting.

"I suppose I should take care of this," I said. "But I may be out of contact. Call Danny with any news and he'll get to me."

"I will. Darling, I have to go. We've got a lot to do."

"Wait," I said, suddenly seized by the urge to tell him everything then and there, or at least the most important thing.

"What?"

"Nothing. We'll talk later."

After we hung up, I sat there with the traffic roaring by and stared out at the abandoned vineyard where a bulldozer was working down in one corner of the field, ripping up the old stumps by the roots, tender young shoots and all.

TWENTY-FOUR

TRAFFIC IS SEGREGATED by speed as it climbs the grade up to Cajon Pass and the high desert of the Mojave. Semis and RV's grind along on the right while high rollers and small-time dreamers fly past in the fast lane, heading for Las Vegas. That left me in the middle and trying to stay out of the way as we wound up the chaparral-covered flanks of the San Gabriels.

Enormous steel towers spanned the cuts and gorges, carrying electricity from the dams on the Colorado into the L.A. basin. In the canyon below, a long freight train chugged slowly up the Santa Fe tracks, at least a hundred truck trailers double-stacked on the rail cars, and I was grateful the freight was down there rather than up here on the interstate.

As I gained elevation I could feel the pressure building in my ears, another reminder of the kidnapping. This was one of the routes we may have taken, but there was nothing to distinguish it in my memory. Still, the vineyard was in the area, too. Something to keep in mind and look into, but right now it didn't mean anything.

Swallowing to equalize the pressure, I tried to shake off the foreboding that had been with me since I pulled off on the Foothill exit ramp, naming it depression instead. And didn't I have a right to be depressed, considering everything?

Trying for positive thoughts, I reminded myself that Erik wanted me with him, no matter the dark hints Charlie was surely dropping. And if Charlie dared to try barring me from the estate this evening, well, I'd deal with that when I got there. For now, I'd concentrate on finding out what I could at the truck stop, then I'd be free to go straight to Corona del Mar. Except for one thing. I'd forgotten all about the session with Alice Carew.

And I had to go ahead with the session, if there was any possibility at all of remembering something that would help find Nicki. Maybe I could even come to Erik with good news.

Past Route 138 now, I saw a huge road sign inviting me to exit for the High Desert Truck Stop. I did, ahead of schedule. The stop offered a large gas station, a small café, and a no-frills motel, ten units housed in a plain barracks-like structure with siding and roof shingles the color of the grayish brown earth.

A buxom, bored, middle-aged woman sat at the reception desk in the tiny office, chain-smoking, dropping ashes on a faded muumuu that was once a hot pink print of tropical flowers, and inking in words on a crossword puzzle in a spiral-bound book of puzzles. She looked at me through a lazy plume of smoke, clearly not impressed by my looks, my state ticket, or my story of looking for a young boy's lost father. The only thing that got her attention was pictures of dead presidents.

A portrait of Andrew Jackson earned me the information that Travis Hall had stayed there in early November. A U. S. Grant got me a look at the registration. Travis had stayed one night, November 2, and paid in cash. The woman recalled no visitors. She did remember that Travis had asked if there was a motel over in Phelan.

"Is there?" I asked.

"Not that I know of," she said. "Anyway, it's not that far. No reason he couldn't come back here for the night."

"But he didn't?"

"Nope." She picked up her pen and returned to her puzzle, her conversation meter having expired.

Rather than pay for directions, I went back to the van and got out a map. The town sounded vaguely familiar. I found it quickly, located about twelve miles away on Route 138 in the direction of Palmdale.

I sat there and debated. It was two-thirty. If I had been flying back to Erik the way I really wanted, I would never have gone on to Phelan, but having decided to see Alice Carew, the appointment became the limiting factor. I could easily drive over to Phelan, scope the place out, and get back to Fullerton in plenty of time for the session.

A few miles back on the freeway, then in light traffic the two-lane road was a fast ride—talk about the middle of nowhere. Enormous uptilted slabs of smooth, pale rock provided an otherworldly look. Familiar, too. Mormon Rocks the outcropping was called, and had often stood in for alien landscapes on the original *Star Trek* series.

Beyond the anomalous rocks, the first of the Joshua trees raised bristly arms above the lower-growing brush. Rain had awakened the desert from a long, dry summer sleep. Cholla wore a celery green fuzz, and emerald shoots pushed up beside sun-dried plants. The area supported a few rough collections of houses and outbuildings that called themselves ranches, although I saw little sign of livestock or anything else warranting the label.

Past the junction with Route 2, the road that traces the crest of the mountains to La Canada, Route 138 curved left and abruptly cleared the foothills. I was on the backside of the San Gabriels now, where the Mojave swept north and east, and a sign pointed me to Phelan, a couple of miles down Sheep Creek Road.

Up against the mountains on the edge of the high desert, the sprawling town was a mixture of trailers, old houses with a low, hunkered-down look, and a sprinkling of newer dwellings. No urban planners had been at work here, directing the haphazard growth.

There was lots of space between homes that were mostly reached by dirt roads. Aside from a few scrawny cottonwoods, few people had bothered with imported trees. Like a cross between an overgrown cactus and a stunted, deformed pine, the Joshuas were the tallest things in the landscape.

At one of the two traffic lights on the main drag through town, progress had arrived in the form of a new McDonald's and two strip malls. I found no motels, but there was a San Bernardino sheriff's substation down among the older businesses.

Enough time to stop and ask a few questions? I decided that there was and that I might as well do it as long as I was here.

The officer manning the desk—J. Krepski, according to his name tag—was a little younger and a much snappier dresser but about as forthcoming as the clerk back at the truck stop motel. I ruled out bribes and settled on low-key persistence.

Any record of Travis being stopped or arrested on or about November 2?

No.

Any accidents around that time leaving patients with amnesia or in a comatose condition?

He couldn't recall any. I'd have to check the hospitals.

Any unidentified corpses, victims of either homicide or accident?

None.

I thanked Krepski for his generous help and left.

So much for those twin demons of intuition and foreboding that had come along for the ride. It was now 3:09

p.m. At least I wouldn't have to rush to make my appointment.

I put the key in the ignition, but instead of starting the engine I just sat there with a new idea quite literally staring me in the face.

Even though parking was certainly not at a premium along the street, immediately in front of the substation big signs had been posted proclaiming: Tow-Away Zone. I had pulled up right next to where the no-parking zone began, so I could even read the fine print on one of the signs that gave the number of the traffic law violation.

It was a long shot, but worth a try.

Rather than spend my time and energy trying to pry information out of Officer J. Krepski, I used my cell phone and let my fingers do the walking. Information even had a number for the sheriff's impound facility in Victorville.

A helpful woman there bought my involved story about my boyfriend leaving his car while he shipped off to the Persian Gulf and how I had to make an extended trip back east, and now I'd come back and found the car gone. Of course, it was possible the car was stolen, but could she please, please tell me whether it had been impounded? The Mustang would have been picked up on—I scanned the local flora—Joshua Tree Drive, Texas plates, registered to Travis Hall, but sorry, no, I didn't remember the plate number.

After a few seconds to check the information, the woman said, "Well, we do have a car here that matches the description, but according to my records it was towed from the two hundred block on Pyrite Street."

"Pyrite? Oh, wait, of course. I remember. I parked it around the corner. Thank you so much. I'll come in and take care of it right away."

Well, okay, so I'd vowed not to tell any more lies. This was work, and didn't count.

3:19 p.m.

If I went out to find the address on Pyrite Street, I would really have to hotfoot it back to Orange County and hope for no jackknifed semis along the way. The fact that Travis's car had been abandoned dimmed any hope I had of giving Brian good news about his father. Still, whatever Travis's fate, he had been gone for two months now. Would a delay of a day or two in checking the address really matter?

Well, it would definitely matter to Brian.

Bloody hell.

I got out of the van, went back inside the sheriff's station, and consulted a town map I had noticed earlier pinned to the wall. J. Krepski watched me, his cynical scrutiny telling me he knew I was a liar and a scam artist and up to no damn good. This was not a person to share your plans with and I didn't.

Pyrite Street was off Sheep Creek on the edge of town, and it was paved, although the asphalt was breaking down into a crazed pattern of geometric shapes and eroding away at the edges. Only a few houses out here—small cookie-cutter homes. The sameness and the paved street made me think this had once been a development sold to retirees as an escape from L.A.

There was nothing to indicate numbered blocks, so I drove slowly and squinted at house numbers. The next-to-last house before the pavement ended in a dirt track had a pine plaque with the numerals 238 burned into the wood and an old Dodge sedan under a carport.

I drove to the end of the street, stopped, and looked at the house that sat about two hundred feet off in the brush.

The place had a shuttered, abandoned look to it that sent a new ripple of unease shivering up my back.

Get a grip, I told myself sternly. A good percentage of the houses in the town probably looked like this one.

I turned around, went back, and pulled off the road in front of 238. The earth was soft beneath my feet as I got out, a mixture of grayish sand and pea gravel. The smell of wild desert brush was strong enough to clear the sinuses. Tan paint on the house was sun-blasted and peeling on the siding, but the block of pine that contained the numbers looked freshly varnished, and some stunted red geraniums bloomed around a small cement slab that served as a porch. Somebody was watching through a window, holding back a lace curtain to peer at me as I walked up a driveway covered with crushed rock.

I stopped just short of the porch and called out, "Hello?" in what I hoped was a friendly, nonthreatening voice.

The curtain fell into place. A second later, the front door cracked open and a woman's voice asked sharply, "What do you want?"

I told her who I was and displayed identification. I doubted she could read it at that distance, but she slipped outside and stood there with her left hand on the doorknob. She did not offer her name. I judged her to be in her late sixties, square and sturdy in jeans and a blue plaid flannel shirt. She had short gray hair, a flat-footed stance in laceless running shoes, and a yellow canister of pepper spray gripped in her right hand.

I stayed where I was and hoped she didn't panic and zap me with the damn stuff.

"The police towed a car from your street back in early November," I said. "A blue Mustang with Texas plates.

I'm looking for the driver of the car. Could I ask you a few questions about him?''

"Don't know anything about him. Never saw the guy. Just the car, sitting there when I got home from the hairdresser. Still there the next morning. I called the cops, and they came and got it.''

"Where was the car parked?''

"Down further, end of the street near the Farrels'. Figured he might have broke in down there, but the sheriff said there was no sign of that.''

"Were the Farrels out of town?''

"Oh, nobody's there, at least most of the time. He died awhile back. She went a couple of years ago. Left the house to her grandson. He's in and out, lets the place go to pot. I thought maybe he was fixing it up a week or so ago and planning to move in. Saw his truck there, and I heard a lot of hammering going on. But now I haven't seen him again. God forbid he should come by and say hello, tell me what he's doing.''

She stopped suddenly, aware of how much she had said and how long she'd been standing on the porch. "That's all I can tell you. Got things to do.'' She backed up, slipped inside, and slammed the door.

I walked slowly back to my van, a confusion of alarms clanging in my head.

Hammering...

No, no, that was crazy.

I was looking for *Travis,* not Nicki. But as I drove down to the house at the end of the street all I could think of was raw wood paneling the walls of our prison room, freshly pounded into place by big shiny nails.

TWENTY-FIVE

STERN LECTURES on logic?

Useless.

The fact that the name *Farrel* was not one I'd heard in recent memory?

Didn't matter.

Every hair on my body rose as I pulled into the crumbling asphalt driveway of the last house on the street.

I stopped about halfway in, facing a one-car attached garage, and shut off the engine. Gripping the steering wheel, I sat and stared out the windshield.

I thought the structure had probably been converted from a standard carport like the one next door and not skillfully done. The house itself looked like an old, abandoned beast crouched in the long shadows of the mountains. Two windows flanked a front door, both dirty and covered with heavy drapes. If I wanted a peek inside, I'd have to try around back. I was also aware that I couldn't see the house I'd just left, number 238—as though I needed one more thing to raise my hackles.

My purse was on the floor next to me. I took out the Beretta and clipped it, in its holster, to the waistband of my jeans. Then, leaving the keys in the ignition for a fast getaway, I climbed out. Having taken the gun, I also left my purse. A quick look, that's all I planned, just enough to quell my overactive imagination.

The sun had slipped westward behind the mountains, and I was wishing for a jacket before I'd gone five feet. The smell of the chaparral was even stronger here, reminding me that I'd smelled nothing like that when the kidnapper took me from his van. It had been raining that night, however. Rain washed the air of odors, didn't it? And there had been the hood as well....

A lone hawk circled overhead, stalking some small creature in the wild brush. I could hear the hawk's wings whispering through the air, the only sound in the eerie silence.

"Shit," I muttered, as I stepped off into rocky earth, drying up now after the rain stopped, earth the color and consistency of the stuff tracked into the prison room by our shoes and the shoes of the kidnapper.

Easy to talk myself into something here, but the truth was, the soil was probably not peculiar to this yard. The chief ingredient was rock from the mountains and while that was certainly not unique, it was enough to crank my heartbeat up a notch or two as I worked my way around the house.

In the overgrown backyard, this was not a simple task. I moved carefully, avoiding nasty cholla barbs but collecting other stickers from plants that had moved in and obliterated anything that might have once been landscaping.

And I tried not to think about all the space out there among the mesquite, manzanita, and Joshua trees—lots of places available for shallow graves—and concentrated on the house. The back windows were also covered, either with drapes or tightly closed blinds. I saw not one possibility of a look inside the building until I completed the circuit and ended up back in front of the garage.

Although there were no windows in this attached structure, poor workmanship had created a wider opening on the left side of the garage door than on the right, a good one-inch gap. I peered through the crack.

It was very dark inside, with just barely enough light to

make out the outline of a vehicle—a van, big and blocky and a dark color, possibly gray.

To hell with logic.

Think, I told myself as I stood there with my mind racing. *Don't get stupid here.*

Maybe the kidnapper was here—Farrel? No, not necessarily his name. He might be in the house, watching me and waiting with the stun gun or something even deadlier. I didn't think he was, though. I thought the old van had probably belonged to his grandparents, that he had taken it out just to use for the kidnapping and to drop me off, a perfect vehicle because it was not his usual one.

I drew the Beretta. Staying close to the building, I went quickly up to the front door and knocked.

No answer.

A padlock secured the big swing-out garage door. The front door looked too sturdy to kick, and it was deadbolted in place. And, as I recalled, the back door also had a deadbolt.

I seized a fist-sized rock from the plentiful supply on the ground and smashed the front window. After knocking out enough glass for an opening, I crouched down and stepped inside, pushing away the drape and crunching the shards under my shoes as I went over the sill.

I was in a living room that looked like the Brady Bunch had once lived here—avocado shag carpet, one of those matched suites of a sofa and chair upholstered in a satiny gold fabric, gingerbread tables, and a brass floor lamp with a fringed shade. The place smelled of mold and sawdust and backed-up plumbing. Somewhere in the house a motor was running, a refrigerator...

Or a fan.

I could feel my heart pounding all the way up in the back of my throat as I went quickly through the dim gloom to a small hallway, a square of space with three doors, all of them closed.

I had gotten only a brief glimpse of the outside of our prison room when the kidnapper dragged me out. But there was no mistaking what I would find behind door number three. It was crudely rehung so the hinges were on the outside and barred with a thick plank dropped into holders that were screwed into place on either side of the door frame.

"Nicki!" I cried as I holstered the gun, pulled the plank up and out, threw it down, and yanked open the door. "Oh, God, Nicki—"

I gagged on the foul odors as I rushed into the small room made even smaller by the paneling of raw wood.

She lay on one of the bedrolls with her knees drawn up, unmoving, her face a waxy white. One of the Sparkletts bottles sat beside her with more than a quart of water left. So she had heeded my lectures on rationing after all. And there was still a Vienna sausage can by the door—the hole I'd worked on now gouged almost through the wood.

I went down on my knees, fearing the worst, but she opened her eyes and looked up at me. I let out a breath that sounded like a sob, overwhelmed with relief because at least she was alive. Alive and breathing, even if there was no recognition at first, just the curious flat stare of somebody who has gone deep inside herself to escape from what has become too dreadful to bear.

"Nicki," I said, "it's Delilah. I've got you now. You're all right. We'll call your dad, get you a doctor, get you out of here, take you to your mom. She's here, Nicki. She came to see me. You won't believe it, but we liked each other."

I keep babbling like that, nonstop, as I grabbed her arms and pulled her up. She flopped over against me, head against my breast, and whimpered. Her skin was hot to the touch, and sweat had plastered her hair against her scalp and her face. She had weighed less than I did to begin with, had lost even more weight. Still, I knew there was no way I'd be able to lift her.

"Come on, Nicki, get up," I said. "Help me, sweetie. Try, okay?"

"You—you—" She tipped her head just enough to look up at me, and I could see a gradual dawning there in the glazed eyes, a swimming back from those remote depths. "You—came—back for me."

"Yes," I said. "Oh, yes, I did. Listen, I'm afraid I can't carry you. I think I'll have to leave you here for just a second, run out and get the phone, get some help."

"No," she moaned and clung to me. "No—don't go— *please.*"

"Okay, shh," I said. "I won't." As a last resort I could drag her out, but I decided to try one more time, got her arm up around my shoulder, and put my arm around her waist. "Hang on to me."

I staggered up, dragging her with me, nearly losing my balance in the process. Once her feet were on the floor, however, she found enough strength to stand on her own, and together we made it out the door into the small square of hallway.

I was concentrating on getting her out of there, of course. And my head was down, bowed under her weight. In addition, I'm sure my brain was working through the impossibility of the situation, making the connections and framing explanations.

Multiplexing, Danny calls it.

With all that going on—too many tasks, an overload— I registered the gust of fresh air as something to be expected, blowing in through the broken window. And so I lost a few precious seconds before I remembered the thick drape falling back over the window when I came in and realized there was way too much breeze...and by then the front door had swung open wide, and the man was charging in.

I thought, *Of course, should've known,* as Nicki saw him, too, and wailed in terror.

Still clinging to me, she tried to run, dragging us both down as I fumbled for the Beretta. I was pulling it from the holster when he got to me, but not soon enough, never soon enough, before the stun gun in his hand hummed and spit a blue arc that bit into my shoulder and licked its way through my body.

My spine arched, my arms flailed wildly, and the back of my head hit the wall as I went down. Through a darkness shot with flashing spots of light I could see Nicki on her hands and knees, trying to crawl away. I heard her thin, high scream and him swearing a stream of curses and then the thud of his boot striking flesh.

And through it all, a cold voice in my head was saying, *See, Erik, I told you she'd be connected to the kidnapper,* Charlie's voice, and only a fraction of what he was bound to say.

And he was right, there was a connection, just enough so he could twist it to suit his purposes, because it was Larry Vogel administering the kick that knocked Nicki down on top of me. Larry, drawn to me through Brian because of what I had done at the mall, and doing just fine without the crutch he'd used to disguise the way he moved. Larry, reaching down to give me another jolt from the stun gun just in case the first hadn't done the job.

My body shuddered in uncontrolled spasms and pain

slammed me down like a fist—and never mind what they tell you about stun guns—stupid idiots, what did they know? Then I was gone, gone in a neural firestorm that burned down the world and buried me in the ashes.

TWENTY-SIX

SOMEBODY WAS HAMMERING off in the distance. *Fixing the place up, planning to move in...*

No, not Larry Vogel's plan at all. He wasn't remodeling his grandparents' house for himself. He was building a prison cell, all snug and cozy. Soon as he was finished he'd get into Grandma's old gray van parked out in the garage and go into L.A., grab himself a rich man's daughter, and one poor loser of a private eye.

No, that wasn't right either. We were already here, Nicki and I. I could feel her lying next to me. She wasn't moving, and her breathing was harsh and uneven. He had kicked her, I remembered that now. Had he used the stun gun, too?

An effort, but I opened my eyes. The light was on in the room that served as our cell. Sixty watts was not a lot of illumination, but enough to see the way she lay curled against me, looking fragile and broken. I'd vowed to protect her, tried to bargain with God, offering my life for hers, but so far, my promises and prayers had been useless. And all along I'd been too busy telling myself that there could be no connection with what happened the day after Christmas at the mall to see the obvious. Too distracted by my feelings for Erik, by the problems with Charlie, to recognize the kidnapper even when he had sat across my desk this morning.

All this time I had been imagining everybody with stockings over their heads, but not Larry, because who would think the poor fellow hobbling around on his crutch capable of the swift, cruel actions of the kidnapper?

Lying next to Nicki with my head angled up against the door frame of the cell, I could see him clearly now. He was at work out there in the living room, nailing some big wooden planks across the window I'd broken.

He had a tool caddy on the floor, one of those compartmented things that fit into the top of a toolbox, and had pulled the heavy drape back to put up the boards. No glass on the avocado shag carpet. He must have cleaned that up already. He'd shucked the quilted vest he wore when he came in and turned up the sleeves of his denim shirt to reveal the ropy muscles in his forearms. Well, I knew about his grip, having seen his hands on poor Brian's neck, and I remembered his strength when he'd manhandled me, dragging me from the van that night he brought us here.

Beside me, Nicki opened her eyes and looked up at me with only a moment of disorientation before reality rushed back along with the pain. I could see a scream coming, so I put a finger against her lips, imploring her with a glance to keep silent and not draw attention to herself.

An effort, but she tilted her head in the slightest of nods. When I moved my finger from her lips and inched my hand down to hers, she gave a shuddering sigh. There was so much trust in her eyes, in those blue eyes so much like Erik's, that I had a moment of daunting terror.

Can't do this.

Yes, you can. You have to.

Only how?

These past few days I'd had a few meals, sufficient water, and a little time to recover, so my strength was already trickling back. What I had to do was to convince him I was helpless, then maybe I'd have the opportunity for surprise.

This would be a lot easier to pull off with the Beretta, but it was gone from the holster. I'd been in the process of drawing the little automatic when Larry zapped me with the stun gun.

I cast a desperate look around, hoping I'd dropped it, that it had landed nearby, that I could summon enough strength to get to the gun. But no such luck because I saw the Beretta—stuck in Larry's belt just at the small of his back.

What else?

If I could get to the van, I would have a cell phone and, assuming he hadn't found it, the .38 in the glove box.

Sure.

Snowballs in hell came to mind.

The board used to bar the door would make a wonderful club, but it was not on the floor where I'd dropped it. Larry was probably nailing it across the window, maybe the reason he hadn't put us back in the room—although I thought he was mostly overconfident at this point.

About the only thing that offered any help was the opened drape baring the window, including the part with the glass intact. Through it I could see my van about half-way down the driveway, the spiky silhouette of Joshua trees looming beyond. And if I could see outside, then somebody else could see in.

Only who was out here to look in this godforsaken place? The next house was too far away, the woman who lived there too scared to stick her head outside without her canister of pepper spray.

And then Larry eliminated that possibility altogether. He hammered in the last nail, pulled the drape closed over the boarded-up window, returning the room to late afternoon dimness, and squatted to put the hammer in the tool caddy.

Pretty good for somebody who was using a crutch just that morning.

I gave Nicki's hand a reassuring squeeze, blinked in what I hoped she understood was a signal, then let my eyelids droop so I could watch him through my lashes. Playing possum, maybe I'd have a chance to come up with something. Taking the hint, Nicki closed her eyes tightly.

But there was no fooling Larry. He got up and turned on the floor lamp with the fringed shade, then came back, limping ever so slightly, and gave my foot a kick that jarred me all the way to the top of my head.

"Come on," he said. "I know you're awake."

"Larry." I didn't have to fake the tremor or the weakness in my voice. "How's the leg?"

"Little bitch nailed me the other night when I took you out," he said. "I was going to turn her loose a lot sooner, but I figured I'd teach her a lesson. This morning, hey, the crutch fooled you, didn't it?"

"Not for long. You know, you ought to get going. Get away. I called Erik. Told him about you."

"Oh, bullshit," he scoffed, calling my bluff. "I saw the look on your face when I walked in. You didn't have a clue about me until then. Anyway, the phone in here doesn't work, and your cell phone's in your van."

He turned his back and went over to pick up the tool caddy, then headed toward the kitchen, although I was pretty sure he wasn't going far. Nicki's eyelashes fluttered open, and she started to speak.

I leaned over and whispered urgently, "*Quiet.* I'll try to get us out of this, but just keep your eyes shut and don't say anything, no matter what. Shh, he's coming."

He returned with a kitchen chair, all tubular chrome and pink vinyl padding, which he turned backward and straddled, positioning it on the carpet just at the entrance to the small square hallway. I noticed now he had the stun gun in the pocket of his western-style shirt. He crossed his arms on the vinyl pad of the chair back as a rest for his chin.

He was in a little island of shadow created by the way the door to the prison room was angled. Backlit from the living room lamp, his face was almost as blank as if he'd drawn the stocking over his head. There was only a defining glint of light off the whites of his eyes, the gold hoop in his left ear, and the pearly snap buttons of his shirt.

"This is really your own damn fault, you know," he said, echoing popular opinion. "If you had any sense, you'd've been cheering up Mr. Moneybags. But you wouldn't stop looking for Travis, so here you are, back in the soup."

"What about Travis? Is he a guest here, too?"

"Nah, he didn't react too well to getting zapped. These things"—he tapped the stun gun in his pocket—"they can act like the defibrillators the paramedics use to restart your heart. Only they can stop it, too. Takes another little zap to get it going again, but Trav, well..." He shrugged, confirming my worst fears for Brian's father. "You know how all this happened? Because I was being a nice guy."

He paused, inviting the obvious question. I knew why. For one thing he wanted to brag a little, to show off what a smart fellow he was. But mainly he was stalling, waiting for darkness to veil his activities, taking no chances that the neighbors would see what was going on when he took us away, when he took our bodies away.

More than willing to play along and delay that grisly possibility, I asked, "What did happen with Travis?"

"Like I told you, I deal in used electronics. Well, sometimes I come across some new stuff."

Was Larry a thief or a middleman? He didn't come right out and say. It didn't matter. Was that why he gave Brian a very expensive VCR for his birthday in October, part of the loot in a truck highjacking? Travis had picked up on the unusual brand name, remembered the robbery, and become suspicious enough to do some checking on Larry.

"Glo told him about the house out here," Larry said. "I mentioned it once, and she's always bugging me to sell it, use the money to buy something in Orange County. Like what, I don't know, the little bit I'd get for this place. Maybe a shack in the barrio. Anyway, I was here when Travis showed up. The idiot saw my pickup parked down the street and tried to sneak in and surprise me. Come to think of it, the two of you got a lot in common, Delilah. Both of you sticking your nose where it don't belong and getting nailed."

His smirky grin was just a flash of teeth under the coarse mustache. "Brian thinks you're such hot stuff. Really thinks you might've killed that guy in the mall. If he could see you now, he'd know what a dumb idea that was. Kid's a shitty judge of character. But, hey, he got us together, right? Soon as I saw that picture in the paper of you and Lundstrom and the girl, I knew it was fate."

So there it was, all spelled out for Nicki. She'd been right to begin with. So had Charlie. I was to blame for this, even if it was in a roundabout way. And something else she had said: *Dad's never going to forgive you.* I thought she was probably right about that, too.

Okay, enough, I told myself sternly.

Lots of time later to beat up on myself. Right now, I had to find a way to get us out of this mess.

"Oh, I don't know, Larry," I said, searching desperately for some button to push while I played the weak, helpless female who could barely hold her head up. "I don't think the kidnapping had anything to do with fate. I think maybe

I worried you. You knew it was only a matter of time until I found Travis.''

"Oh, yeah? Let me tell you about this area. My mom used to ship me off in the summer to stay out here with Gram and Gramps. Talk about bored. I roamed around a lot. Found some interesting spots, lots of old mine shafts. Those places—if things go in, they never come out. Like this yappy little poodle Gram used to have. Nah, I wasn't worried about you finding old Trav. I go with the flow. Little Miss Rich Bitch was too good an opportunity to pass up.''

"Sorry," I said. "I don't buy it. Kidnapping's a fairly major gamble. You were running scared, and you risked everything for one big score because you were afraid I'd catch up with you.''

"Well, you didn't catch me, did you?" he said softly. "Just to show you how much I appreciate it, tell you what. If you're nice and don't make trouble, I'll use your little gun to put a bullet in your head first before you join old Travis and the pooch.''

Nicki whimpered, unable to control her terror. I gave her hand another warning squeeze, sending her a silent message to shut up and lie still.

"She waking up?" Larry asked. "Or she been faking it all this time?''

"No," I said. "She's out of it, Larry. She's sick, burning up with fever. You got your money. And she's not going to remember you. So why not let her go?''

"I'm thinking about it," he said, although I was fairly sure he was lying.

Takes one to know one, as they say.

"If you hadn't screwed things up," he went on, "I might've just dropped her off tonight at that McDonald's where I left you. Now, I'm not sure there's enough time. I have a plane to catch.''

''Wherever you're going, Larry, it's not far enough,'' I said. ''No place will be. You think you can kill Erik Lundstrom's daughter and get away with it? There'll be a reward on your head so big the bounty hunters will be lining up. I give you six months, tops.''

''First they have to figure out it was me,'' he said, but he was rattled at last.

''I figured it out.'' Well, I hadn't, not exactly. But I had been getting there. ''You were careless, Larry. You left Travis's car sitting around.''

''Didn't get back in time,'' he muttered. ''Damn old biddy next door is so nosy, didn't want her to see me driving it away in the daylight.''

''But she called the police anyway, and they impounded the car. There's lots of loose ends like that this time, Larry. I've been around asking questions today. People are going to remember, like your neighbor and the deputy down at the sheriff's station, to name a few. Only a matter of time until there's an APB out on the two of us, and the TV starts broadcasting pictures. You'll be identified, all right.''

No more careless relaxation, leaning on his arms. He straightened up and gripped the chromed tubular supports of the chair. A control freak, I'd been right about that, and apt to become mean and unpredictable when things got out of hand. That last thought started another drumbeat of panic. Maybe I was playing this all wrong, pushing too hard.

''Of course,'' I said, ''you could leave us here and take off. I'd see to it Erik knows what you did and that he's grateful.''

''Yeah?'' he said scornfully. ''And what about the cops?

They going to see what a nice guy I am and forget about kidnapping charges?"

"Erik did what you said. He never called them in. Why would he do it now? He won't be eager to put his daughter through all that publicity, the stress of a trial if they ever caught you. No, you play your cards right, I think you've got a good chance of walking away free and clear."

He hunched forward, considering, and I would have given a lot to be able to look into his eyes.

Nicki squeezed my hand tighter, and her face grew even more tense. Praying, I'd bet. I thought she was holding her breath, too. I know I was.

After a long moment he said, "What about Travis?"

"What about him? I found his car, that's all."

"You won't have them looking down mine shafts? You'll just let poor little Brian whine and cry about finding his daddy and never say a word? Give me a fucking break."

He stood, picked up the chair, and set it aside in the living room with a thump. I'd been concentrating on him. Now I saw beyond him and noticed the deepening shadows in the corners of the room. The sun had set. There would be a moon later, but right now there weren't even any streetlights to mitigate the darkness outside.

And I wasn't ready, not ready at all, still too weak and not a single plan of attack mixed into the doomsday scenarios swirling in my brain.

"We need to talk about this some more," I said, making no attempt to hide the desperation in my voice. "Please, Larry, we can work this out."

Let him feel superior. Let him feed his sadism on our helplessness. I didn't care, because he was reaching into his jeans pocket to take out some long strips of black plastic with square lock tabs on the end that I recognized as cable ties.

"Nah," he said, "I'm done talking."

Then he removed the stun gun from his shirt pocket with the other hand, and I knew time had just run out.

TWENTY-SEVEN

I MUST HAVE telegraphed my fear to Nicki. She pulled away and scrabbled up with a moan of pure terror. On all fours she was suddenly an obstacle for Larry as he came at me with the stun gun.

I'm sure his plan was to take care of me first, then Nicki, and it cost him a second or two to shift gears. He hesitated, saying, "Son of a *bitch*," in a tone of betrayed surprise, then bent toward her.

No way to stop him. The blue light flashed, licking her back just above her shoulder blade. I could only try to get out of the way as her spine arched and her body bucked with the electrical shock. She was still between Larry and me, both a help and a hindrance in the confined space of the small hallway.

Nothing to do but retreat.

No place to go except the prison room.

Nicki—I thought of Larry's horrifying story of Travis Hall's death and knew there was no way to help her if she was having the same reaction to the stun gun.

All I could do was scramble backward, still down on the floor, my weakness not a pretense after all. I banged into the door and sent it crashing against the wall. The shock of the collision jolted through my body, but I was full of adrenaline now, the pain blocked, held in reserve to assault me later.

I wasn't thinking clearly—hell, I wasn't thinking at all. I was operating strictly on instinct: evasion, avoidance, escape. And doing a damn poor job of it, forced into the cell, and Larry only a step or two away after he simply and brutally shoved Nicki aside.

I still wasn't up on my feet, either. Well, I was trying, but mostly I was crab-crawling, scuttling on my butt—and that's why I was looking up, toward Larry, who was coming at me, swift and agile, and toward the inside of the door frame with the gouges that marked our pitiful attempts at escape.

I'd noted the splintery grooves earlier, gratified that Nicki had continued to work on the wood. And that she had saved the sausage can. It was there on the floor against the wall.

Larry thrust the stun gun at me. I lunged sideways to avoid it, and my fingers closed on the smooth metal of the can. Larry was moving too, jamming the stun gun down as I was twisting and rolling. The thing connected for just a second, a quick beesting on my thigh that jarred through my system, but I was already swinging the can.

About two and a half inches high, two and a half inches in diameter, a good six or seven ounces of pork, chicken, corn syrup, fillers, and artificial flavorings.

Gripped and used as a weapon, the can worked as well as I had imagined. It hit high on Larry's left cheek with a bone-crunching sound and sent him reeling backward with a shriek of pain and blood pouring down his face.

One could hardly ask for more—except maybe for him to drop his weapon or fall down unconscious, and neither was happening. I thought of grabbing Nicki up—impossible, who was I kidding? She lay unmoving, but her eyes were open, and I was sure she was still alive. So I did the only thing I could do. Dodging around Larry, around Nicki, I stumbled toward the front door.

No, I was not just simply in a flight mode, saving myself. I was the mother bird, pretending to have a broken wing and luring the predator away from the nest. Only I didn't have to pretend much because I could barely stay on my feet.

Larry lumbered after me with a roar that was a combination of pain and rage. I was only three steps ahead of him as I turned the knob and yanked. The door stayed firmly closed.

Deadbolt.

I fumbled it open, threw back the door, and heard the bug-zapping hum of the stun gun close to my ear as I ran outside. The heavy drapes and the boards dimmed the big front window. Mostly there was light spilling from the open doorway to illuminate the concrete slab that served as a front porch. Beyond was a night as black as the cell had been when the overhead bulb went off. Clouds covered the stars, and there were no streetlights out here. The distant glow from scattered houses and the town only made the darkness seem more complete.

My van was a big, blocky mass down the driveway. A cold wind picked at my clothes as I ran with Larry so close on my heels I could hear his wheezy breathing and thick curses. Blood in his sinus cavities. I hoped he choked on it.

I skidded around the front bumper, wrenched opened the van door, and jumped inside. Slammed the door shut and hit the lock button. I was beyond the reach of the stun gun, but not the Beretta, my little gun Larry had stuck in his back belt. Twenty-two caliber ammunition doesn't have a lot of stopping power, but it can do some real damage, and there were nine bullets in the magazine, one in the chamber.

I don't know why he didn't use the little automatic. Maybe he wasn't used to having a real gun at his disposal. Maybe he just forgot it. More likely he was still trying to keep the noise down and not alert the neighbors. Instead he banged with his fist on the window, his head an anonymous blob up close against the glass.

As for me, my first thought was for the .38 Smith & Wesson locked in the glove box. There was a moment, however, when I considered the other things I could do, would have preferred to do: dig out the cell phone and call the cops, start the car and drive over the son of a bitch. Shooting and killing George Mendel was still fresh in my mind, and I had no desire for a rerun of that scene in the mall.

But Larry was dipping down out of sight and then bobbing up, his arm swinging toward the window. Even though I couldn't see the rock in his hand, I knew it was there. My mind was screaming *move, move,* even before he smashed the glass.

I snatched the keys from the ignition and dove across to the passenger's side as an explosion of glass pellets showered me in a hard, stinging rain. While I stabbed at the glove box lock with the key, Larry kept up a mantra of curses and fumbled with the door—a ghastly replay of that day on Coast Highway. The dome light came on as the door opened, giving me a precious moment of illumination to ram the key into the glove box lock, turn it, and grab the .38.

He was climbing inside the van and reaching out with the stun gun as I clutched at the passenger door handle, yanked it open, and tumbled out. I fell on the broken asphalt and made an awkward, bruising roll with no thought of anything but to get away and hold on to the revolver.

I was back at the rear of the van, stumbling to my feet, when he came sliding out behind me.

"Hold it," I yelled. "Stop right there."

He froze in the open door for a second, an incredulous

look on the ruined face quickly giving way to renewed rage and contempt. Who could say what went through his mind? Could be his ego would only allow that my smashing his cheekbone with the can was a lucky fluke, that I certainly didn't have the guts to shoot him. Whatever it was, he was moving, eeling around the door and bolting toward the house, toward Nicki.

"Stop," I cried.

But he wasn't stopping. He plowed toward the open front door, a moving, weaving target in the shadowy darkness. I ran after him, wanting to end this somehow without more bloodshed, already afraid this was impossible.

"Brian was right, Larry," I called. "He was right about that guy at the mall."

I was shaking with cold, with nerves, as I crouched and leveled the .38. Amazing how rock steady my weapon was, gripped in both hands and aimed just the way my firing instructor back at the academy had taught me.

"Stop, please," I said. "Don't make me kill you, too."

He didn't listen, or didn't believe me, just kept barreling ahead. If he got inside, got to Nicki, God knows what he would do—hold her hostage at the very least, maybe kill her for spite.

Then he reached the doorway and was framed for an instant there by the light. Inside, Nicki began to scream.

"Dammit, Larry," I said, overwhelmed by feelings of sadness and waste and absolute inevitability as I pulled the trigger.

The first shot slowed his headlong rush to a stagger, the second dropped him like a stone. Yelling to Nicki to stay put, I approached him slowly with the .38 ready. He'd fallen face first. From the position of the entry wounds in his back and the amount of blood already staining the stoop beneath him, I knew a third shot wasn't necessary.

TWENTY-EIGHT

SHOOTING SOMEBODY when you're in imminent danger of dying yourself is one thing. Shoot somebody in the back while he's running away from you and the cops will want to have very long in-depth conversations, which could lead to an indictment for murder.

I left a hysterical Nicki long enough to retrieve the cell phone and called Erik on his private line right after I called 911. By then I was holding his unconscious daughter in my arms and listening to sirens in the distance.

As soon as I assured him she was alive, that I thought she'd be all right, I said. "Listen, I don't have much time. I killed Larry—the kidnapper."

I told him where we were—told Charlie, too, of course, because by then he was on the line snapping questions. "I've no idea where they'll take Nicki—or me. You'll have to find out. Just get here, okay?"

I had to end the call because the police arrived, guns drawn, taking in the carnage. They were quickly followed by the paramedics. After I gave them Erik's name as next of kin for Nicki, I watched them take her away in an ambulance. Then I went docilely in handcuffs to be interrogated for hours in a bleak little room, too physically and mentally exhausted to lie about anything—even when it was for my own good.

Well, I did manage to restrain myself from telling them about killing George Mendel back at the mall. At that point I only said that Larry was connected to me through a client.

I told them about the kidnapping, about Travis Hall being murdered and dumped somewhere in a mine shaft, about shooting Larry because I was afraid he would kill Nicki. And I emphasized over and over how I was sure Larry would've murdered both Nicki and me if I hadn't hit him and made a break for the van. All this got me was the skepticism learned by all cops through years of listening to suspects' endless excuses and litanies of blame. It didn't help that the shooting I'd been involved in the year before was also in San Bernardino County.

Surely they had other investigators talking to Erik and to Nicki, if she was conscious. Just a look inside that house at the prison room should confirm much of what I was telling them. Still, I knew they would see this as their one big opportunity to squeeze me dry.

Erik's first priority would be Nicki, so I didn't expect him to ride to my rescue. But I did think he'd send an attorney to look out for me, to hold the police's feet to the fire. When it got to be two in the morning and no lawyer appeared, I could guess what had happened: Erik had delegated the job to Charlie.

Which meant I was on my own.

"Okay, that's it," I finally said. "You either charge me or release me."

Acid test—I got up and headed for the door. I really didn't think I'd make it outside; I figured I'd be spending the night in jail. If that happened, at least I'd be allowed a phone call.

After a brief consultation, the detectives let me go, with warnings to stay available for further questioning. My guns would be kept as evidence. My van had been impounded, probably taken to the same lot as Travis Hall's blue Mustang.

Out in the squad room, I spotted Charlie bullshitting

with one of the detectives. He ambled over to intercept me, his black eye almost gone but not forgotten.

"Finally cut you loose, huh?" he said with such malevolent glee I knew he hadn't done a thing to speed up the process.

"No thanks to you," I said. "How's Nicki?"

"Cracked rib and a nasty bronchial infection, but the doctors think she'll be okay."

He tagged along as I found my way past the station's front desk. Locating a rental car might not be an easy task out here in the middle of the night. I could always take a taxi, but Charlie was waiting, and, like it or not, he was the logical source of transportation.

"Now that you've had your fun," I said as we went out in the raw night air, "you can get me to the hospital."

"You look like hell, Delilah." He eyed my dirty clothes and tangled hair. "You sure you don't want to go home first?"

I clenched my hands to keep from renewing his shiner and landing myself in jail for sure this time for assault.

"Positive," I said. "Now, let's go."

Charlie—the coward—had brought somebody along so he wouldn't have to be alone with me. Deke—or Dirk—the guy who had picked me up in the vineyard that night after I'd delivered the ransom—snoozed in the car. Out of Charlie's earshot, he said softly, "Good work," as he held open the door for me.

That made one person who thought so. The important people waited in a private room in a hospital in Victorville.

A nurse was coming out of that room as I walked up. I stopped to let her leave, put out a hand to hold the door ajar. Through it, I could see Nicki in a narrow bed, her blond hair spread over the pillow. The side rails were up on the left side. On the right Erik and Margaret sat, holding hands, watching their daughter sleep.

At that moment all I wanted to do was walk away, call Rita, and have her come and take me home. I might have done it, too, except that Erik saw me and came hurrying out to grab me and hold me tightly against him.

"Delilah, thank God," he said. "Everything's square with the police? Did you get checked out with a doctor?"

"Everything's fine," I said, avoiding his questions and pressing my face against his shoulder to keep from seeing Charlie's knowing eyes. "Nicki's really okay?"

"She will be."

"Do we have to keep Charlie any longer?" I asked.

"Oh, I can stick around," Charlie said.

"No, it's late," Erik said. "You've done enough. Thanks for helping Delilah."

"My pleasure," he said.

I waited until he was heading down the hall to say, "I don't know what he's told you, Erik. I did bring Larry Vogel to Nicki, but it was such a remote connection, I swear to you I never once suspected the guy."

"The important thing is you saved Nicki's life, and you're all right. Right now, nothing else matters."

So Charlie hadn't laid out his nasty little scenario after all. He was undoubtedly plotting to go to Plan B of his threats, but let him. I could handle Charlie. Hanging on to Erik, I told myself the worst was over.

Famous last words.

TRAVIS HALL'S body was found in a mine shaft ten miles from the house in Phelan, along with the skeleton of a small dog. The other two bedrooms in the house that once belonged to Larry's grandparents contained stacks of new and used electronic goods, some of them from the truck highjacking.

Brian had been right about his father. While the attempt to find out if Larry Vogel was a criminal was a big mistake, Travis was no deadbeat dad. He died trying to protect his son. And maybe he'd had some kind of premonition, because he'd taken out a $500,000 life insurance policy shortly before his death. The money provided a college fund for Brian, plus a small condo for him and his mom, with enough left over so that Gloria could work part-time and be home after school for her son.

One would hope that the mess with Larry would have taught Gloria to be more selective about men. It didn't. Within six months she had hooked up with another borderline-abusive sleaze bucket who even looked a lot like Larry. It took a private talk with me and a friend who was big enough and mean enough to convince the guy he was never going to get his hands on Brian's money and if he laid a finger on either of the Halls he was in for a world of trouble.

Brian finally stopped playing hooky from school. He still comes by once a week after class to say hello and play checkers with Harry. He even lets Harry win once in a while.

The ransom was found in a Louis Vuitton bag in Larry's pickup. The bonds had been cashed, and the money was all there except for what he'd spent on the bag, the new wardrobe inside, and a first-class ticket to the Cayman Islands.

The story of the kidnapping was perfect media fodder, especially for the tabloids. I don't know how Erik kept the story quiet, but he did. He also got my van released, sent somebody out to get it, and had it brought to me with the window replaced and all the broken glass vacuumed up from the inside.

In the weeks and months that followed, fixing the rest of my problems would be a different story. Even though the San Bernardino County district attorney finally decided not to press charges against me, I lost my permit to carry a concealed weapon. Worse, the state sent me a letter advising that my PI license might be suspended or even revoked.

Charlie, of course, making good on his promise.

By then he had even more reason to have it in for me.

THAT MORNING after I found Nicki, I went back to the hospital after a few hours' sleep at a nearby motel. There I got profuse thanks from Margaret, and Nicki put her arms around my neck for a fierce squeeze while she whispered, "We didn't let the asshole win, Delilah."

"Damn straight," I whispered back.

She was responding quickly to some high-powered antibiotics. That afternoon the doctor let her go home with a prescription for rest, love, and a good therapist to help her deal with the trauma. A few days later, when Erik suggested I could use some of the same treatment, I quickly made excuses.

He didn't push. I even thought he might be relieved that I didn't take him up on the offer.

By then, you see, I'd begun to notice a difference in the way Margaret looked at me. And although it was not so apparent, I felt some of the same reaction from Erik. How could they put aside the fact that I'd brought the kidnapper into their lives like the plague? How could they forget I'd killed a man, even if it was to save their daughter's life?

As for Nicki, the kind of ordeal we had gone through forges a bond, no doubt about it. But I had brought the horror to her, after all. In any case, the closeness between us soon turned awkward and strained.

Did Charlie have a hand in this? Easy enough to blame him because he was in and out of the house, but I honestly didn't know.

Just then I had other things to worry about. The diamond ring Erik bought the day Nicki and I were kidnapped, for example. Was he still saving it for my birthday, which was fast approaching? And if he was, what was I going to say when he offered it to me?

And no, I still hadn't told him how I felt, I had not fessed up to the shooting at the mall, and I hadn't told him about Charlie. I guess I was waiting for the right moment for all these things, a moment that never seemed to come.

Well, okay, all things considered, I had decided that I couldn't tell him about George Mendel, not after having turned my hedging into a bare-faced lie when he asked about my other secrets.

Anyway, it was hard to have a discussion with Erik because he and I simply didn't spend a lot of time together. I tried not to think of chasms opening in the earth and told myself that mainly this was my fault because I wouldn't stay at the house with him. And, my God, if I couldn't do that, what was the point of wondering about engagement rings?

So he spent as much time with Nicki as possible, and I slept in my apartment with the lights on. In addition, I had an office to run, a living to make. The really bad stuff was yet to come, but, meanwhile, the business out in San Bernardino County kept dragging on, requiring endless trips and miles of paperwork.

Then that last week in January, everything caught up with me, and on top of everything else, I felt like I was coming down with something. When Erik called to make plans for my birthday, I had a perfect excuse: I didn't want to pass a cold or the flu along to Nicki—and sincerely hoped this was really the case.

It was more than a week later when I had to admit to myself that what was wrong with me was probably not contagious, and that I could no longer put off that talk with Erik. I called to make sure he was home, the call reminding me of that day I'd sat on the ramp on I-15 overlooking the abandoned vineyard, desperate just to hear his voice.

He said yes, of course, come now. It was going to rain. Nicki had wanted hot chocolate. He'd have a fresh pot waiting for me.

I made one stop, then rehearsed what I was going to say to him during the rest of the drive—at least a half dozen different versions. But every one of them flew out of my head as I drove up the winding road and parked in front of the house, because Charlie's car was on the circular driveway.

A cold front had moved in, bringing the first hard droplets of rain and a wind that was especially bone-chilling up on the exposed hill. The afternoon was quickly turning to stormy night as I got out and ran for the front door.

Erik was in the big family room with Charlie. Oak logs blazed in the fireplace. The huge windows offered a panoramic view of the swirling masses of sullen clouds and wind-whipped trees. Erik hugged me and took my wet jacket while behind him Charlie gave me the kind of grin that comes with a dagger hidden in a sleeve.

"Charlie called right after you did," Erik said. "He's got some wrap-up stuff to tell us about. Hot chocolate, as promised, darling," he added, gesturing to a big silver pot and mugs on a cart, although I would have known because the room was filled with the heavy, sweet smell.

I shook my head, knowing I'd never be able to keep the

stuff down. I followed him over to the three sofas, waited for him to sit opposite Charlie, then took a seat, alone, on the third couch.

Erik looked at me and then at Charlie, realizing something was wrong.

"I know what he's going to tell you," I said, hugging myself and shivering in the warm room. "Get it over with," I said to Charlie.

I'd waited too long, as usual, so I just sat and didn't say a word in my defense as he laid out the whole disgusting scenario for Erik. The story was just as absurd but even more persuasively detailed, this time with the big clincher that I'd shot Larry to look like a heroine and to keep the truth from coming out.

Erik didn't say anything, either. He just waited, silent and unmoving, the way he had that day Charlie played the recording of Gary Hofer spilling the beans about Turk Rizzo.

If Charlie was willing to take such an enormous risk, I knew he had an ace in the hole. He did.

"In case you have any doubts about how capable Delilah is of deception," Charlie said, "I have something you should see."

His briefcase was under the square coffee table. He opened it and took out a videotape. There's a television and a VCR hidden behind sliding doors in a bookcase on one wall in the room. Charlie went over to open the doors, turn on the TV, and plug in the cassette.

I recognized what was being shone instantly: a grainy surveillance tape of Main Street mall on the day after Christmas. God knows how many miles of tape from how many cameras Charlie had sifted through. The stuff is usually recycled, but this had probably been saved because of what had happened that day.

There was no footage of me shooting Mendel, of course. Just as I thought, no camera had been pointed at that particular spot. Otherwise, things would've happened very differently. But some expert editing told a coherent story all the same. There were glimpses of Isabel and me making our way down the mall to the lemonade and hot dog stand, followed by some quick clips of Mendel as he began his bloody work along the same route, the silent, chaotic realism more graphic than anything Hollywood can produce.

Then there was a scene of the big glass container exploding, of me grabbing Isabel and Brian and shoving them down. Mendel again, from a camera that caught him on the other side of the mall, but from an angle showing that he was approaching the lemonade counter. Somebody ducking out of the door to the storeroom, just the quickest glimpse that might have gone unnoticed, except that Charlie had done a freeze frame, and then a computer enhancement, so there was no doubt that the person was me. A little added footage from some news coverage established the location of the counter in relation to where Mendel's body had been found.

Nobody said anything as Charlie stopped the tape and hit rewind. He brought the cassette back and sat down with a smug look on his face.

Erik held out his hand for the tape, and then in the iciest tone I'd ever heard him use, he said, "You're fired, Charlie. I expect you to cover security for the next few days until I find somebody to replace you, but after that I never want to see you or hear from you again. And if I ever find out you passed on copies of this tape or repeated that ridiculous, insulting pile of bullshit to anybody, you'll never work for another company in this state again. Now, get the hell out of my house before I have you thrown out."

You'd think I would've been cheering as Charlie beat a hasty retreat, but I wasn't.

"You didn't believe him," I said. So why was I filled with free-floating dread instead of relief?

"That you could have been part of the kidnapping? No, of course not. But he's right about this, isn't he?" Erik put the videocassette down on the table between us. "You killed that man."

"What would you have me do?" I asked. "I had to stop him, Erik. I was pretty damn sure he was going to kill Isabel and Brian—and several other people, including me."

"But to do something like that and keep it to yourself, to outright lie to me—my God, Delilah."

I hunched forward, still hugging myself, wondering if I'd ever be warm again. "I couldn't face the fallout, I guess. Imagine what your friends—whatstheirnames—the Weylands would think. Or Nicki. Or you, the way you're looking at me. I took what I thought was the easy way out. Boy, was I wrong about that one."

"You could've told *me*," he said. "In Vermont. Here, when I asked you. You were right. It really wouldn't have led us to Larry, but what if you were wrong?"

"I know," I said miserably. "I'm sorry. I warned you— I'm not always a nice person."

I got up, banging my leg on the coffee table as I made my way through all those damn sofas. The smell of chocolate was overpowering and sickeningly sweet. I thought I'd never drink the stuff again.

Erik got up and came after me. "Where are you going?"

"Home—if I can find my coat."

I saw where he'd put it, on a chair by the door. I headed for it, but he caught up with me, saying, "Wait," and grabbing my arm. "This is important, Delilah. We have to talk."

"What's there to say?" And how could I say it when I felt as though I had a huge stone hung up between my throat and my chest? "Later maybe. I can't do this now."

I tried to pull away, but he gripped both my arms and swung me around to face him.

"Listen," he said. "I didn't plan to tell you this way, but I'm leaving in a day or two. Margaret's sick of hotels. She's going back to New York and taking Nicki with her. There were times Nicki needed me, and I wasn't around. I have to be there for her now."

Should've seen it coming, but I hadn't. I had to force myself to say, "Yes, of course, sure, I understand."

"No, you don't. I don't want to have to worry about what crazy chance you're taking while I'm gone, or what wacko you're getting mixed up with, or whether I'm going to get a call that this time I'll be visiting you in the morgue. I love you, Delilah, you must know that. I want you to leave this dirty, violent business and come with me."

I thought about Gloria Hall, all the poor souls desperate for this kind of offer, and never mind what you give up when you accept it.

"Sorry," I mumbled. "Wouldn't work. Safe trip," and tried again to pull away, but he held me tightly.

"I don't believe this," he said fiercely. "You're going to just walk away? Can't you at least for Chrissake *say* it?"

I couldn't, not with him touching me. But when he let me go, well, there was just so much hurt in those eyes of his, I said, "I love you, too."

Then I left quickly, running out the door into the rain.

And I drove away and never told him about my stop at the pharmacy on the way over or the pregnancy test I bought and would take when I got home.